Sign up for our newsletter to hear
about new and upcoming releases.

www.ylva-publishing.com

OTHER BOOKS BY CHEYENNE BLUE

A Heart Full of Hope
Switcheroo
I Do
Not for a Moment
For the Long Run
The Number 94 Project
All at Sea
A Heart This Big
Code of Conduct
Party Wall

Girl Meets Girl Series:
Never-Tied Nora
Not-So-Straight Sue
Fenced-In Felix
The Girl Meets Girl Collection (box set)

Cheyenne Blue

SOMETIMES
WE FLY

DEDICATION AND ACKNOWLEDGEMENTS

I remember the first time I rode a motorbike. It was Sydney, Australia, and I had a Sunday job in a nursing home. With no public transport to get there, my housemate would get up at stupid o'clock and take me on the back of his motorbike.

It wasn't the safest thing in the world. The bike was something large and blue, but the pillion seat was small and scarily close to the road. I'd be wearing a nurse's dress hiked high on my thighs to straddle the bike, bare arms and legs, and shoes, not boots. At least I had a helmet.

That hour on a Sunday morning meant little traffic. My housemate would open the bike up as we flew over Sydney Harbour Bridge. Every Sunday for a few months, I'd have the sun, wind, or rain on my face, and the incredible high of speed: low to the road, weaving around slow Sunday traffic, and the throaty roar as he let the bike rip. The blue, blue harbour below, the sky above.

Magic. Pure magic.

And now, as I so often do, I've written a book about something I love. This time it's motorbikes. I hope you enjoy it.

As always, huge thanks go to the crew at Ylva Publishing, my editor Sarah Ridding, and every wonderful person who helped get this book out in the world. My long-suffering betas Sophie, Marg, Jan, Elle, and Erin—thank you for keeping me under control Thanks, Lee, for enlightening me on DVRs. Also, a shout-out to my neighbour Russ, who will never read this—thanks for answering hundreds of questions about bike terminology. Next tapas evening's on me.

Cheyenne Blue
Queensland, Australia

CHAPTER 1
THE LATE NEWS

MAREN TOOK ANOTHER MOUTHFUL OF the baked salmon, closing her eyes in appreciation as the subtle flavours of lemon myrtle and Tasmanian pepperberry mingled in her mouth, enhancing the taste of the succulent fish. The new catering company was excellent. She'd certainly use them again for her next dinner party.

Next to her, Ethan, the producer of Channel 12's six o'clock news, sliced a potato with his fork. "Channel 12 is well-placed to lead the national news ratings into next year. TVEast's format is looking tired; their presenters are losing their edge."

Across the table, Maren's co-presenter, Luka Dokic, lifted his glass of wine. The pale liquid clung to the glass as he swirled it. "While we're hitting our stride."

Maren's lips twitched. Luka was just finding his form; she, as the veteran of the team, had been on point since before Luka had joined the station. But that was okay—they had sparkling chemistry together, and the viewers liked them.

Across the table, Zoey Hammond curved a practiced smile on her face. "Ratings have improved since you joined the team, Luka. Nothing against Rob, of course, but bringing in a fresh face can do wonders."

Ethan held out his glass for Maren to fill. "We were lucky to get Luka when Rob retired." He raised his glass to the younger man. "But the public's trust needs to be earned when it comes to the news. Rob built that trust over a decade at Channel 12. Maren, too, has a high approval rating. The two of them easing Luka into the second anchor position went a long way in retaining that trust. And of course, Luka is doing a magnificent job."

Zoey inclined her head. "We all are learning from the best."

Maren noted the slight stress on the "we". Spidey fingers twitched on her back again. Zoey was younger—in her mid-twenties to Maren's own forty-six—and possessed a willow-slim elegance and coolly beautiful face. Impeccably styled chestnut hair framed her smooth, olive-skinned face and dark eyes—a face made for the camera, as Ethan liked to say. *And a body made for TV*, Maren added silently. Zoey's role combined outside stories with studio fill-in if either Maren or Luka were away, and she'd made no secret of her ambition.

"That's it, isn't it?" She smiled at the younger woman. "We all keep learning in this game."

Zoey toyed with a piece of broccolini and slanted a swift glance at Maren. "I consider myself lucky to have joined this team. I hope it's my place for a long time to come."

Maren inclined her head and raised her glass in response. *Play nice.* "I'm sure it will be."

She glanced around the dining table. Apart from Zoey, everyone was eating with gusto. The only couple at the table, the weatherman Cliff and his wife Sula were too intent on their food to join the conversation. Maren suppressed a smile. Cliff loved his food—he was always the first to dive into the biscuit tin or fill his plate at the station lunches. No doubt, on Monday, he'd be complaining his pants were too tight again.

The soft—and flattering—lighting in the dining room added a warm and intimate feel to the dinner. Maren knew it added highlights to her dark hair, smoothed the faint crows-feet bracketing her eyes and mouth. She swept her gaze over the table. The messmate timber gained a softness in the light and set off her china with its bold geometric design. White linen napkins, and a rack of votive candles completed the scene. Maren was the only member of the news team to host regular gatherings at her home—and she liked it that way. It subtly reinforced her place as lead news anchor and senior member of the team. Although "senior" at only forty-six seemed wrong, it was preferable to "veteran".

She rose and went to the sideboard, before returning with a fresh decanter of wine. "I haven't forgotten the red wine drinkers. This Nero d'Avola goes beautifully with salmon."

Cliff nodded. "Your wine pairings never disappoint, Maren."

She found him and Sula fresh glasses, and, leaving the decanter at their end of the table, returned to her seat.

She'd just picked up her cutlery again when the door opened, and her housekeeper slid into the room. Maren shot her a glance. Although Janelle lived in, her only role in Maren's dinner parties was the cleanup the next morning. Maren felt the part of a competent and gracious host was better played if she gave the appearance of effortlessly arranging everything.

Janelle came up and leaned to whisper in Maren's ear. "There are callers for you. In the hallway. They say it's urgent."

Maren frowned. "Thank you, Janelle, but I'm not expecting anyone. Please ask them to come back tomorrow."

Janelle's hand gripped Maren's forearm, then slid down to grip her fingers. "It's the police. I think you should come."

Maren had to strain to hear her soft words, but when she did, her heart froze. The *police*? Had something happened to Orli? Then her muscles unclenched. Orli was in her room, no doubt watching TV or chatting online with her friends. This was no accident or incident.

Janelle's fingers shook. "You need to come now."

Janelle's words fell into a sudden silence, as conversation paused. Luka's and Ethan's faces wore quizzical expressions, and Zoey's intense gaze flickered between Maren and Janelle. Cliff helped himself to potatoes as Sula poured more wine.

"Excuse me for a moment." Maren stood and set her napkin on the table. "Something I have to attend to. I won't be long." At least, she hoped she wouldn't. "Please, help yourselves to more food and wine." Her heels tap-tapping on the timber floor, she preceded Janelle to the door.

Once in the hallway, she turned to her. "Did they say what it was about?"

Janelle shook her head. "No, they wanted to speak with you. But they seem serious. I would guess it's not a noise complaint or the like."

"Thanks. Hopefully, it's easily sorted, whatever it is." She hurried down the long hallway to where two uniformed police waited by the front door. Anxiety pushed insistent fingers into her throat.

The officers wore sombre expressions, and the thick belts, weighed down with firearm, radio, baton, and handcuffs, seemed out of place in the elegance of her hallway.

She forced her mouth wide, letting it soften into her trademark serene smile. "Good evening, officers. How may I help you?"

Both officers held out their ID. "Maren McEvoy?" one asked. At her nod, he continued, "I recognise you, of course, from the news, but I have to ask. I'm Senior Constable Peter O'Grady and this is Constable Maria Castillo. It's about your daughter, Orli Coffey."

A gasp caught in Maren's throat before she could subdue it, and her breath shuddered. A hundred scenarios ran through her head before she could suppress them: an accident, a kidnapping, maybe Marcus had made a complaint... That last one caught her up short. Marcus wouldn't do that—their relationship was solid, still each other's best friend, even with Rick now a part of Marcus's life. And Orli was upstairs. She swallowed away the panic and asked, "What about her?"

Castillo stepped forward. "I'm sorry to break this to you, but she's been arrested for joyriding in a stolen car. We're holding her at Richmond Police Station. She refused to make a call, but as she's a minor, we can't interview her without a responsible adult present."

Ice stole through Maren's abdomen, and she wrapped her arms around herself. "You must be mistaken. Orli is upstairs in her room. Obviously, the person you arrested has given you a false name."

The officers exchanged a glance. "We'll wait while you check upstairs," O'Grady said.

Their composure rattled her again, and Maren spun on her heel and stalked toward the stairs. Orli would be in her room. She'd deign to let Maren enter, and she'd find Orli sprawled on her queen bed, wearing her shapeless baggy jeans and a too-large T-shirt, the heating cranked as high as it would go to keep out the Melbourne cold. She'd raise her head from her phone, say, "Chill for a minute, my mum's just come in," to whoever was on the call, then she'd put the phone face down on the bed so Maren couldn't see who she was talking to. "What?" she'd say to Maren with a long-suffering sigh.

Orli's door was closed. Maren knocked twice. "Orli, can I come in?"

Silence. Orli must be listening to music on her headphones. She banged louder. "Orli, if you don't answer in ten seconds, I'm coming in."

She waited fifteen, the curl of annoyance growing in her chest. The least Orli could do was respond. Then she'd know. Know that this whole thing was a huge mistake by the police.

Still no answer. "Orli, I'm coming in."

She pushed open the door. Inside was dark, curtains drawn. But even the low light from the hall was enough to show the empty bed. She flicked the bedroom light on. Maren clenched her fists. Orli would be in the bathroom. That's where she'd be. There was no way she was in a police cell several kilometres away. Not her daughter. Not her Orli. Joyriding? She may be a brat, but she wasn't a lawbreaker.

But the en-suite door stood ajar, the room its usual mess of damp towels on the floor and spilled shampoo in the shower.

"Orli? Orli?" Her voice rose, and she took a deep breath. *Calm, blue oceans. Think of calm, blue oceans.* She pulled her mobile from her pocket and pressed Orli's number. There was no sound of it ringing in the room. The call rang off.

She lifted her chin. Okay, so she had to return to the officers and tell them her daughter wasn't in the house. But that didn't mean she was at Richmond Police Station.

But what if she is?

Slowly, she descended the stairs. Castillo's soft gaze rested on Maren's face, while O'Grady's eyes shifted away to stare at a point above Maren's head.

"She's not here," Maren said.

Castillo nodded. "We are sure we have Orli in police custody. We arrested her and two of her friends; a fourth teenager escaped arrest by fleeing the scene."

"What friends?" Maren asked. Her voice cracked, but she lifted her chin, gave Castillo her best cool newsreader stare.

"I can't tell you that, ma'am. Will you drive yourself to Richmond?"

She nodded once. "I just have to let my guests know I'll be absent for a while."

A movement to one side of the hall caught her eye, then Zoey emerged from the direction of the bathroom. How much had she heard?

Maren closed her eyes. Orli was her priority; she wouldn't waste time on Zoey.

"Is everything okay?" Zoey came across to where Maren stood and rested a hand on her arm. She wore her concerned, empathetic newsreader face, the one she pasted on whenever she had to report on a heartbreaking story. The expression that dropped like a final-act curtain once the cameras panned away from her.

"Fine." Maren let out a breath and relaxed her shoulders, summoned what she hoped was an easy smile. "Nothing major, but something I have to sort out. Please, return to enjoy your dinner."

Zoey's eyes raked her face, searching for the cracks. She mustn't have found any, as after a moment, she removed her hand. "Let me know if there's anything I can do." Her voice oozed false sympathy. "It's stressful when a child is involved."

"Everything's fine," Maren repeated. She turned back to the officers, shutting Zoey out, waiting until she heard the tap-tap of her retreating feet, and the soft thunk of the dining-room door closing. "I'll be a few minutes, but I'll meet you there."

O'Grady nodded. "That's fine, ma'am." The officers turned away to the front door.

Maren waited until they'd left, then sank onto the ottoman in the hallway. Her fingers trembled, and she clenched her fists to stop the movement. She sucked a breath, forcing herself to take the slow, deep breaths her yoga instructor insisted upon, then she rose and looked at herself in the mirror.

Wide, panicked eyes stared back at her, and she ran her palms over her hair, restoring her smooth, elegant bob. She smiled so it reached her eyes, then relaxed again. *Better*. After a final deep breath, she went to the kitchen to update Janelle, and then to the dining room to let her colleagues know she had to leave, that Janelle would look after them, and they should enjoy the rest of their meal. That she hoped to be back in time for coffee and liqueurs, but these things could take an annoyingly long time.

She brushed away Luka's and Ethan's genuine concern, and refused Zoey's offer to accompany her, "so you have someone to lean on."

Then, thanking her lucky stars she'd barely had any wine with dinner, she snatched up her car keys and went out to the garage.

CHAPTER 2
BREAD AND WATER

Nearly four hours later, Maren pressed her lips together as she stalked along the corridor of Richmond Police Station. Orli slouched by her side, hands stuck in the front pockets of her baggy jeans, hoodie covering most of her face. She had yet to say a direct word to Maren.

"Excuse me, Ms McEvoy." A young policeman approached. "There are some reporters outside. We didn't call them, but sometimes they listen to the police radio."

Or Zoey gave them the tip.

"You can't get to your car without going past them. Do you want me to call a taxi for you? It can collect you from the rear compound."

"Thank you. That would be kind," Maren said.

Orli huffed, and throwing her hood back, she mooched her way to the front entrance of the station.

"Orli!" Maren's voice was sharp. "We will leave through the back."

It was as if Orli was suddenly as deaf as her father's goldendoodle. She pressed the green button by the door, and it slid open.

Maren gritted her teeth. Of all the stupid, unthinking things to do. Orli should have known that Maren would want to keep this on the down-low, and out of the press. She hurried after her, catching up with her outside the security doors. And as Orli waved and gave a thumb-up to the press, grinning for the cameras as if she'd just won an Olympic medal, Maren realised that Orli had indeed known what Maren wanted.

Taking her daughter's arm, she tugged her toward her car, opened the passenger door and all but pushed her inside. Orli yanked her hoodie back up, slumped in the seat, and pulled out her phone.

Maren waited until they were driving along Punt Road before she spoke. "Why?"

Orli flicked her a glance. "Why not? I was bored."

"And stealing a car, endangering the public and yourself by driving over the speed limit, is a cure for boredom? Most people watch TV. You can't even drive."

Orli shrugged. "Obviously, I can. And I'm not 'most people'."

"You'll be very bored if you end up in juvenile detention."

A flash of worry crossed Orli's face. "But I won't, will I? Your rich-bitch lawyer friend will get me off."

"Helena might manage it, yes. Or the judge might want to make an example of you. Either way, it won't be pleasant. Even if you escape detention, you'll have bail, community service. Serious restrictions in your life."

"Yeah, yeah. That's just words. You got me out. You coulda bailed Raz, Eboni, and Leesh, too. Their parents aren't as rich as you."

"They're not my responsibility."

"Unlike me." Orli's voice held a bitter tinge. "I bet you wish you could have left me there—would have saved you having to *be responsible* for me."

Maren inhaled sharply as Orli's comment bit deep. "If that's what you think, you're wrong. You're my only child, and I love you deeply." She summoned a smile. "To the moon and back."

"I'm too old for that sentimental shit. I'm a woman, not a child."

"You're still a minor; if you want to be treated as an adult, you need to start acting like one." She reached out a hand and gripped Orli's knee. "We'll sort this out in the morning, but I'll be wanting some changes and promises from you."

Orli pressed her back against the door and stared out of the windscreen. "And do I get to ask the same of you?"

"Right now, I'm the one calling the shots." The illuminated clock on the dash ticked over to 2:00 a.m. "We'll talk about this in the morning. Over breakfast."

"Bread and water?"

"No, you can have your usual waffles, if that's what you want. Or something healthy for a change. But, Orli…" She waited until Orli turned to look at her. "We will talk, and you will give me answers and assurances."

There was no answer from the passenger seat. Maren pinched the bridge of her nose and wished hard for the night to end.

"Talk," Maren said.

Orli continued pretending to read the back of the waffle packet. "Yada, yada, yada."

"Very funny. Tell me exactly what you did last night."

"Nothing. The usual."

"The *usual*?" An ice block slithered down Maren's spine. "You're telling me stealing a car and nearly wrapping it around a lamppost is *usual* for you on a Saturday night?"

"Not every Saturday night. Sometimes, we just hang in the city." Orli shot her a defiant glance.

"And that would be the nights you tell me you're at Leesh's house? Studying."

"I don't study. And not at Leesh's house. Not often, anyway. Sometimes it's just me and Raz." She jammed two waffles into the toaster.

"And you steal cars?"

"Borrow," Orli said. "We only borrow them for a short time. Sometimes, we don't even go far. We just park up, smoke some weed."

Drugs. It was getting worse by the moment. "And where do Raz's, Leesh's, and Eboni's parents think they are?" She'd met them, of course she had, and they seemed decent people, parents who would know where their kids were.

"Here. They're delighted, of course, that their kids have made such a nice friend." She made finger guns at herself. "That's me, in case you're wondering. The lovely daughter of Australia's most famous newsreader, the popular Maren McEvoy."

"I'll be calling their parents. You're grounded, and you're not to have anything more to do with those kids." She glared at the sliced avocado and tomato she'd intended having on toast. Her stomach was churning like a washing machine; there was no way she'd keep anything down except coffee.

"Gonna be difficult when we sit together at school. What you gonna do? Tag around after me?" Orli hit her forehead with her palm. "Of course, you can't do that, as you'd have to take time off work to spend with your daughter."

Guilt slashed Maren like a knife through butter. She should have made more time for her daughter, but Orli always seemed so content. She had her friends—although not the good kids Maren had thought they were—her online chats, and she loved to read. Did she still do that? The pile of books in her room didn't seem to have changed much the past few months. "You could find yourself suspended from school. And you're not seeing your friends, full stop. Not in the evenings, not weekends. No more 'study sessions', no more hanging out in the city, and certainly no more weed. It's not legal for recreational use in Victoria, and you're too young even if it were. At least you didn't have it on you when you were arrested."

"Guess they didn't search the car properly."

Maren pressed her fingers to her temples where a headache threatened. "It's getting worse by the minute. You'll have to go to court, you know. It's anyone's guess if they'll put you in a youth justice centre. Anything else you want to tell me?"

Orli shook her head. For a moment, she stayed staring at the coil of smoke coming up from the toaster.

Maren held her tongue. Now was not the time to nag Orli about setting off the smoke alarms.

Orli turned to face her, and her eyes glistened with moisture. Her lips trembled and she pressed them together. "I won't go to jail, will I? I mean, your lawyer will get me off. All the rich kids get off. I'll just die if I have to go to prison."

Was it like this for every mother? The need to make things right for their kid, even when making it right was so very wrong? She bit back the automatic words that she'd do everything she could to keep Orli out of juvenile detention, that it was a first offence, nothing had gone terribly wrong, that it would be okay— *No.* Smoothing the path wasn't the best way forward here. That was the first step down a slippery slope. "It's called 'justice' for a reason. It may not be perfect, but it doesn't matter who the person is; people are judged on what they've done, not who they are."

A single tear trickled down Orli's nose and dripped off the end. "But you'll try to help me?"

Her heart expanded, and she took two steps and wrapped Orli in a tight hug. "Of course, I'll try. Everyone deserves a second chance. But there will have to be changes, Orli. Major ones. You're at a crossroads, and the choices you make now could affect the rest of your life."

Her daughter sniffed and wriggled to free herself.

Maren released her and stepped back, watching as Orli dashed at her eyes with the backs of her hands, then pulled the waffles from the toaster. Orli wrinkled her nose at the burnt edges and threw them in the bin, then reached for the packet again.

Maren watched, her heart alternately expanding with love and contracting with horror. Her daughter. How had it all gone so wrong?

And, what did she need to do to move past this?

"I'm pregnant." Orli stood in the doorway of Maren's bedroom two days later, arms folded across her chest.

"What?" For a few heartbeats, time stood still. Maren clutched the freshly ironed shirt in front of her and stared at Orli. She searched her memory for anything in the past few weeks which might have indicated a pregnancy but drew a blank. Orli had asked for tampons a few weeks ago—how many weeks? She couldn't remember. She ate well, looked in peak health. Maren's breath huffed in shallow waves. Her sixteen-year-old daughter, pregnant. So not what she'd hoped for her. Not at this stage of her life.

Orli's mouth curled up at one side. "I said, I'm pregnant. Aren't you going to congratulate me?"

"Who's the father?"

"Raz. I haven't told him yet."

"Your boyfriend?"

"Boyfriends are so last year. He's just someone I hook up with sometimes."

Maren closed her eyes. *No judgement.* "Okay. I guess the first question is: are you sure? When did you do a pregnancy test?"

"I haven't. But my period is nine days late. I'm never late."

"There could be other reasons for that. Worry, stress—"

"I'm chill. No worries in my life."

Maren laid the shirt on the bed, went over to Orli and held out her hand. "Come sit with me and talk."

For a moment, she thought Orli would sneer and turn away, but after a long second, she put her hand in Maren's and allowed herself to be led over to the bed where she flopped on her back on top of Maren's ironed shirt.

"Orli, you've been arrested, suspended from school, and have a court date next week. Pretty much anyone would be stressed in that situation."

"Not me. My vibe is chill." Orli rolled over and propped herself on one elbow and stared back, one eyebrow arched.

The expression was exactly like Marcus's. Questions and comments churned through Maren's mind: *You're too young for this. What about your future? Why didn't you use contraception?* She suppressed them all. Those weren't the immediate issues.

"Well, whatever your vibe is, the first thing is to do a pregnancy test. Whatever you decide to do, you'll need the result." She tugged her shirt out from underneath Orli. It was wrinkled, not the pristine look needed for national television. "I'll pick one up on my way to the studio."

"What, and have your adoring public speculate you're pregnant? Divorced from your husband and all? Oh, the scandal."

She shrugged. "Do you think that's important?"

"No, but you do."

The words cut deep. Orli was right, and a shaft of shame knifed Maren's gut. Even as she'd said the words, she'd wondered if anyone would recognise her, whether some fabricated story would be plastered over the internet. It had been hard enough suppressing the story of Orli's arrest, even though juveniles weren't supposed to be named.

"I'll cope," Maren said. "I'd say for you to buy your own, but of course you're grounded. But no bread and water—Janelle's cooking pasta tonight."

"Of course she is." Orli's voice was strangely flat, as if all the sneer and fight had drained out of her. "Sometimes, when we're eating at the kitchen table, and she's asking me about my day, I pretend *she's* my real mother."

The breath left Maren's chest as if she'd been slammed against a wall. The words hadn't been said to wound, more a statement of fact. And that was what hurt. She sucked a breath and waited until she could speak without her words shaking. "Janelle is a loving, caring, person. We're lucky to have her with us."

"You mean you're lucky." Again, that expressionless voice. "If she wasn't, you'd have to, y'know, parent me. Pretend to love me." Orli levered herself off the bed. "You'll be late for work. Buy the test or not; I don't care."

"I do love you, Orli. So very much. And you know that—I tell you most every day." She rested her hands on her daughter's arms, even as the bile sat thickly at the back of her throat. Did her daughter really hate her this much? Or was it the defiant words of a scared teenager? "And if you're pregnant, I'll help you decide what to do. And whatever your decision—*whatever* it is—I'll support you." She pulled Orli into a hug.

For a moment, Orli stood like a plank, hard and unyielding, then like a sapling in the wind, she leaned against Maren's shoulder with a sigh.

The clock on the wall ticked on. She'd be late at the studio. But there was no way she could leave now. She shifted her position to cradle Orli's head.

With a sniff, Orli pulled back. "Yeah, well, let's see if you'll support me when it comes down to it. Maybe Janelle will drive me to the abortion clinic or hold my hand while I'm in labour. Pretty words, but you haven't been here for me much lately." With a jerk, she tugged away from Maren's hands and stomped out of the bedroom.

The slam of her bedroom door echoed down the landing.

Maren's knees buckled, and she sat heavily on the bed. Tears pricked at the back of her eyes, and she pressed her palms to them so they didn't fall. Makeup wouldn't be happy if she appeared in the studio with puffy, red eyes.

For a moment, she thought of calling in sick, pleading an emergency. Ethan would understand. Hell, if this wasn't a family crisis, she didn't know what was. But the slamming of the door echoed in her head. Orli wouldn't be receptive to anything else tonight.

And she had a pregnancy test to purchase.

With a sigh, she pulled a fresh blouse from the wardrobe and donned it, before going downstairs to speak with Janelle.

CHAPTER 3
LINES ON A PLASTIC STICK

IT HAD BEEN HARD IN the studio to push thoughts of her daughter from her head. To banter with Luka, make the cross to Zoey in Federation Square, and keep the calm, professional façade she was known for. She thought she'd managed it, though.

"Are you okay, Maren?" Luka leaned across the console in a break. "You seem a bit on edge tonight. Is everything all right?"

Okay. Not so calm and professional then.

She pasted a fake smile on her face. "I'm fine. Everything's fine. I'm just tired."

Luka's eyes searched her face. "If you say so. Is Orli okay?"

She managed a shrug. "Is any sixteen-year-old ever okay? There's always drama in their lives."

"And Orli's more than most," he murmured. He knew about the arrest, of course. Zoey had seen to that, spreading the story around the studio under the guise of concern for Maren, and some papers had run guarded mentions without naming names. To Maren's charged gaze, it was obvious who they were referring to.

She managed an eyeroll at Luka. "Ain't that the truth, buster!"

He laughed. "Your American accent isn't getting any better."

Then the producer signalled they would be back on air, so she composed her professional face, and glanced at the teleprompter for the updates on the Minister of Foreign Affairs's visit to China.

Once home, Maren snuck into Orli's bedroom and left the pregnancy test on her bedside table. For a moment, she stood, watching her daughter. In sleep, Orli's face was softer, more child than woman.

How had it come to this?

She turned away. It was late. She needed sleep, because who knew what fresh horror tomorrow would bring?

Maren was on her third coffee of the morning when Orli appeared. Her dark hair stuck up in tufts, and she had pillow creases on her face.

Janelle rose from the table, murmuring something about needing to prepare the grocery order.

"Stay," Orli said. "You're as much my family as Mum is."

With an apologetic glance at Maren, Janelle subsided into her chair.

Maren summoned her composure and waited as Orli poured a coffee, and put waffles in the toaster, then grabbed butter and plum jam from the fridge. *Did you sleep well? It's a lovely morning. Have you got what you need for school?* Inane questions that had no part of this morning. Besides, the school had suspended Orli. Unless they allowed her back, Maren would have to arrange a private tutor.

Her heart slammed against her ribs. Whatever Orli said now, there would need to be changes, adaptations. A way forward found, one that would bring them closer together.

She already knew Orli wouldn't like it.

Orli threw a plastic stick on the counter. "Negative. You can start breathing again."

Negative. Thank god.

She closed her eyes for a second. "How do you feel about that?"

For a moment, Orli's tough façade cracked. "Relieved," she whispered. "I was so scared. I don't want to be a mother. Not now. Maybe not ever."

Maren rose and went to her, taking her in her arms. One part of her mind registered that this was the second time in twelve hours.

Before that, when had she hugged her daughter? Guilt shafted as she realised she couldn't remember.

"It's okay." She smoothed Orli's hair back from her forehead. "I've got you. I've always got you."

Orli sniffled and burrowed closer.

The door clicked shut as Janelle left them alone. Maren pressed a kiss to the top of Orli's head. There were still hard words to be said, and tough decisions to be made. Decisions that would surely catapult them back to their previous state of detente. But for now, it was just the two of them, mother and daughter, and the unbreakable, but oh so fragile, bond between them.

"It was negative, Marcus," Maren said. "Orli was obviously relieved." She pinched the bridge of her nose. "I'm in a holding pattern, wondering what the next crisis will be."

"Do you want me to come down?" Marcus asked. "Spend time with her? Talk with her? Oh, not as the big He-Man sweeping in"—he laughed self-deprecatingly—"but to take some of the pressure from you. It's times like these I feel doubly bad I'm not on the doorstep."

"It's up to you," Maren said. "But please talk with her. Right now, she's not listening to me. I'm trying to strike a balance between scaring her as to consequences and supporting her."

"I'll call her tomorrow. And you… How are you doing?"

"Not well." She sighed. "This…everything. Things Orli said…that I didn't want her around… That hurt. So much. And it's forced me to think hard about a few things. My career, mainly."

"Don't be hasty. Orli has two parents, even if I'm not close by. There's nothing that says you should sacrifice everything you've worked for because of our child."

She pictured him holding the phone, brown hair falling over his eyes, maybe biting a thumbnail. "There's nothing that says I must do that, but I feel I've failed her. For Orli's sake, I have to make some changes."

"I'll support you in whatever you decide," Marcus said. "Rick, too. He loves our troublesome daughter as well."

"You're lucky. You found a good man." She sighed. "I'll let you know, of course. I may need your help."

"What are ex-husbands for? You have it, Maren."

Ethan shuffled papers on his desk, then fixed his gaze on Maren.

She kept her newsreader easy smile on her face as she waited for his answer.

"And you're sure this is the best thing to do?" Ethan leaned forward. "A year's a long time in this industry. Right now, you're at the top of your game—in twelve months' time, who knows? Lots of eager, young things out there, lining up to take your place."

Like Zoey. This news would make her week.

She spread her hands on the desk. "I have to take that chance— I've given my career my all these last years, but it's been at the expense of Orli's wellbeing. That has to change—for her sake. I'm trusting that at the end of the year, I'll be able to slot back in."

Ethan's face softened. "There'll be a position, of course. If it were up to me, your existing one would be open for you, and this would simply be a career break. But the higher-ups will look at ratings, popularity of your successor, and so on."

She kept the smile fixed on her face. "Of course. I understand."

"It can only be for a year," Ethan warned. "Past that, you'd either have to formally apply to work from Sydney or resign."

"I understand. I'm hoping a year will be long enough to help Orli balance herself again."

"Maybe you can treat this break as an opportunity to reevaluate. Not that I want you to go, but you could court other offers. Many newsreaders move across to the current affairs programs. I've always thought you'd be a good fit for that."

"Maybe." That progression had been in the back of her mind, flickering away like a candle, for some time now. But the current affairs slots were even more tightly held than the lead newsreader ones.

"How is Orli taking this?" Ethan came around the desk and took the chair next to hers.

Maren sighed. "Not well, as you'd expect. But she has no choice. I have no choice. I need to take her away from Melbourne. Give her a fresh start where no one knows her. A new school."

"She'll aways be known as your daughter."

"There's nothing I can do about that. The hearing..." She hesitated, wondering if, despite their friendship, she should tell Ethan. She plunged on. "My lawyer friend, Helena, represented Orli. She was sentenced to a period of community service and nine months' probation—all her friends were." Maren heaved a breath. "She's completed her community service over the last three months, and I've applied to have her probation moved to New South Wales."

"She's lucky." Ethan looked down at his polished shoes. "It could have been worse. So, what's the plan?"

"I've bought a house in Suttons Bay, in southern Sydney. It's a quick settlement. We'll move in two weeks in mid-November so that it's close enough to the end of the school year that Orli needn't start school until the new school year in February. And, of course, Marcus and Rick live in inner Sydney. So, when Orli decides she can't stand me, she can stay with her father."

"And what will you do? You're not the type to go all hippy-dippy earth-parent. You can't watch Orli twenty-four hours a day."

"Marcus found the house for me, and from the photos I've seen, it needs a fair bit of work. I'll have to oversee that. Past that, I don't know. Lots of yoga maybe—I certainly need the calm. Right now, my priority is Orli. It has to be. I've left her alone for too long. Now I must show her she's the most important thing in my life. And hope she accepts it."

"Good luck," Ethan murmured. "You might need it."

CHAPTER 4

BEER AND HIGH-VIS UNDIES

THE CLIENT DISMOUNTED FROM JAC'S motorbike and straightened once both feet were on the ground. She swayed and grabbed Jac's shoulder. "Sorry. Motorbike legs must be like sea legs. I feel I should lean into the corners."

Jac removed her helmet, shook out her short curly hair, sweaty after the hot day, and took her client's helmet. "Many people say the same. Rubbery legs and euphoria are the most common reactions."

"Certainly that." The client—Eva—smiled back and raked a hand through her short, blonde hair. "I'm euphoric enough that it's worth even a severe case of bike-helmet hair."

Her hand remained on Jac's shoulder. It was hard to tell through the leather jacket, but she thought she felt a squeeze and a rub of the thumb. She'd noticed the queer vibes when she'd picked up Eva at her harbour-side accommodation, and had deflected her subtle flirting when they'd stopped for lunch at a cliff-top hotel at the midpoint of the motorbike tour.

The pressure on Jac's shoulder increased. When she glanced at Eva's face, her eyes held a sparkle that Jac would bet her bottle of Patron Anejo tequila wasn't entirely due to the thrill of swooping around the twisty roads north of Wollongong and over the Sea Cliff Bridge.

Eva's tongue touched her upper lip.

Jac's gaze followed. Eva was gorgeous and exuded the sort of hot MILF vibes that Jac loved. And she was obviously out and proud. Confident. And sexy as hell.

With a sigh, Jac turned around to the pannier to retrieve Eva's bag. The movement dislodged Eva's hand from Jac's shoulder. No matter how much Eva's eyes screamed "up all night and multiple orgasms", Jac just wasn't feeling it. Tonight, the prospect of beer and pool with her best mates was more appealing.

"I hope you enjoyed the day," she said. "I appreciate any review you care to leave. Please tell your friends."

Eva took the bag and hitched it over her shoulder. "I will. Thank you, Jac. You've turned my last day in Sydney into something to remember."

Here it comes. Jac settled her expression into her I'd-love-to-but-I-can't one.

"If you're free tonight, I'd like to take you out for dinner." A quick smile. "Breakfast, too, if you want."

She rested her hands on the fuel tank in front of her. "Any other time, I'd take you up on that offer. Both offers." She let her gaze drift in a lingering perusal of Eva's lean body, from mussed hair to sturdy boots, to soften the refusal. "But I'm sorry, I can't tonight."

Eva offered a wry smile. "I thought you'd say that, but you can't blame a woman for asking."

"Of course not. I appreciate the directness. But I really do have something on tonight. If you're back in Sydney again, I hope you'll take another bike tour with me."

"Count on it. Thanks, Jac." With a last smile, Eva turned away and took the steps to her hotel two at a time.

A pang of regret at turning down Eva's offer thrummed in Jac's chest. A hot, older woman, someone who knew what she wanted. Maybe she would have been the person to loosen the knot behind her ribs, the knot Talia had tightened when she'd left.

Jac started the bike and moved off into the slow-moving traffic. Rush hour was less of a problem on a motorbike, and soon she was flying over the Sydney Harbour Bridge, her concentration on the heavy traffic, but peripherally aware of the joy of the ride, and of

Sydney Harbour far below, ferries and yachts criss-crossing its blue water. She weaved in and out of traffic on the freeway, passing around the international airport and alongside Botany Bay until she turned off into the major suburb of Cronulla.

She pulled into a service station to fill the bike ready for the next day's tour. Leaving her helmet on the seat, she went to pay. She was halfway to the counter when she saw her. Jet-black hair twisted in a thick plait that hung nearly to her waist. A long-sleeve top and loose pants draped over her slight frame. Jac's feet dragged to a halt. For a second, she thought it was Talia standing there paying for her fuel, as if conjured by Jac's earlier thoughts. But Talia had moved away with her new husband, up to Port Macquarie. Jac took a step forward, and then the woman turned her head to say something to someone on her left.

Jac's breath froze in her lungs. *Talia.* And the person she was talking to, now handing her two cans of soft drink, must be her husband. The husband she'd married because her family had wanted it.

Talia and her husband conferred for a moment, then she finished paying for the fuel and turned to leave.

I can't let her see me. Jac ducked behind the display of lollies, and put her head down, staring unseeing at the packets of Minties and red liquorice. Out of the corner of her eye, she saw Talia and her husband walk out together and get into a compact sedan. They were laughing as they fastened their seatbelts before driving away.

Jac watched until the sedan turned onto the main road. She pressed her lips together. Talia's family lived in Cronulla—she must be down for a visit. Jac hunched her shoulders, remembering when Talia's visits hadn't only been to see her mum.

She went to the dairy cabinet and grabbed a litre of milk, then went to pay.

Talia wasn't her concern anymore. She hoped she was happy. It appeared so, but who really knew how other people's lives went? She certainly didn't.

She stowed the milk in the pannier and headed for home.

A few minutes later, she turned up her driveway, passing alongside her old brick house and on to the large shed at the rear.

Home. Her space.

Once she'd put the bike away, she entered the house, shedding her jacket, gloves, and other paraphernalia of the ride along the way. The black-and-white photo of her gran stared down at her from above the hall table. Her gran's wicked smile shone from under her curly hair, so like Jac's own.

Jac touched the photo with her fingertips. "Love you, Gran."

She continued along the hall, skirted the heavy, wooden furniture that had been her gran's, now swathed in bright material Jac had brought back from her backpacking trips to Asia. In the kitchen, she put the milk into the fridge. Low fat, she noticed with a grimace. She must have been distracted.

She looked longingly at the beer fridge. A beer would dull the shock of seeing Talia again, but she resisted. Soon, she'd be sharing beers with her besties, and that beat any solitary beer on her veranda.

Jac gripped her cue as Kyra lined up a shot. Out of the corner of her eye, she saw Liz creep up behind Kyra to grab her arse just as she hit the white ball. Kyra jerked, and her shot went wild, spinning around the table until, by chance, it nestled up against one of her striped balls.

"Lucky! Jac nearly got two shots," Liz said with a grin.

Kyra stuck her tongue out, watching Jac as she stalked around the table, picking her shot. She bent for a shot on the green, straightening with a jerk as Caitlin, beer in hand, sauntered up behind her.

"Don't even think about it." Jac thumped the cue on the floor. "I don't want beer on this shirt."

Caitlin arched an eyebrow. "Would I?"

"Of course, you would." Jac waited until Caitlin had stepped back before she lined up her shot once more. As she drew the cue back, a splash of cold liquid hit her bare back below the T-shirt. But this was an old trick, and the green ball fell into the pocket.

"Bitch." She rolled her eyes at Caitlin, who flicked the beer from her fingers.

"Didn't put you off, though. I'll make it half the schooner next time."

Eventually, and with many distractions and interruptions, Jac and Liz won the game, and the four of them retired to their usual table in the corner to order food and drink more beer.

"Anyone got anything to share from the wild world of lesbian dating?" Kyra asked. "I'll go first: no. Not a cracker. I'm the epitome of the invisible middle-aged woman. If I walked down Pitt Street in my undies, no one would notice."

"I'd see you," Jac said. "Especially if you were wearing those high-vis boxer shorts. You could see them from the space station."

"Still wouldn't improve my chances." Kyra took a mouthful of beer. "What's a forty-four-year-old butch got to do to pull around here? Metaphorically speaking. You all are not my types."

"That's not what you said when we went to Canberra to watch the soccer. The time the motel stuffed up and gave us a room with one queen bed," Caitlin said.

"I was drunk!"

"So was I. Lucky we stopped at kissing," Catlin said.

They looked at each other for a long moment.

"Would have been a bad, bad thing—" Kyra said.

"—If we'd fucked," Caitlin added.

Their laughter mingled in the high-ceilinged bar.

"I got hit on today by my customer," Jac said. "Is that news?"

"Not really." Liz propped her elbows on the table. "It seems every other one does that. But as you're here and not in some hotel room, I guess you turned her down. As usual."

Caitlin touched her arm. "Were you tempted? At all?"

Jac sighed. "She was gorgeous. Maybe mid-forties, and I'd definitely have noticed her walking down the street, even without high-vis undies."

"Not helping," Kyra muttered.

"Sorry." Jac rubbed Kyra's arm, and her beer spilled on the table.

"Still not helping. You should give me lessons in general flirtiness. I don't know if a woman's interested in me or if she just likes my shirt."

"It's been a few years since you came out," Liz said. "Haven't you got the hang of it yet?"

"There isn't an app that records their responses and tells me if they realise I'm flirting. Not yet, anyway. Caitlin should develop one."

"Programming databases is a long way from app development. You'd be better off following Jac around for an evening." Caitlin raised her glass in salute to Jac.

"Tried that. They climbed over me to get to her." Kyra threw up her hands. "I'm doomed."

"So, your perfect fling flung herself at you today and you turned her down." Caitlin propped her chin on her hand and stared at Jac. "One day, Jac, one day soon, you're going to shove Talia back in the closet where she belongs and get yourself out there again."

"I saw her today," Jac said. "Talia. In the servo. With her husband."

Everyone turned to stare at her.

"What did you do?" Liz asked.

"I hid." Jac stared down at her beer. "What could I do? What could I say? I doubt her husband knows she dated a woman—so what purpose would it serve to approach her except to stress Talia that I was going to out her?"

"You didn't do that in the two years you were dating," Kyra said. "Why would you do it now? You're not that kind of person."

"I know." Jac's face slackened, as if all feeling and expression had drained away. "But still. It was…unsettling."

"The next hot MILF who propositions you," Caitlin said, "promise us you'll at least think about it?"

"And if you don't, then give her my phone number," Kyra added.

Their laughter snapped Jac's apathy, and she smiled and nudged Kyra with her shoulder.

"It's not dating news, but I do have something interesting," Liz said. "Guess which celebrity goddess has moved to southern Sydney?"

"Cate Blanchett? Margo Robbie?" Jac asked.

"Not that great, but all the same, she's a sapphic fantasy. Think dark hair, elegant figure. Seen every night on Channel 12 purring into the camera, making the share market report sound like an invitation to dinner and after."

Kyra's eyes opened wide. "Not Maren McEvoy?" She fanned herself with a drink coaster. "Holy hotness, girlfriends, if she's moving here, she's all mine."

"Better buy those high-vis undies in bulk," Jac said. "But why would Maren McEvoy move here and not somewhere in inner Sydney with glitz and glamour?"

"No idea," Liz said, "But I read it online this morning."

"Must be true then," Caitlin muttered.

Kyra elbowed her in the ribs. "Don't destroy my fantasy. She's around the same age as me. We're a match made in heaven."

"Except she is—was—married to that rugby player, Marcus someone, so it's likely she's straight," Caitlin said.

"A butch can dream." Kyra flapped the coaster faster.

"Maybe she's bought the house next to you, Jac," Caitlin said. "Didn't you say the sold sign went up a couple of weeks ago?"

"Dream on." Jac snorted. "If 'Australia's most popular newsreader'"—she made air quotes—"has bought next door to me, then she's in for a shock. She won't be prancing over a manicured lawn for cocktails and canapés by the pool. More like pushing through my jungle for a beer on the deck with a bag of cheese-and-onion chips."

"The house is lovely, though, just old-fashioned," Liz said. "I remember when we went to the open for inspection for a stickybeak. It could be her sort of thing." She grinned. "As long as she loves the sound of motorbikes in the morning."

"It won't be Maren McEvoy," Jac said. "The moving truck arrived a couple of days ago, but I've seen no one yet. My new neighbours will be rich hipsters with two kids who don't look up from their mobile phones, and a golden retriever which never gets walked and barks all day. Who else can afford to buy a house in Sydney these days?"

"Don't be such a cynic." Caitlin nudged her hard enough to make the beer slop over her glass. "Until you meet those hipsters, I'm going to assume your new neighbour is Maren McEvoy."

"Not sure that would be any better," Jac said. "She'd probably try to shut down my business."

"Well, when you get to the neighbourly drinks on the deck, you are totally inviting all of us," Kyra said.

"Sure." Jac laughed. "The hipsters will love you, hi-vis undies and all."

CHAPTER 5

WHAT TO DO WITH THE RICE COOKER AND THE SULKY DAUGHTER

DESPITE HAVING MOVED IN OVER a week ago, the house was still disorganised, with cartons stacked everywhere, and the pots and pans still in boxes on the floor. At least the bedrooms were set up, and Janelle, who was a whiz with electronics, had got the TV and internet going.

Maren stared at the screen where Luka and Zoey were wrapping up the six o'clock news hour. Zoey made a perfect rectangle from the papers in front of her and tapped them on the desk, smiling at Luka as they exchanged the customary scripted banter. She looked relaxed in the anchor seat, and the chemistry with Luka worked. But Luka was a golden-retriever of a bloke—he got along with anyone.

There goes my job. Maren's mouth pressed into a thin line. Not that she wanted Zoey to fail, but despite what Ethan had said, she was counting on stepping back into her role in a year's time.

She turned from the screen and went back to the kitchen, where Janelle was staring at the kitchen cupboards.

"There is no way all this"—Janelle waved at the dozen boxes on the counter—"will go into those few cupboards."

She was right. Maren mentally added "kitchen renovation" to the list of things she needed to do to make the house work for them. Right behind "resurface driveway" and "pest control" for the wasps' nest under the eaves. She slung an arm around Janelle's shoulders. "Unpack what you can. The essentials. I'll figure out the rest in time."

"I'll stick a list of local takeaways to the fridge," Janelle said. "Unless 'learn to cook' is on your to-do list, you won't need much in the way of kitchen gadgets once I leave."

"Maybe you could teach me in the weeks you're here?"

"Maybe. But that wasn't on our list of priorities." Janelle rolled her eyes at the loud, thumping music coming from Orli's room. "Maybe add, 'better soundproofing' to that list."

Maren squeezed Janelle's shoulder and released her. "Have I said how grateful I am you agreed to give us these weeks to help Orli settle in? I'm sure if it was just us, the homicide squad would be breaking down the door. Although whether to arrest her or me, I'm not sure."

"You'll get there." Janelle turned back to the boxes and lifted out the rice cooker and air fryer and set them on the counter. "And it's no problem. I'm happy to stay the extra time."

"And delay your world cruise."

"The world will still be here in six weeks' time. I hope."

"Come back anytime," Maren said. "While we're here in Sydney, when we move back to Melbourne. There's always a place for you with us."

Janelle's rather stern face softened. "I know. And thank you. But my sister and I have wanted to do this for a long, long time. But it's not good-bye. We'll stay in touch."

The sound of a door crashing back came from the end of the house, and stomping feet, as if the Australian army was on the march, came along the corridor. Then Orli stood glowering in the kitchen doorway. "This place is a shithole, and I'm totally, like, bored and we've only been here, like, a week. How am I going to spend the rest of my life here? I'll die. Even convicted killers are allowed friends."

"Not the rest of your life." Maren clenched the countertop with both hands and managed to keep her voice even. "Just a year. And you'll make friends when you start school, if not before."

"That's months away—"

"Just over two."

"—and the only people I've seen here are, like, eighty."

"Not true. And even if it were, maybe they'd have grandkids."

"If we had to move to Sydney, why couldn't we have gone somewhere like Bondi or Newtown? Or near Dad and Rick. At least they live somewhere that's not totally dead."

"You know why, Orli. Suttons Bay is thirty minutes from your dad, near the beach, and forty minutes from the centre of Sydney by bus. You're hardly in the outback."

"Feels like it." Orli hunched her shoulders. "What am I supposed to do all day?"

"You always wanted to learn to surf. The beach is ten minutes away. We can look into a surf school."

"And the other twenty-three hours?"

"The amount you sleep and eat that shouldn't be a problem," Janelle said.

"Get ahead of next year's schoolwork," Maren suggested. Even as the words left her mouth, she knew they were the wrong thing to say—even if true.

"What's the point?" Orli sneered. "Maybe I'll leave school. You can at sixteen. Or maybe I'll find some bogan kid with a big dick and get pregnant."

Maren forced herself to breathe normally. This was Orli intentionally trying to hurt her. Maren had seen the fear in her eyes when she'd thought she might be pregnant. She was just lashing out.

"Or you can stay in school, decide what you want to do with that gigantic brain of yours and get yourself a decent life," Janelle said. "It's not all terrible, hen." She came around the counter and swept Orli up in a hug.

Orli sniffled into her shoulder. "It's just so boring here."

"Give it time. It takes a while to settle somewhere new."

A stab of something twinged in Maren's chest. Jealousy, she realised. Orli talked to Janelle, allowed her hugs. Why couldn't she be more like that with Maren?

Janelle met her eyes over Orli's head. Rueful, sad. Carefully, she released Orli. "Maren and I are going to make biscuits. Your favourite—white chocolate and macadamia. Want to help?"

"I'm not six," Orli muttered, but her lips lifted in a tiny smile. "Guess I'll sort out my room."

"Decide what colour you'd like it painted, then we can choose new bedding for you," Maren said.

"I need new sneakers." Orli kicked the bottom of the counter.

"We can get them too."

Her daughter's back bristled as she stalked out of the room.

Maren turned to Janelle. "She's so angry. What if I've made the wrong decision bringing her here? Maybe I should have bought somewhere closer to the centre of Sydney. But I thought she'd be less likely to get into trouble here."

"That one'd find trouble in the middle of the outback."

"Maybe the inner city would have been a better choice."

Janelle rubbed her arm. "Time will tell. But, for what it's worth, I think you've made the right one."

Later that evening, Maren sat on the back deck with a gin and tonic. Janelle had gone to visit an old friend, and Orli had declined the offer to go out for ice cream and was now sulking in her room.

Maren took a sip of her drink and looked across the overgrown garden. Grevilleas, kangaroo paw, and a climbing purple vine mixed with old rosebushes, a few windblown flowers still clinging to the bush. Weeds choked the entire garden. She added "find gardener" to her mental list.

Lights from the house next door shone through the line of lilly pilly on the boundary. The highset house was older than hers, built of yellow brick. The block was large, but nearly as overgrown. Patchy lawn surrounded the house, and there was a tarmac area in front of a large double-bay shed at the rear. Obviously, there was no point asking her neighbour for recommendations for a gardener.

As she looked, a figure came out on the upper deck and leaned on the railing. The person lifted a bottle of something to their lips. The moonlight showed a trim figure with short hair. A woman? Maybe.

Maren sipped her own drink. She should call Marcus, vent about Orli, maybe ask his advice. Certainly, he and Rick would have ideas for entertaining a sulky teen during the holidays.

Right now, though, she was content to sit and listen to the night. Sip a rather fine gin and tonic and try to push her worries about Orli from her mind.

The move was done. And for the next year, they had to make the best of it. Rebuild what she'd lost with her daughter while she'd focussed on her career. Encourage Orli to find a fresh path, one that didn't lead to jail. Show her she was loved, no matter what.

And then? When the year was over? She didn't have a clue.

CHAPTER 6
LATE AT NIGHT

THE MORNING SUN WARMED JAC'S shoulders as she ambled down to her workshop to get the Honda Goldwing ready for the next day's booking. She reached the shed and stopped. The sliding door was open a few centimetres—just as it had been two days prior. Then, she'd figured she hadn't closed it properly—the door was heavy and if she didn't get it just so, it would stick—but this time, she knew she'd shut it all the way across. She glanced around the surrounds. Nothing appeared out of place. Her small sedan was still parked next to the shed, and the overgrown planter boxes were the same as ever.

She yanked the shed door hard, and it slid all the way open. Her three motorbikes waited under their dust covers. The Goldwing on the left, the BMW in the middle, the vintage Norton on the right. Jac flicked on the light. Nothing seemed amiss, although her nerves jangled like a badly tuned piano. A thief would have gone for one of the valuable bikes, or the power tools that were neatly arranged on the side wall. But they were all in place.

Maybe a homeless person seeking shelter had looked around, or an opportunist-would-be-thief who hadn't recognised the worth of the bikes. Her glance fell on the chest freezer against the back wall. Yesterday, she'd left cleaning clothes and the seat cover for the Goldwing on top, ready to wash them. Now, they were pushed aside, as if someone had looked inside the freezer.

She went across. Sure enough, on the dusty concrete, a couple of footprints showed. Not her own motorbike boots with their distinctive tread, but the narrow tread of a sneaker or running shoe.

The inside of the freezer seemed undisturbed, her bulk meat still in place.

Why would someone prowl around her sheds, but not take anything? Even the most unobservant of thieves would have found something worth stealing.

She should buy a padlock for the door. And she should also take Liz's advice and get a security camera. She'd take a trip to the hardware later and get both. If someone was prowling around regularly, she needed to stop them as soon as possible.

A couple of nights later, the phone alert jerked Jac out of sleep. For a moment, she didn't recognise the sound, then the bright screen of her phone caught her eye. She picked it up and looked at it. Almost two in the morning. The screen flashed an alert for the security camera she'd installed at her shed. Heart pounding, she flicked over to the camera feed.

The shed was in darkness, but she could clearly see a light bobbing around. A beam of light flashed over the Goldwing at the front of the shed ready for her client. Jac clenched the phone. Was this a vandal, about to graffiti her bike, or tip sugar in the fuel tank? Or just knock it over, doing expensive damage?

She should call the police. Her finger hovered over the call button, but then the intruder moved the torch and their face was briefly illuminated. Jac caught her breath. The person was young, short hair mostly hidden by a hoodie. She hesitated. Call the police or not? The obvious thing—the sensible thing—was to dial triple zero and report an intruder. But what if it was a young person, homeless maybe? An arrest wouldn't help them. And so far, she'd seen no damage or anything missing.

Jac swung her legs out of bed and reached for her shorts. She left on the oversize T-shirt she slept in and thrust her feet into runners.

She stole out of the house, pausing only to pick up a thick chunk of timber that she hoped she wouldn't need.

The sliding door of the shed yawned open. Inside, the torchlight bobbed, then steadied. The intruder appeared to be looking at the Norton.

With a deep breath, Jac gripped the timber, stepped inside, and turned the light on.

A crash echoed, followed by, "Oh shit!"

The young person she'd seen on the security camera turned to her, eyes wide in a white face under the hoodie.

Jac glanced around. The crash seemed to have been one of her bike helmets falling to the ground. Her lips tightened. She'd need to get it checked over—lucky it was an old one. "Got an explanation for why you're here?" She made her voice dark and menacing.

"Uh, I'm sorry. But I'm not doing any harm. Just looking around." A girl, going by the voice.

"You're trespassing. And it's not the first time."

"You didn't lock the shed."

Jac cursed the fact that she hadn't installed a padlock on the sliding door. "That's no excuse. You shouldn't be here in the first place."

"You're a business, right?" A flash of belligerence, and the teen pushed her hands into the front pocket of her jeans. "Businesses welcome customers."

"Not at 2:00 am. Not unaccompanied. This is a workshop, not a lingerie store." Her gaze wandered up and down the teen. Tall, lanky body, wearing baggy jeans and a shapeless hoodie, but her sneakers were an expensive brand, and the clothes were clean, apart from a smear of dirt she'd probably got brushing against something in the shed. So most likely not a homeless person then. But that didn't mean she wasn't in trouble and running from something. Or just trouble. "I could call the police. Lock you in here while we wait for them. Or you could give me a sensible answer."

A flash of something—fear perhaps—came and went on the girl's face.

"Let's start with your name."

"Orli." A mutter.

Jac frowned. "Like the airport in Paris?"

"Spelled different. With an 'I' not a 'Y'."

"Okay, Orli-with-an-I. Can you push that hoodie back so I can see who I'm talking to?" Jac set down the timber she'd been holding. Her gut told her Orli wasn't a threat. What she was, she still needed to find out.

Orli lowered the hood to reveal a pale face, grey eyes, and short, dark hair mussed from the hoodie.

"How old are you?" Jac leaned against some crates and crossed her legs at the ankle.

"Sixteen."

She looked older. Maybe it was the bristling attitude.

"And the real reason you're in my shed?" She didn't see any spray paint cans or anything to suggest vandalism.

Orli shrugged. "I'm bored. Your shed has, like, cool things to look at. Do you know there's a black snake in the back corner under the tarp? I left it alone. It doesn't bother me."

She hadn't known, but with the overgrown garden and the bush reserve behind, she wasn't surprised.

"What else?"

"I like your bikes. A Norton. I googled it. That's a cool bike. When was it made?"

"1973." It was a cool bike, and her favourite.

"That must be worth a bit."

Jac shrugged. It was, but she wasn't about to tell Orli that, in case the bike went missing. "Do you live somewhere?" she asked instead.

"Of course." Orli frowned.

"It's not a given," Jac said gently. "Plenty of kids have nowhere to go, or a bad situation at home. Is that you?"

A silence while Orli looked at her feet.

"The truth."

"I live next door. My mum and I just moved in. And she's boring and doesn't trust me, but it's not *bad* bad, as you mean it."

"Does she know you're out now?"

An abrupt laugh. "What do you think? I just sneak out the back door."

Strange kid, all prickles and defence. "So, you can get back the same way?" At her nod, she continued, "Well Orli-who-lives-next-door, you don't seem to have done any damage, so I won't call the police."

Orli's shoulders dropped and some of the tightness left her body. "Thanks."

"But if you come back, I will. Okay? I can't have you prowling around my workshop any more than you can have me prowling around your house in the middle of the night."

"Will you tell my mum?"

Jac considered. Would she? It was the responsible thing to do. Most parents would want to know if their kid was roaming around, breaking into buildings. But she wasn't sure if telling Orli's mother was the way to go here. If the woman was as boring and untrusting as Orli said, telling her wouldn't help. Jac snorted. Seemed the mother was right not to trust her daughter. "Not this time. But if I catch you again or you show up on my security cameras, then I'll be next door for a visit with your mother, right before I call the police. Got that?"

"Yeah. I'll go home now."

"That's a good idea." Jac stood aside so that Orli could leave. She'd expected her to leave down the driveway to the road, but her slouching figure mooched off into the overgrown area between the two houses. Her phone torch bobbed its way through the bushes, then stopped and pointed at the ground.

Jac waited to see if she called out, but after a minute she moved on again. What was so interesting there? Jac remained still, catching flashes of the torch through the thick vegetation as Orli made her way back to the dark house. Another couple of minutes, and a light came on in a room at the back. The kid must be home.

Jac went back to her own house. It was now two-thirty, and she had to be up in four hours to get ready for the next day's booking—Roy, an elderly nursing-home resident who was one of her regulars. She yawned. What a strange kid Orli was. Defensive, belligerent, but somehow vulnerable as well. If her family were her new neighbours, well, she supposed she'd find out about them soon enough.

CHAPTER 7
GARDENING IS NOT ALL ROSES

As ALWAYS, ROY'S TRIP WAS pure fun. He was too frail to ride pillion on the normal bikes, but the armchair-like seating of the Goldwing kept him safe. Jac took him through Royal National Park, and to a quiet pub near the beach where they had a break. She turned a blind eye to his beer and peanuts—both forbidden in the nursing home—before they rode back. His whoops of delight over the Bluetooth headset as they cruised across the Harbour Bridge on the Goldwing never failed to make her smile.

She handed him back to the care of a smiling nurse, then rode home. She put the bike away, settled the dust cover over it, and left the shed. She looked across at next door. Now that she knew where to look, the narrow path of trampled vegetation—the way Orli had gone home last night—was obvious. What had the kid been looking at? Probably nothing. But it wouldn't hurt to check. Treading carefully, she followed the winding trail around bushes, ducking under spider webs, and avoiding the worst patches of spiky grass seeds. She needed to attack this jungle and turn it back into a garden.

Jac pushed on until a circle of brown dirt where the ground had been disturbed caught her eye. She bent to look. A dozen small seedlings stuck up from the earth. There was no mistaking what they were. Jac tightened her lips. She had no issue with people smoking weed— even though it was illegal for recreational use in New South Wales—

but she had a huge problem with someone growing it on her land, where she would be the one to get prosecuted and fined if discovered.

A few quick yanks, and then she crushed the plants in her hand. She hesitated, staring at the house next door. This wasn't something she could let go. Jac continued along the trampled path, coming out in her neighbour's overgrown back yard. She found a cracked concrete path and followed it around the side of the house to the front door.

She pressed the bell and waited. Soft music played, but no one answered. She rang again, holding the buzzer for longer.

"It's okay, Janelle, I've got it." Footsteps sounded, and then the door was pulled open. "Hi."

Hi indeed. Dark hair in a chin-length bob framed an oval face with clear grey eyes. The woman wore faded jeans and a white T-shirt tucked in on one side. Bare feet. No makeup. Even without Orli there for comparison, this was obviously her mother. And it was equally obvious this was Maren McEvoy, Australia's favourite newsreader. Jac's lips twitched. Kyra would lose her shit over this and when she heard about it, she'd be camping on Jac's veranda with a pair of binoculars.

Jac sucked a shuddery breath. How would Maren McEvoy take to being told her daughter was growing weed and trespassing in the middle of the night? Guess she was just about to find out.

"Hi, I'm Jacinta Fowler, your neighbour. I live there." She jerked a thumb toward her house.

Maren inclined her head and smiled a gracious meet-the-public smile. "It's nice to meet you, Jacinta. I'm Maren McEvoy. I've just moved here from Melbourne with my daughter."

Jac shuffled her feet. Maren's poise and outward friendliness were disarming. Jac steeled herself. Maren held celebrity status in Australia—although would that fade now she was no longer doing the news? That was a puzzle for another day. Right now, Jac had to focus, not get distracted by Maren's superficial friendliness. "Actually, I've already met your daughter."

"Oh?" Maren's smooth brow wrinkled momentarily. "I wasn't aware."

"No, I'm sure you're not." She grasped for the words she had to say. "Look, can I come in? I have things to say that are better not said outside on your porch."

Maren hesitated. "Why don't we sit here?" She indicated a setting of a low table and four chairs on the front deck.

Jac shrugged. "If that's what you want. Is Orli home?"

A nod. Maren's outward friendliness was evaporating fast, a protective mama-bear wall going up brick by brick. This wasn't going to be easy. Maren waved again at the chairs, and Jac moved across to sit. There was no offer of tea or a cold drink.

She waited until Maren had sat as well before she dropped the crumpled handful of marijuana seedlings on the table. "Do you know what these are?"

Maren leaned forward to look, then sat back. "Of course. I'd appreciate if you'd remove them from my property. I'm not interested."

Jac left them there. "I'm sorry, Maren, this will not be a pleasant conversation. Last night, I met your daughter. She was trespassing in my workshop in the middle of the night—and it wasn't the first time. She didn't do any damage, and I agreed not to involve the police, as long as she didn't do it again."

She glanced at Maren. Her face was a stone mask, blank, giving nothing away, but her eyes bored holes in Jac's face.

"This morning, I followed the path Orli took to return to your house, and I found those, obviously deliberately and recently planted in a small patch of cleared ground on *my* land."

Maren gasped and for a second, a look of worry flashed across her face.

"Yes, *my* land, not yours. Orli obviously knows that if the crop is discovered, the police will first look to blame the landowner."

"What are you going to do?" Maren asked in a low voice. "She's only sixteen."

"Old enough to know growing weed is illegal. Old enough to know not to do it on your land. I should go to the police."

"She's *sixteen*, Jacinta."

Jac forced her shoulders to relax. "I realise that. I made allowances for her...last night...and she promised not to enter my shed again.

But I'm not sure I should overlook this." She leaned forward, resting her elbows on her thighs. "I don't use marijuana, but I have no issue with adults smoking weed. I'm sure Australia will eventually make it legal. Orli is sixteen though. I also question why she planted a dozen seedlings. Is she planning on dealing?"

Maren looked away. Her face was a glacial shade of pale. Her mouth opened, then closed. She squared her shoulders and looked Jac in the eye. "How do I know you're not the one growing the weed, and Orli discovered it? Maybe you're trying to wriggle off the hook, forestall *me* going to the police. Growing an illegal crop is one thing, knowingly planting it where a minor could stumble across it is another."

Jac raked her hand through her hair. "I have CCTV footage of Orli in my shed. Both of our properties are overgrown near the boundary. If you beat your way through your backyard, you'll see the trampled path where Orli has pushed through. You'll see the cleared area where these seedlings came from. And you'll see the trampled path continue onto my land. The path is more used on your side. If I was the one growing it, you'd expect there to be a better-used path on my side. Come and see for yourself." She offered a tight-lipped smile. "I won't have you arrested for trespassing."

Maren stood and paced over to the railing and gripped it with both hands.

"Or maybe we could both talk to Orli—before the police do," Jac said.

Maren's shoulders hunched, and tension shimmered around her body.

"Look..." Jac tried for a softer tone. "I've seen you on TV and I know who you are. I didn't know you were Orli's mother, though, until just now. You probably want to keep this out of the news. I'm not a mother, so I don't know how serious you consider this. I don't know if Orli's a good kid who's struggling to adapt to a new city, or if she's a hellion on her way to a lifetime in jail. What I want is for my property to be left alone. I don't want to find my bikes vandalised, my sheds covered in graffiti, or a meth lab on my boundary."

Maren snorted. "You've formed a low opinion of my daughter very quickly."

"She was difficult and argumentative in the middle of last night. That's all I have to go on. All the same, I accepted her word she'd leave my property alone. Seems that trust was misplaced."

"I'll send her around to apologise to you properly and ensure she stays away from now on. I'll also hire someone to tame the wilderness between our houses. If you want your side done, I'm happy to pay for that." She lifted her chin. "If all that is done, will you consider giving her another chance?"

Jac hesitated. Was this an entitled mother flashing money to get her daughter out of trouble? Or a new neighbour, genuinely apologetic, smoothing the path to cordial relations? Orli's narrow face flashed into her mind. The kid had been belligerent, rude, and argumentative. But behind the front, Jac was sure she'd seen a touch of insecurity. The kid had been dragged up from Melbourne, and, it seemed, left to fend for herself.

Maren licked her lips, and the movement snapped Jac's gaze to her. She focussed upward on Maren's clear eyes.

"That came out wrong," Maren said. "I didn't mean to sound as if I was buying Orli's way out of trouble. I was going to get the garden tidied anyway, and I'm happy to include your side, especially as Orli did some creative gardening of her own."

"Maybe you could redirect her to tomatoes," Jac said. "Seeing as she has a green thumb and all."

Maren laughed, a low, husky sound that sent a ripple down Jac's spine. It was one thing hearing Maren laugh on TV with her co-presenter; in person, the sound was deeper, more intimate. More sensual.

"The move from Melbourne is for Orli's benefit. To be closer to her father. She's been a bit rudderless in Melbourne. Didn't make the best friend choices."

Jac frowned. Was Maren being overprotective? Or was there a valid reason for policing Orli's friends? She flicked the thought from her mind. *Not my problem.*

"I've taken a leave of absence from work to focus on Orli. TV is a swamp. It pulls you in, takes a bit more from you every day, and then sucks you down. It's not fair to her. I'm not telling you what to do"—her eyes shot icy sparks—"but I am asking you to consider giving a teen who's had a hard time lately, a chance."

Jac smoothed her jeans over her thighs and longed for a drink of water. It was distracting, having the face she'd seen many evenings on TV focussed on her. And while she'd thought Maren appealing on TV, in the flesh, she was more intense, still like a pool of cool, clear water. Jac hunched her shoulders. It wasn't like her to be so fanciful. But she'd give Orli another chance. She had done no damage, after all. And Jac had got rid of the marijuana before anyone else had found it. Sixteen was a turbulent time for kids—heaven knows, she'd been no angel at that age.

"Thank you. I'll accept the offer of taming my side of the boundary over to the driveway. I won't report this. But I'd like an apology from Orli herself and another assurance she won't repeat this. I'll leave the security camera in my shed, though."

Maren's shoulders dropped a centimetre and her eyes closed for a moment. *So, not so cool and calm then.*

"I'll send her around later today. After I've talked with her. Thank you, Jacinta."

"Please call me Jac. Everyone else does."

"Jac, then." A flash of a smile. "I appreciate your understanding. I hope once things have settled down, we'll be able to see our way past this and get to know each other as neighbours."

She settled for a nod. It was too early to agree to that. First, she had to be sure Orli would not cause more trouble. She stood. "I should get back, and no doubt you've got things to do."

Maren stood as well. "Unpacking." She grimaced. "I'll let you know when the garden cleanup crew are coming."

Jac stood for a moment, taking in Maren's slim figure, hands pushed into the front pockets of her jeans, her narrow hips, lean thighs. "See you around."

She took the steps two at a time, without looking back.

CHAPTER 8
GERMINATION

MAREN BLEW OUT A BREATH as she watched Jac descend the steps. The nervous tension that had swamped her when Jac had thrown down the marijuana seedlings still jumped in her throat like a frog in a sack. The wilting plants lay on the table. She'd have to get rid of them.

She poked them. The slender green shoots were young, but even so, Orli must have germinated them in Melbourne and brought tiny seedlings in the car with her to Sydney. That took serious planning. Maren pinched the bridge of her nose. Already, the thought of the talk she had to have with her daughter had her stomach wound in knots. She huffed a laugh; if anyone could see her now, her calm reputation would be shot to smithereens.

A noise behind her made her turn.

"I heard voices." Janelle stepped out onto the deck in cotton shorts and a loose top. "Everything okay? I didn't want to interrupt."

"Let's just say I've had better days."

"I've got coffee on. Come inside and have a cup." She glanced at the seedlings. "Are those what I think they are?"

Once she was sitting with Janelle at the counter, Maren wrapped her hands around the mug and related what Jac had said. "Orli told Jac she wouldn't trespass again. She neglected to mention she was using her land for her growing dope." She shook her head, but the headache blooming behind her eyes persisted. "How can I trust her now? I thought she'd learned her lesson in Melbourne. That she'd take advantage of a fresh start here. We've been here, what, ten days, and she's already committed two acts that would breach her probation. Does she not realise the trouble she could be in—or does she not care?"

Janelle shook her head. "I don't know the answer to that. But it's obvious she's bored. Staying in her room all day and then roaming around at night."

"She's not the sort of kid who likes structured time," Maren said. "I could send her to surf school, horse riding classes, sign her up to volunteer at the library, but she just skips out of anything she doesn't want to do. At least she did her court-ordered community service in Melbourne."

"She's going to Marcus and Rick's house next weekend?"

"Yeah. Maybe inner Sydney would have been a better choice after all."

"Where she'd be able to get herself into worse trouble than this. You have to let that idea go, Maren. Orli has the best of both worlds here. Space, and the city a bus ride away."

The deep growl of an engine cut through their conversation. Through the side window, a massive motorbike, all shiny maroon paintwork and chrome, rumbled down Jac's driveway. Maren couldn't make out the rider's face behind their full-face helmet, but the wiry body, encased in leather, was obviously Jac. For a moment, she wondered if Jac lived alone. She'd seen no one else there, but it wasn't as if she'd been paying much attention. Until now.

The bike paused at the end of the drive, then turned left, accelerating smoothly up the road. Maren followed it with her gaze until it disappeared out of sight. That was some transport. She must keep it in the shed, the one Orli had wandered through.

She turned back to Janelle. "I have to talk to Orli. Wish me luck. Grounding her—again—probably isn't the answer, and I can't weld myself to her side until school starts. Maybe I should implant a GPS tracker under her skin."

At Janelle's raised eyebrow, she added, "Only joking. That's so wrong. But I'm running out of actual options."

"You'll think of something."

"I guess. We'll muddle through as we always do."

Jac bent over the pool table and lined up a shot on the red ball. Once potted, she moved to take the purple, which she missed.

She returned to sit at the table while Caitlin took her shots.

"So," Kyra said. "Don't keep me waiting. Have you met your neighbour yet?"

"You know I have. Tom and Bec took my bins in yesterday and gave me a couple of their home-grown lettuce."

Kyra swatted her arm. "You know I don't mean them. Your *other* neighbour. Spill. Is it Maren McEvoy?"

Jac sipped her beer. "You're obsessed. Why would she move here?" In less than a minute, Kyra was going to go into orbit once she found out Maren was indeed living next door.

Liz finished potting her balls and lined up on the black. When that, too, was in the pocket, she returned to them. "Is your new neighbour female, single, and hot?"

Jac suppressed a smirk. "Two out of three, but I don't know if she's single."

"So, you met her." Caitlin nodded. "Spill."

"She's pleasant. Friendly, in a distant sort of way."

"What's her name?" Kyra asked.

Jac set down her beer so it wouldn't spill when Kyra leaped up. "Maren."

Kyra shot up like a rocket. "No *way!* You're having me on. *The* Maren McEvoy?" She slumped back on the stool and stared at Jac.

"It is, yes. But keep your voice down. No point telling everyone."

"So, is she having you around to dinner? Are you going to take power-walks through the neighbourhood together? Bottles of wine on the deck?" Kyra asked. "You're inviting me over if so."

"None of that. She's pleasant. We chatted. That's all. I'm not sure what you expect."

"Gossip." Kyra leaned forward. "Who's visiting? What cars stay overnight? Does she have expensive tastes? What's her daughter like? Anything really."

"Calm the obsession," Jac said. "I just talked with her for a few minutes on her front deck a few days ago. No gossip." But there was. Kyra would lose her shit if she found out what Orli had done. Maren hadn't asked her to keep it quiet, but it didn't seem right to blurt out Orli's midnight expedition to the biggest gossip in southern Sydney.

"Did you meet the daughter?" Caitlin asked.

"Briefly, yeah." Jac shrugged. "She didn't say much."

"Apparently, the daughter's the reason Maren shifted to Sydney and put her career on hold." Kyra waggled her eyebrows. "One of the gossip sites hinted about her getting into trouble in Melbourne. You can't name minor offenders, of course, so they didn't actually name her or say what she'd done."

"I wouldn't know." Jac took a swallow of beer. Maren had mentioned something about Orli and her poor choice of friends, sure, but she'd bet it was exaggerated on the gossip site. She certainly wasn't going to add anything.

"Are you going to invite her over for a friendly drink?" Liz stuck her elbows on the table. "To meet some local people. Like us." She waggled her eyebrows. "We'll keep Kyra in order."

"Just try it," Kyra said. "Maren McEvoy's my forever-and-always. You tell us when to come, Jac, and we'll be there."

"Don't hold your breath," Jac said. "She seemed very private. I don't think she's up for rowdy friends."

"You mean us?" Caitlin batted her eyelashes. "Why, you can't get a more subdued and decorous bunch of people than us!"

They all broke up laughing as Jac threw beer coasters at them.

CHAPTER 9
HALF-ARSED

The next day, Jac unfolded the note left in her mailbox.

> *Landscapers coming tomorrow to clear the jungle on both sides of the boundary. Expect to be here all week. Is that okay with you?*

Jac reached for her mobile before remembering she didn't have Maren's number. Presumably, she was cautious about handing it out. Instead, she found a pen and wrote, *No worries. Will be out most of tomorrow, so tell them to go for it. Thanks.* She went around to Maren's mailbox.

"Hi," The greeting made her look up as she dropped the note in the box.

Maren was sitting on the deck where they'd had their conversation the previous week.

Jac gave a short wave. "Hi. Just letting you know that's fine about tomorrow."

Maren stood and came over to lean on the railing. The angle gave Jac a fine view from her bare feet up her slender legs to the hem of her shorts. *Nice.*

"That's good." She hesitated, then glanced back into her house. "Would you like to come up for a drink? My horrible daughter is in her room, so we'll be undisturbed."

"Sure." Curiosity tickled. Maybe she'd get to see inside Maren's house and would have some harmless gossip to share with Kyra. She went up the stairs to the deck.

"What can I get you to drink?"

"Just a beer would be good, thanks."

"I think there's some IPA that Marcus, my ex, left. Is that okay?"

"That's fine."

Maren waved at the Balinese wooden couches. "Have a seat. I won't be a moment."

Jac sat on one end of the high couch. For a second, she thought of shucking her shoes and curling up against the cushions, but that seemed presumptuous. With a sigh, she tried to rest back, but the couch was too deep, so she leaned on the arm instead.

Maren was gone for a few minutes, but when she returned, she held a tray with a beer, what looked like a gin and tonic, and a wooden board with a soft cheese, crackers, and some olives. She set it on the low table in front of the couch, then shed her shoes and curled into the opposite end of the couch from Jac, pulling her feet up onto the cushions.

She looked across at Jac. "You don't look very comfortable. The only way to relax on these things is to put your feet up. Go for it."

"I'm not going to argue. I've wanted to do that since I sat." She slipped out of her Birkenstocks and relaxed into the couch in a mirror posture to Maren's. "I promise I've showered since removing my motorbike boots. I wouldn't do this otherwise."

"I've seen you ride off on a couple of different bikes. Do you always ride to work?"

"That is work. I run City and Coast Motorbike Tours. I take people on trips through Sydney, along the coast and through the national parks. Mostly as a pillion passenger, but if they have their own bike, as an escorted tour."

Maren propped her chin in her hand and regarded her with clear grey eyes. "Have you always done that?"

"For the last three years. Living here made it possible. Before that, I was a park ranger, worked bar, the usual sort of manual jobs." She huffed a laugh. "Well, probably not usual to you."

"Don't put yourself down. I worked my way through uni like most people." Maren raised a shoulder. Her loose T-shirt slid down her other shoulder, revealing a delicate curve of neck, the line of collarbone, and a snow-white bra strap. Jac's gaze snapped to it. *Nice.* She thought of her own rather practical sports bras and smothered a smile. That movement would not be half as appealing if she did it, with her more weathered skin and utilitarian underwear. Maren had to be several years older than her, but their lifestyles were reflected in their skin.

Maren hitched up the T-shirt and a twinge of disappointment went through Jac. It had been a particularly pleasant view.

"So, who are your customers?" Maren asked. "Younger people, I guess. Those who haven't yet learned their own mortality."

"Not at all." Jac grinned. "I have several older clients who like to relive their youth—and nothing does that better than leaning into a corner, watching the scenery rush past, feeling the sun, and smelling the sea air. Roy, one of my regular clients, is in his eighties, but he still loves to go out. I take him on the Goldwing now, though, as it's more stable for him."

"Have you ever had an accident?"

"With a client, no. By myself, yes. A car didn't see me coming and continued through the give way. A classic case of a driver not looking properly. I wasn't too badly hurt, but my bike was a write-off—and the car was very banged up. My clients have to wear sturdy high-vis clothing, leather boots, and so on."

"I've never been on a motorbike," Maren said. "I'm not sure I would— I'm too much of a worrier."

"It's not for everyone, that's for sure, but it's a much more immersive experience than driving a car. If you ever change your mind, I'd be happy to take you."

"Thanks." Maren took a sip of her drink and stretched her legs along the couch. There was enough room that there was still a gap between her and Jac. Her legs were as soft-looking and pale as her shoulder.

Jac dragged her stare away from those legs with difficulty. When she raised her eyes back to Maren's face, she wore a slight smile, as if she knew exactly what Jac had been thinking. *No, she wouldn't have noticed. That's just her professional, polite smile.* She searched for something to say. "Are you enjoying living here? You've come from Melbourne, haven't you?"

"Yes, and yes," Maren replied. "I grew up in the Illawarra...on the north side of Wollongong, in Thirroul. I'd have moved there, but although I'm on a career break at present, it's more practical for me to live in Sydney rather than an hour down the coast. And of course, there's Orli to consider..." Her gaze unfocussed for a moment, then snapped back to Jac. "Did she apologise to you?"

Maren didn't know? That was odd. "Not yet, but it's been less than a week, and I haven't been home much."

Maren's lips thinned. "No time like the present. She's in her room. I'll get her." She set her drink down and rose, then went back inside the house.

Jac shuffled on the couch. A forced apology was worse than none in her book, but she wasn't the child-rearing police. It was up to Maren how she raised her daughter—and she obviously had a battle on her hands. She sensed there was more to the Sydney move than Maren was saying. Maybe Kyra had been right when she'd said Orli had been in some sort of trouble.

She took a couple of swallows of beer, relishing the frosty brew.

The glass door slid open once more, and Maren stepped out, followed by Orli. The teen's hair stood on end, and, despite the warm evening, she wore a hoodie with *Fuck the Patriarchy* emblazoned on the front.

Maren resumed her seat on the other end of the couch, picked up her drink and took a sip.

Orli remained standing. She licked her lips and focussed on Jac. Her eyes were a clear grey like Maren's.

"I'm sorry for planting weed on your land," Orli said. "I won't do it again."

Jac waited a beat. That was it? The apology? She shot a glance at Maren, who was studying her drink. "Thank you. But you apologised for breaking into my shed before and said you wouldn't do that again.

It seems your apologies are very specific—what am I going to find next?"

Orli's face was a blank. "What are you expecting?"

"I hope, nothing. I hope I have pleasant neighbours, and my property is undisturbed."

"And I hope I get to go back to Melbourne and my friends," Orli shot back. "Maybe one of us will get what we want."

At the other end of the couch, Maren's fingers clenched on the glass.

Orli flipped her hoodie up, so it shadowed her face. "Can I go now?"

"That's up to Jac," Maren said. "If she's okay with your apology, you can."

Shit. Talk about putting me on the spot. "I think Orli has agreed to leave my property alone. So that's fine by me." She smiled at Orli. There was no point making things worse; forcing a more heartfelt apology out of the girl was doomed to failure.

"I'll be in my room." Orli turned and shuffled back inside.

Maren sighed. "I'm sorry about that. You can probably tell things are tough right now. She's the main reason for the move from Melbourne."

Jac waited for her to say more, but she was again looking down into her glass as if the answer was in the clear liquid.

"Is there anyone who can help? Maybe counselling…?"

"She refuses to go. I'm just trying to keep her occupied. Tomorrow, we're going to pick a colour scheme for her room, get paint, curtains, bedding and so on. She's going to paint it herself while she's grounded. I only hope she doesn't choose all black like a pit of doom." She sighed. "Later this week, she's going to spend a couple of days with Marcus—her father. He lives in Paddington. Hopefully, being in the inner city will be more exciting for her. Although that's not without its own concerns."

Marcus. Jac searched her memory for what Kyra might have said about him. Nothing she could remember except he had been a professional rugby player and he and Maren had divorced a couple of years ago.

"Our housekeeper, Janelle, moved from Melbourne with us. Well, she's a friend more than an employee. She'll be with us for another few weeks before she takes her retirement cruise. Orli loves her." A flash of a smile. "I might dump Orli on Janelle for a few days." She ran her hand over her smooth bob. "That's a joke, although I wish it weren't. My daughter is my responsibility. Thank you for accepting her half-arsed apology."

Jac shrugged. "I'm fine with that, as long as she honours the promise."

Maren swung long legs to the floor. "Can I get you another beer?"

Jac set down her empty bottle and stood. "Thank you, but no. I need to finish up from my day and get ready for tomorrow's clients. I have a couple wanting the bike and picnic experience. You probably have things to do as well."

"Janelle's made fish pie, so I just have to reheat it. I'll have to get her to teach me how to cook more than spaghetti bolognese before she goes on her cruise. Thanks for coming around, Jac. I hope you return home to a less overgrown yard tomorrow."

"It can hardly be worse. See you around, Maren." She descended the stairs from the deck. She glanced back as she walked to the front gate. Maren was leaning on the rail, watching her leave. With a raise of her hand, Jac returned to her house.

CHAPTER 10
HOW NOT TO STEAL A MOTORBIKE

JAC JERKED AWAKE IN THE middle of that night to an alert on her phone. The security camera! She sat up in bed, heart pounding, then swung her feet to the floor, reaching for her shorts, toes groping for her shoes.

The roar of a motorbike engine split the night. She ran to the back of the house. Moonlight illuminated her workshop, and the sliding door stood wide open. Her stomach burned white-hot with acid, and she smashed a fist on the windowsill. She would bet her prized Norton that Orli was prowling again. Worse than that, she'd fired up a bike.

The engine revved again, and Jac recognised the sound of the BMW touring bike. If that little shit Orli damaged her bike, she—or more likely, Maren—would pay. She ran to the back door and down the steps before jumping back as the BMW weaved mere centimetres from her, way too fast for the short, narrow driveway. The revs were high. Orli obviously didn't know how to change gear.

Prowling around her shed without damage was one thing, but this was an entirely different crime. Stealing a bike—and riding it dangerously without a licence. Jac lifted her phone to call triple zero for the police when the screech of brakes followed by a crash and the sound of metal grinding along the tarmac stopped her.

The fucking idiot's crashed. Jac's heart smashed against her ribs, and she sprinted toward the sound. If Orli was trapped underneath the heavy bike, if she'd hit her head—there had been no sign of a helmet when she'd raced past—she could be seriously hurt.

The BMW lay on its side in the driveway. Orli sprawled on the ground a short distance away. She'd hit one of the concrete gateposts and the front wheel of the bike was buckled, the petrol tank dented, and the handlebars twisted. Jac closed her eyes for a second, then hurried over to Orli. As she reached her, the teen groaned and sat up. Jac ran her gaze over her, assessing. No obvious injury to her limbs. As she crouched next to her, the reek of bourbon reached her. Orli was absolutely shitfaced drunk.

She leaned to one side and vomited. It splashed her jeans and Jac's shoes.

Jac sucked a deep breath of air and touched her shoulder. "Take it easy, Orli. Don't get up, take your time. What hurts?"

Orli's slack face stared at her, and the smell of bourbon and vomit made Jac sit back on her heels.

"Nothing hurts." Orli laughed, a high, hysterical sound.

"I'm going to check your limbs, okay? Tell me if anything is painful." Without waiting for an answer, she propped her phone where the torch would illuminate Orli and ran her hands gently over her head, down her neck, shoulders, and arms. No bumps, minimal blood from a long graze on one arm, and a scratch on her forehead. Carefully avoiding Orli's torso, she continued on to look at her legs. No blood, no obvious break. No shout of pain.

"Look at me," she said, and held up three fingers. "How many fingers?" Was this the right thing to do? The kid was so stonkered she probably couldn't count anyway, regardless of any potential head injury.

With a groan, Orli lay back on the driveway. "I'm fine. Stop fussin'."

"Tell me your full name and date of birth."

Orli groaned. "Orli Louisa Coffey, the rest's my business."

"Turn on your side." She had no idea if she was going to lose consciousness, but at least she'd be in the recovery position.

Orli shuffled over. Jac reached for her wrist and felt her pulse. It beat fast, but steady and strong. She watched her chest rise and fall. She didn't appear to be hurt—just rotten, stinking drunk. Did that merit an ambulance? She looked at the bike. The damage was superficial—but expensive. Orli must have slowed before hitting the post—or maybe she'd fallen off before then and the bike had continued without her.

She'd get Maren. If Maren wanted an ambulance, that was her call. Jac had seen far worse injuries from riders falling off on dirt trails. They got back on and continued without a second thought.

"I'm going to call your mother, okay? Don't move."

Orli pushed herself to a sitting position. "Don't get her. Lemme be an' then I'll go home."

"Not an option. It's your mother or the police. Your choice."

"Neither."

"Right, I'm calling the police. Stealing a bike is a major offence."

Orli swallowed. "'Kay. Mum then."

Jac hesitated. Maren would be next door, but… Jac couldn't leave Orli. If she passed out, vomited and aspirated, or staggered off down the road it would be far worse. "What's her number? If you give me the wrong one, I'll call the police."

Orli reeled off a number.

Jac entered it and pressed call. The phone rang off. Likely, Maren either had it on silent at night or didn't answer unknown numbers. "Give me your phone," she said to Orli.

Orli fumbled in the pocket of her jeans then handed it over. The cracked screen still lit up when she activated it. She handed it back to Orli. "Unlock it."

As she'd thought, a button on the home screen said *Mum*. She pressed that. Three rings later, Maren's voice said, "Orli, what the hell? Where are you?"

"It's your neighbour Jac. Orli stole one of my motorbikes and has crashed it in my driveway. She appears unhurt and doesn't want an ambulance."

A gasp. "I'm coming." The line went dead, and a light appeared in the house next door.

In less than two minutes, hurrying feet announced Maren's arrival.

"Oh my god, Orli." Maren dropped to her knees in the grass at Orli's side. "Are you okay?"

"Yesh." Orli nodded, then lay back on the grass and closed her eyes.

Maren's nose wrinkled. "Is that...?"

"She's stonkered," Jac said. "But other than that, appears unhurt."

"Stonkered?" Maren glanced up.

"Smashed, pissed as a newt, hammered, shitfaced, trollied, jarred, maggotted—"

"I know what it means," Maren snapped. "And I can smell bourbon. How that happened is for another day."

Orli opened her eyes. "Booker's bourbon. S'good."

Maren's lips thinned.

"She has good taste," Jac said. The Booker's was over one hundred bucks a bottle.

"Not helpful." Maren brushed the hair back from Orli's face.

"I can't find any broken bones, significant blood, or anything a litre of water, two ibuprofen, and a Berocca won't fix. She asked me not to call an ambulance—and I can't overrule that lack of consent. Your call."

"Have you rung the police?" In the moonlight, Maren's face took on an alabaster paleness.

"Not yet. My priority was making sure Orli wasn't seriously hurt." Jac took a deep breath. "But I should call the police. Breaking and entering—I padlocked my shed after the last time she broke in—stealing a motorbike, damaging both the bike and private property, riding without a helmet, and unless I'm mistaken, no licence, and under the influence."

"Don't need no lish-ence." Orli curled into a ball, her hands underneath her head. "No amb-lance."

"At least she didn't get out onto the road." Maren rested a shaking hand on Orli's shoulder. "I'll take her home. Check on her overnight, get her to hospital if need be. Otherwise, she can go to the GP in the morning when she's sobered up. Stand up, Orli."

"Sleep here."

"Stand up, or we'll drag you."

With a groan, Orli rolled to a sitting position. Maren put a hand under her arm, and Jac moved to the other side. Together, they hauled Orli to her feet. She swayed.

"I think you need a hand getting her home." Jac lifted Orli's arm over her shoulder and wrapped her own arm around Orli's waist, waiting as Maren did the same.

Together they half-carried, half-dragged her to the steps.

"It's tempting to leave her here." Jac gazed up at the dozen steps she'd bounded down so easily the day before.

Maren's jaw tightened. "I think we can do it."

A light came on in the house, and an older woman's voice called, "Maren? Is that you? What's going on?"

"Can you come and help us with Orli, Janelle?"

A stocky woman wearing pyjamas came down the steps. She swept her gaze over Orli, and without a word, lifted her feet. Carrying her like a hammock, the three of them mounted the stairs and continued through the house. Jac had a fleeting glimpse of polished wooden boards, a gleaming, older-style kitchen, and wooden furniture that had a look of polished elegance. It was all a far cry from her own inherited furniture and op-shop finds.

They entered Orli's room, stepping over the clothes on the floor, and put her down on the unmade queen bed. She rolled onto her side.

Maren went across to where a sleek, silver laptop rested on a desk by the window. She tapped the spacebar and the screen came alive. Whatever she saw made her lips tighten.

Janelle tugged off Orli's shoes. "She'll get blood on the sheets."

"It's minor," Maren said. She stared down at her daughter, an unutterably sad look on her face. "She can wash her own sheets when she's sobered up." Maren moved Orli's hair back and bent and kissed her forehead. Then she scooped the laptop from the desk and went back to the living room.

Jac lingered for a moment, looking at Orli. On the surface, this kid had everything: a comfortable home, a mother who loved her, no family financial worries...yet something was obviously wrong.

Janelle gave her a small smile. "You're Jac the neighbour? Orli's mentioned you."

"Right now, I'm not sure that's a good thing."

"It's not been easy lately. But now, I think we let her sleep."

Jac took the hint and returned to the living area.

Maren was in the kitchen. "I'm about to have a cup of mint tea. Something soothing. Can I get you anything?"

Jac hesitated. It was now nearly two in the morning, and she had to be up early. Luckily, the next day's client was booked for the Honda Goldwing and not the BMW. She sighed. "Honestly, it's tempting, but I have a damaged bike to move, my workshop to secure, and an early start in the morning."

"I understand." The kettle boiled, and Maren pulled down a mug. "You want one, Janelle?"

"No thank you, hen. I'm back to my bed. I'll check on Orli in a couple of hours."

"Thank you." Maren squeezed Janelle's shoulder as the older woman passed.

Her gaze moved to Jac. "I'm so sorry this happened. I thought Orli had learned her lesson the last time she trespassed on your property." She bit her lip. "I realise it's late, but before you go, I need to ask what you intend to do about this." Her hand waved in the air. "About tonight."

"This is more serious than Orli wandering around my shed. Beyond a few marijuana seedlings. This time, Orli has damaged my property—the shed lock and door, and importantly, one of my bikes, which affects my business. I won't know how much damage there is until I have it fully checked over. I take paying customers on that bike; it has to be mechanically sound."

"Of course." Maren took her tea and went to sit on the couch.

"Then there's the broken promises. Orli has repeatedly trespassed. Twice, she's said she'll respect my property. Twice, she's broken that promise, and each time is worse than the one before. Obviously, I can't trust her. If she promises a third time to stay away, what will she do? Burn down my house?"

Maren gasped. "She wouldn't do that."

Were all parents the same? Determined to think the best of their kids, no matter the evidence to the contrary? "Neither you nor I can know that. The first two incidents weren't major, but this is thousands of dollars' worth of property damage and lost business income. Plus, I'll have to put in more security measures to ensure she stays away. More cameras. Barbed wire and Dobermans."

"That seems extreme."

"Chicken wire and a poodle then." She wished she'd accepted the tea. "Seriously, though, this is a criminal act. I'll need to file a police report to get my insurance to pay. And it goes beyond that for me. The BMW will be out of action for a while. I'll either have to cancel clients or work around it. That's time and money. My insurance premiums will hike." She studied Maren's down-bent head.

"I was hoping we could come to some arrangement." The words fell softly into the room.

Jac's lips tightened. *Right. The rich mama bear wants to protect her offspring.* Surely, that was the wrong way to go about things. Surely, Orli had to have some punishment for her actions. If she didn't, maybe she would burn down Jac's house. She huffed. "I'm not sure that's the best way. You protected her last time, and look what happened."

"Will you hear me out?" Maren pressed the heels of her hands to her eyes. "I want nothing more than to go to bed, too."

A lick of flame ran over Jac's thighs, but she suppressed it. *Go to bed.* Yeah, that would be something, having Maren McEvoy, Australia's favourite newsreader, in her bed. All pale skin and slender body. Those full lips curved in a smile before— *Enough.* Jac slammed that door shut in her mind. She must be tired as all hell to be fantasising like that over someone she barely knew, and who hadn't given her the slightest hint she was interested—either in her specifically or women in general.

"I'm listening," she said.

"Orli is… Orli has…" Maren dropped her hands and focussed on Jac, her grey eyes now stormy. "What I'm about to say is between us, right?"

Jac nodded, intrigued despite herself.

"Last year, in Melbourne, Orli fell in with friends who got a kick out of rebellion."

That sounded like every other teen in existence, but Jac nodded.

"She was sneaking out of her room many nights and going joyriding. Inevitably, they were caught and arrested. She's still on probation. There was also a pregnancy scare. The move up here and my career break are all about her: to get her away from her friends, so that I could spend more time with her, and so she could spend more time with Marcus, her father. She accused me of ignoring her. That's not entirely untrue."

She dragged a shuddering breath and stared down at her fingers. "If the police charge Orli with whatever you press charges on, she will likely end up in juvenile detention. She needs to be punished—I'm not arguing for her to walk away with no consequences—but Australia's juvenile detention is a hard place, and I don't think it's the right place. Not for Orli. Not for most kids, to be honest."

Jac sifted through Maren's words. "You're asking me not to go to the police because your daughter can't take the punishment?" *Hell no*. Maren was doubtless right about juvenile detention, but a slap on the wrist wouldn't work here. "Orli obviously thinks she's Teflon, and nothing she does will have major consequences. She could have killed someone—both with her carjacking and tonight on the bike."

"She could have," Maren agreed. "But I'm asking you not to go to the police. I'll pay for all the damage she's caused, and an agreed amount to cover the inconvenience to your business. As for Orli's punishment…it would be fitting if she came to work with you making good that damage. Oh, not skilled work, but a sort of direct community service fixing what she's broken. You could give her the dirty jobs, the hard manual jobs. She could clear your yard, clean your shed. Fix the lock. Clean and polish bikes. Whatever you want, as hard as you want, as long as it's not dangerous."

Really? Jac rolled her eyes. "And who is going to supervise her? There's only me in my business, and a friend when I need a second escort. I haven't time to monitor someone who almost certainly will resent being there and need close supervision. If you want a childminder, Maren, you'll have to employ one."

"When you put it like that, it is an imposition," Maren said in a low voice.

But it was a fitting punishment, a hard one that might make Orli reconsider her ways. The thing was, did she want to commit to that?

"I'll reimburse you for your time."

That was a sweetener, but it wasn't the reason for her hesitation. "That helps, but it's more than that. It's responsibility, insurance, it's having Orli around my workshop. It's not a McDonald's playground; there are power tools, motorbikes, heavy things, sharp objects, trip hazards. I've seen mice. There's apparently a red-bellied black snake around, too. What if she hurts herself?"

"I'll put in writing that you bear no responsibility."

"If you want her to do something dirty, physically hard, and out of her comfort zone, she'd be better off volunteering. A homeless charity, or an aged care home."

Maren leaned forward and placed both hands on Jac's knees and gripped. For all that it was an urgent touch, in no way sensual, the trickle of flame she'd felt earlier spread out from each of Maren's spread fingers.

"She harmed you and your business. This way is more direct, more of a learning experience for her. And you...surely you've got some revolting jobs you've been putting off? Emptying the shed, cleaning, degreasing, whipper-snipping. Filling potholes, painting walls. Anything you want, as long as it's safe."

Jac closed her eyes, and a yawn threatened. The clock on the wall had ticked past 2:30 am. "I can't answer you now. I need to think about it. Sleep on it."

"I understand." Maren removed her hands and stood. "Thank you for at least considering it. We can talk in the morning." Her lips twisted. "Ideally, when Orli is sober, and after she's been to the GP. I need to lock my drinks cabinet, too."

Jac stood as well. "That was a waste of good bourbon."

"Can I ask that if you decide to go to the police, you let me know ahead?"

The yawn bloomed. "I'll do that. Goodnight, Maren. We'll talk tomorrow."

Jac went down the steps and back to her house. The BMW still lay on its side at the end of the driveway. She heaved it upright. The stand hung loose, the front wheel was buckled, and the left side was a patchwork of scraped paint and minor dents.

With difficulty, she pushed it under the front of her house. She'd deal with it in the morning. Turning on her phone torch, she went down to her workshop and shone the beam around. Apart from the space where the BMW usually sat, nothing else appeared disturbed. She pushed the door closed, chucking the broken padlock to one side. Orli must have used bolt cutters to remove the padlock—that required forethought. Where had she got them from?

She entered her house and shed her shoes so she could fall backward on her bed. What a stinking mess of a night. What a horror of a teenager. And Maren wanted Jac to supervise her. She shook her head. It would have to be a no. She didn't want the responsibility, or the drama Orli would surely bring.

Her mind conjured up the image of Maren's face: the sadness and worry that had lined it when she'd talked about her daughter.

Still not my problem.

Jac's eyes closed. She'd figure it all out in the morning: about the police, about Orli, about Maren. Although what was there to figure out about her, other than how gorgeous she was, how her fingers had trembled for that small moment before she'd clenched them on Jac's knees.

How that had made her feel.

Jac rolled over. She wouldn't think about that one. There were already enough complications with her new neighbour.

CHAPTER 11
AN APOLOGY

MAREN STARED DOWN AT ORLI. Mid-morning sunlight filtered through the curtains, but she still slept on, lying on her side in a loose curl. One hand was tucked underneath her pillow, the other lay fingers up next to her cheek. Tear tracks cut through the grime on her face.

Maren's heart turned over. How much of this was her fault? Parenting wasn't simply giving birth and hoping the kid turned out okay; it was being there for them, guiding them, raising them, as well as loving them. She'd thought she and Marcus were doing okay with that. But then their relationship had changed—hardly surprising given the circumstances, and a possibility they'd both allowed for—and Marcus had moved to Sydney, leaving her to manage Orli and her own soaring career.

A noise in the doorway made her turn around. Janelle walked over and looked down at the sleeping girl. "Poor wee hen."

"She's not badly hurt, I think."

Janelle glanced up. "I meant you. Orli has to take some responsibility for her own life. You've got the harder job."

Maren slipped an arm around her waist and leaned on to Janelle's shoulder. "You're the wise one. How lucky we are to have you."

"None of the sentimental stuff." Janelle hugged her back. "It's worked well for both of us."

"If you don't like the cruising life, you're always welcome to return. Either as our housekeeper, or else you can just live in the apartment rent free and hang out with us."

"Thank you." Janelle kept her gaze fixed on Orli.

"She left her laptop open last night. She'd been chatting with her friends in Melbourne. Raz accused her of going soft and dared her to steal the bike." Maren sighed. "I've taken her laptop away, but I can't police all her online activity."

"What are you going to do?"

"Drink more gin? Cry? Enrol her in the navy and hope they knock the rebellion out of her?" At Janelle's startled glance, she added, "I'm joking about the navy. The first two options are still a possibility."

"I'll join you in the gin bottle," Janelle said. "Is ten in the morning too early?"

"Not if you mix it with orange juice." Maren left the room. "But in the meantime, there's coffee."

How long until Jac decided what to do? And what would happen if she reported Orli to the police? Maren pressed her lips together. She couldn't blame Jac if that's what happened. She knew little about motorbikes, but the blue-and-chrome bike had looked expensive. Beautifully kept—apart from the Orli-inflicted damage—and she'd seen the BMW insignia on the tank. She could pay—that wasn't the issue. The concern was keeping Orli out of detention, yet scaring her enough as to what could happen. Making sure she had some joy in life. Was it possible for all of those things to exist simultaneously? Or was she living in fairy-floss land, on pink clouds of sugar and fantasy?

Jac stood on her front deck with a beer and stared over at Maren's house. Now that the landscapers had cleared the worst of the undergrowth between the houses, she could more clearly see her neighbour's. She'd intended to get back to Maren before evening, but her client had loved the trip on the Goldwing so much that he'd asked to go for longer. Then she'd arrived home to an empty fridge and no milk, so she'd had to go grocery shopping. Then a beer.

There was no sign of anyone out the front of next door, which was lucky, as she still had no clue what to do.

She took her beer to the back deck where she wouldn't chance seeing Maren and slumped into the chair.

What to do about Orli? The sentence hummed in her mind on repeat. How was she supposed to supervise someone who didn't want to be there, almost certainly didn't want to work, and had shown nothing other than a sullen personality? And the big one: Orli hadn't demonstrated Jac could trust her.

At all.

Jac had trusted her once, had laid out the deal, and Orli had shattered that most spectacularly. Maren's confession that Orli was already on probation had only reinforced her belief that the girl was in no way trustworthy or honest.

What was the expression about fool me once, shame on you; fool me twice, shame on me? Well, this was three times for Jac and four for Maren. Maybe now was the time to pick up her mobile and report the crime.

Still, she hesitated. Orli would likely go to juvenile detention if she pressed charges. She'd read the stories, heard about the conditions. The number of repeat offenders. There had to be a better way.

But… *Still not my circus. Still not my monkeys.*

A sound below her in the garden made her tense up. It had sounded like a cough. Quietly, she set her beer down and went to the top of the stairs that led down.

"Hello, Jac?"

Oh, for fuck's sake. Not again. What part of "stay away from my property" didn't the kid get?

"You promised me, Orli, that you wouldn't trespass on my property. Of course, you smashed that promise into smithereens."

"I know. But there was no answer at the front door, and I knew you were home as I saw you arrive." Orli's voice drifted up from the dark garden. "I've come to say sorry."

"Did Maren send you?"

"No. She doesn't know I'm here."

"And it didn't occur to you that, now of all times, you should have remained grounded?"

A shrug. "What's the point? Until we moved here, she didn't know or care what I did. Why should things have changed now?"

Jac pressed her lips together. Maren's actions last night had been that of a very caring parent. But now wasn't the time to say that. "What's the point of you apologising? You said sorry before, promised me you'd stay away. I don't put any worth on your promises anymore."

Orli put a foot on the bottom step. "Can I come up? I'll go as soon as you tell me. That Beemer was one lit bike. I'm sorry it got damaged."

"Not sorry you broke in again? You planned it, too—I saw the bolt cutters. Not sorry you stole the bike and rode it blind drunk? Not sorry that, had you got onto the road, you could have hurt or killed someone? Just sorry the bike got damaged. Well, Orli, I don't accept your apology."

She bounced her hand on the stair rail. "I guess I could have said it differently."

Jac sighed. "Come up then. You've got five minutes, not a second more, after which you're going home."

Orli took the stairs two at a time. She lounged at the rail, the hoodie half-covering her face. "Don't suppose I can have a beer?"

"That's a hard no. Please put that hoodie back so I can see your face."

Orli did so. "Look, I really am sorry. I only did it because I was drunk and not thinking straight. I don't like it here, and there's nothing to do. Mum wanted to get me out of Melbourne, away from my friends, but I haven't made new ones." She hunched her shoulders. "Your bikes are rad. They're so beautiful. It must be, like, so cool to fly along, so free. Will you take me out some day?"

"That's also a hard no." Jac folded her arms. "So far, all I've heard is you were bored and drunk and love my bikes. Tell me why I shouldn't go to the police."

"You haven't yet? Oh. Mum said—" She swallowed. "I swear on my mother's grave I won't come around again, unless you invite me.

I'll take up lawn bowls or something. I won't steal Mum's booze—I can't anyway; she's locked it away."

"Locks haven't stopped you so far. And you can't swear on your mother's grave as she's still alive."

Orli shrugged again. "I guess... I dunno... It's just..." She chewed her lower lip and stared out at the dark garden.

Jac waited. Something about the girl's slumped figure, the unutterably sad look she had when she thought she was unobserved, tugged at her.

"It's just nothing." Orli pushed away from the rail. "I really am sorry for what I did. I won't come near your place again. I know I said that before, but I mean it this time. If you don't go to the police, that would be cool, but I guess I wouldn't blame you if you did. I think Mum will pay for the damage. She'll take it out of my allowance for the next hundred years, like she is for the car I wrecked in Melbourne." She hunched her shoulders. "And I'm grounded. I'm allowed out with Mum to get paint and then I have to paint my room, but I can't go anywhere else. She's still deciding the best punishment for me. And she told my dad, and he called and ripped into me. So, I know you don't believe me, but I'm really sorry. And if I ever, like, get any money of my own again, I'll pay you to take me out on the bike. That would be everything."

She flicked the hood back up to hide her face and jammed her hands in the pocket of her jeans. "Thanks for listening. Bye." She turned, and with dragging feet, went down the steps.

Jac watched as she went back to her side of the garden and blended into the shadow of the house.

What a strange girl. So much sullenness and sadness...but so much wistful longing when she talked about what it must be like to ride a bike. Jac stared at the house next door, an unsettled feeling in her stomach. Maybe, just maybe, Maren's idea was a good one. Give Orli a purpose, something she might actually want to do. If she loved the bikes that much. If she kept her word about no more damage. If she didn't expect to be riding a bike or doing any interesting tasks. She'd have to do the hard yakka, the dull and repetitive things.

Jac finished her beer in long swallows. She shook her head as if clearing her ears. What was she thinking? It would be a massive responsibility, a huge amount of time and commitment. She'd tell Maren she couldn't do it.

But Orli's downcast gaze, the slump of her shoulders, and her longing for the bikes wouldn't leave her.

CHAPTER 12
CONDITIONS

MAREN CAST A GLANCE AT Orli's closed bedroom door. In the two days since she'd smashed Jac's bike, apart from their trip to the hardware store, Orli had barely left her room. She'd picked dark-purple for her walls, and black bedding. Orli had shut down Maren's suggestion they decorate the room together, and from the glimpses Maren had seen of the room, it looked like a moonless night at midnight.

She put her bare feet up on the couch. Janelle had gone to visit a friend, and she and Orli were alone in the house. Maren had knocked on her door to ask what she wanted for lunch and had received a "whatever" in reply. She'd been tempted to serve up dry bread and water, but had figured that would only make the tense situation explode once more.

She rested her mobile on her knees as she talked to Marcus on WhatsApp. "So that's how it is," she concluded. "Sorry to be the bearer of bad news, but you and Rick should know how Orli is before you collect her later."

Marcus's handsome face stared back at her. His bent nose—one result of playing professional rugby league—only enhanced his good looks, giving him a ruggedness he might otherwise lack. "I don't know what to say," he said. "You and I are both reasonably intelligent. How come our daughter is such a bloody idiot?" He sighed. "Don't answer that. She's got the brains. We just have to figure out what's going on in her head. Did you set a punishment other than grounding her?"

"I'm still waiting to hear if Jac will let her work off some of her debt. In the meantime, Orli has limited internet, and you or Rick will need to supervise that. I'm paying Jac for the damage she caused."

Marcus whistled. "Added to the damage she caused in Melbourne, Orli won't have any allowance for the next fifty years."

"I think this is my fault," Maren said in a low voice. "Since the divorce, she's spent more time apart from both of us. You in Sydney, me putting effort into my career."

"Don't say that," Marcus said. "If either of us has to take the blame, it should be me. Starting the divorce. Moving to Sydney. Giving her an instant stepfather."

"You're living your life, Marcus. You have to do what's right for you. I don't think you—or Rick—is the problem here. She's accepting of our divorce, and she loves Rick."

"When are you going to find your happiness? Our reasons for remaining closeted were similar, but your industry has always been so much more accepting of queer people than professional rugby league."

"I know that. It's not only career keeping me closeted; it's Orli. One gay parent, fine. Two? She'd then have to accept we were both living a lie to some extent with our marriage, and then she'll wonder how she came about. She's in enough of a turmoil right now as it is; I don't want to add to that. There'll be time in the future to tell her."

"Our marriage wasn't a lie. I loved you. I still do. And we loved each other enough to create Orli. Her generation, too, is less black and white about sexuality." Marcus touched the screen. "She'll come to realise that, whatever you decide to do."

"I hope so. But equally, now isn't the right time." She shrugged. "And it's not as if there's anyone I want to date right now."

Marcus glanced away for a second. "Rick wants to say hello."

His partner's face filled the screen. "Maren, honeybun, I'm sorry, I overheard that. But since I did, I want to say that you're a total catch for anyone of any gender, and Orli will just have to deal when you start dating again. You'll be there for her, we'll be there for her, and we'll always be there for you, too. Now I'm gone. Love you." He blew her a kiss and waggled his fingers, then pressed a kiss on Marcus's lips.

"Want me to get Korean BBQ on the way home this evening? Orli likes that."

"Sure," Marcus said. "And some of those fabulous dumplings."

"Love you, my little dumpling." With a last kiss, Rick disappeared.

"You two are such poster boys for love." Maren pushed down a twinge of jealousy. Not of Rick. She and Marcus had started as best friends at university. A couple of years later, when a vindictive ex-lover had threatened to out Rick, Maren had wanted to protect her friend. After all, strong friendship was a better foundation for marriage than many couples—and it would save Marcus's career. There were so few gay athletes in Australia, especially in the more macho sports like rugby. Neither of them had expected the marriage to last eighteen years—but it had.

"I want what you have," she said to Marcus.

"Rick's taken." He winked. "But I'm sure we can find you a chiselled investment banker of any gender with expensive tastes in suits, who sings off key, and farts in the shower, if that's your thing."

She laughed. "No. I want your level of ease with each other. And comfort. And hot sex."

"Love?" Marcus asked.

"And love."

"I'll do it." Jac stood on Maren's front deck the next morning, arms folded. "Orli can work for me a couple of days each week." She swallowed, wishing she could take the words back. But Orli's wistful face and forlorn figure had tugged at her. It was something she could do, and maybe it would make a difference to the girl.

Maybe.

"But there are conditions."

Maren closed her eyes for a moment and her shoulders dropped a centimetre. "Of course. Name them."

"An insurance claim would hike my premiums for years to come, so I'll take up your offer to pay for the repairs to the Beemer and the door of the shed. I'll get a couple of quotes…but it won't be cheap. Orli can repair the damage to the grass and repaint the gatepost."

"That's fine. Anything else?"

"This is Orli's absolute last chance with me. If she commits any further criminal act against me or my property, I *will* immediately call the police. If she does anything at all that negatively affects my business, the arrangement ends, and I'll call her probation officer. No more chances, Maren."

"That's understandable, and I'll make sure she's aware of that."

"I'll also need both of you to sign a disclaimer. My workshop has hazards, and I'll make sure she knows about them, but I don't want a lawsuit on my hands if she injures herself."

"Again, fair enough. I can ask my lawyer to draw one up if you'd like."

Jac nodded. Maren's easy acceptance of her conditions made the tightness in her chest ease a little. "Last one. If this doesn't work for me, if it takes up too much time, if Orli is difficult to deal with, then I will end it."

"Understandable. I hope that won't be necessary. Is that all?"

"All that I can think of right now." Her heart thumped. Maren in close-fitting, faded jeans and a tie-dye T-shirt was very different from the Maren she'd seen on TV many nights. More approachable, less professional, more relaxed. *Even more attractive.*

"Then I want to add a couple of conditions of my own." Maren tilted her head. "The first is that if I think Orli is at any risk, then this ends immediately."

At Jac's nod, she continued, "And I'd like you to let me know how she's going. Report in. I want to know what she does for you, and, more importantly, if she's still being difficult."

"I'm not a psychologist, or anything like that." Jac pushed her hands into her hair. "I've had little to do with kids or teens. To be honest, that was a major reason I nearly refused to do this. But I'm not sure reporting to you will help build Orli's trust—and she has to trust me if this is to work."

"I'm not asking you to break any confidences, but I need to know she's okay."

"You could just ask her."

Maren stared down at her feet—bare, narrow feet, high-arched, with unvarnished, neatly trimmed nails. Jac had never found feet a sexy part of a woman, but Maren's were elegant, like the rest of her.

"She's not the chatty sort. Not with me, anyway."

Jac considered. It shouldn't be too onerous, talking with Maren for a few minutes a couple of times each week. "Okay, that's fine then. But anything she tells me in confidence stays that way unless it's something dangerous or illegal."

"Thank you. I really appreciate this." She approached Jac and held out her hand. "Looks like we have an agreement."

Jac took her hand and gave it a brief pump. Maren's skin was soft, but her grip was firm, and when she looked up, her intense grey eyes held Jac's.

She couldn't look away. Maren still held her hand—or was it the other way around? She was still gripping Maren's fingers, acutely aware of the warmth of her palm. Jac relaxed her fingers, slid them away.

Maren still stared at her, lips parted. "I'll...I'll get my lawyer to draw up an agreement. Hopefully, she'll be able to do that today. Assuming it's all fine, what day suits you to start?"

"Wednesday? Right now, I don't have clients booked so it will be a good time to start with Orli. Say, eight?"

Maren wrapped her arms around her middle. "I'll let her know when she returns from her father's house. And Jac, I'll pay you for your time."

"I'll send an invoice." She turned.

Maren's steady gaze was making her uncomfortable. It was too direct, too all-knowing. It was as if she knew how Jac's world had tilted when she touched Maren's hand.

"I'll be seeing you, Maren."

She descended the steps, acutely aware of Maren watching her leave.

Maren pressed her palms to her cheeks. What had just happened? Her fingers still tingled from the touch of Jac's hand. What had started out as a brief business handshake had scrambled her thoughts, licked flames over her skin, and left her fumbling for words.

In her professional life, she shook hands all the time: with celebrities, powerful people, some of the most beautiful people on the planet. But she'd never had that electric moment of connection she'd had with Jac.

Jac wasn't even her type. Her last—her only—steady girlfriend had been a classically beautiful femme, who wore full makeup for the hundred-metre walk to the milk bar. Nothing like Jac, with her old clothes, rather nondescript short, curly hair, and skin that had seen too much sun and wind. Jac probably considered Chapstick a full beauty regime.

But her face lit up when she smiled, a rather quirky, slightly lopsided smile that showed even, white teeth. She had a freckle underneath her left eye, and she wore no jewellery that Maren had seen except a silver ring on her thumb.

She's attractive in a way, but she's so not my type.

This attraction to Jac had to be because she was bored. Since the move to Sydney, she'd had no career to focus on, and, despite her efforts to spend time with Orli, she didn't seem to want her company. It was time to find a yoga studio and put some effort into modernising the house. Maybe she'd do the painting herself. Sugar soap, rollers, and paint charts should keep her occupied and take her thoughts away from her neighbour.

She hung onto that thought as she went back inside.

CHAPTER 13

WHAT NOT TO WEAR TO WORK

"Hi."

Jac looked up from where she was sorting the high-vis vests.

Orli stood in the doorway, hands jammed into her pockets, her ever-present hoodie hiding her face.

"Great, you're here." She pasted a smile on her face. No point making this difficult for them both.

"What do you want me to do?" Orli advanced into the workshop and scuffed the concrete with the toe of her Docs.

"First, I need to tell you some safety things. That hoodie has to go. There are many protruding objects here, sharp items. You'll need your peripheral vision. And the hood could catch on something, make something fall, or get you hung up."

"Seems extreme." Nevertheless, Orli shrugged out of the hoodie and left it bunched on a crate by the door.

Jac glanced at what she was wearing. The embroidered T-shirt looked new and was certainly not a chain-store purchase, and the faded jeans had tears that a designer had probably placed there. "I'm glad you're wearing heavy boots, but the clothes will end up filthy. Do you want to borrow a pair of overalls?"

"Nah. I'll just get new clothes."

Jac suppressed an incredulous stare. Guess this was how the other half lived. "Suit yourself." She ran through safety procedures for the workshop. At least the kid seemed to be paying attention. Then she led Orli across to the BMW. She'd wedged it upright, using a concrete block to replace the broken stand. "I'm taking this to get repair quotes tomorrow, but it needs a clean first. Get the dirt and oil off, clean the damaged parts, and polish any undamaged paintwork and the leather. Take your time. I'd rather you took all day and did a good job than rushed it."

She led Orli over to the rack where the cleaning kit was. "Here you go. Shout if you're unsure of what to use. I'll be doing an oil change on the Norton."

Orli nodded. "Okay. I guess."

Jac left her studying the polishes, pastes, and rags, and went over to the Norton. The oil change went smoothly, and she replaced the plugs as well. She glanced at the clock on the wall. Two hours had passed, and Orli had been very quiet. She walked back to the BMW.

Spilled chrome polish and patches of mud dotted the concrete, and a puddle of water surrounded the bike. The bike, however, was clean. More or less. Orli wasn't in sight. Surely she didn't think she'd finished?

Jac walked outside and found her sitting on a camp chair, swishing flies with a eucalyptus branch. "How are you going with it? You've made a good start."

Orli looked at her feet and muttered something.

"I didn't catch that."

"I've finished. It's clean."

"It's not. There's still mud and grass in the chain guard and the fork. You've done a good job on the chrome, but the seat is still dirty. When you're done, you'll need to clean up the surrounds, too."

"Don't I get a break?"

"How long have you been sitting here?"

"Five minutes."

She doubted that, but there was no point alienating the kid completely. "Sure. We'll have a cup of tea, then you can finish." She went over to the workbench and flicked on the electric kettle. "There's biscuits in that tin."

Orli followed her and lifted the lid. "No chocolate ones?"

"No. Just plain."

Orli replaced the lid. "When do I get to do something more interesting?"

Jac's mouth hung open for a moment. "Like what?"

"Change the oil. Go for a ride."

"You don't until you've proved yourself with the tasks I give you."

She sighed and shuffled her feet. Her once pristine T-shirt had a smear of oil on the stomach and mud on the shoulder. "Then I'll get on with it. I don't want tea. Thanks, though."

She ambled back to the BMW.

Jac blew out her breath. It was going to be a long summer until school started.

Maren glanced over at Jac's house. It was nearly eight, and the sun was finally going down, glowing orange through the trees behind their houses. Was Jac going to come around to let her know how Orli had done? It didn't seem as if she was.

But then, she probably was waiting for Maren to come to her. After all, Jac was the one putting herself out to take Orli.

Janelle was in the kitchen, puttering around, making dinner. The rich scent of basil and tomato filled the air. Some sort of pasta, she guessed. She rose and went down the steps and around into Jac's front yard. Up close, Jac's house was shabbier than she'd thought—the window frames and railings could do with a coat of paint. Jac had said she'd inherited it from her gran; maybe the house hadn't had maintenance for many years.

Indie rock was playing inside the house as she knocked on the door. After a minute, the door swung open and Jac stood there. She wore soft cotton shorts and a brief singlet that clung to her upper body, leaving her shoulders bare. One hand held the door, and her taut biceps and shoulder muscles drew Maren's gaze.

"Hi, I hope I'm not intruding. I wondered how things went today."

"We're both still alive." Jac swung the door wider. "Come in, if you like. I'm cooking."

Maren followed her down a long hallway with scuffed polished boards glowing chestnut. A narrow hall table and coat stand stood to one side. The kitchen was large but old, with dated countertops and cabinets.

Jac went over to where a chopping board with various vegetables waited. An opened beer sat on the counter. "Can I get you anything? Tea, coffee, beer, water? They're the only choices."

"Water would be great, thanks."

Jac found an old-fashioned, coloured-glass tumbler and filled it from the tap. Maren snorted softly. To think she thought her kitchen with its black marble counter tops was dated.

She perched on a bar stool watching as Jac sliced cauliflower and onions, before dumping them in a wok with an array of spices. A rice cooker bubbled away next to it.

"Are you vegetarian?"

"No, I eat most things, although I happen to be making a vegan curry tonight."

It smelled delicious. "I should get the recipe. Orli announced she wanted to go vegan a couple of weeks ago, although so far she's still eating everything."

"She said that this morning." Jac stirred the wok and added a handful of frozen peas and a tin of coconut milk. "Then I offered her a salad sandwich for lunch, and she asked if she could have some of my chicken."

Maren fidgeted on the stool. "I'm sorry. I didn't realise she'd still be with you at lunchtime. She could have come home. It's hardly a strenuous commute."

"She sat with me. I offered the sandwich. She ate it. It wasn't a big deal."

"Still."

"I'm not sure what you want to know, to be honest." Jac dumped a handful of cashew nuts in the wok and turned the heat off, covering it with a lid. "Orli's prickly, but after a slow start, she cleaned the BMW up fine." She grinned. "Hope you've got a good washing machine. I offered her overalls. She's refused them. Her T-shirt could be a rag now."

"I already found it." Maren grimaced. "It was *my* new T-shirt. Guess she's still angry with me." She took a deep breath, letting the simmering annoyance subside again. Orli had just shrugged when confronted with the T-shirt. "Was she any trouble?"

"Not really. Just a few sharp comments. But I'm not used to other people in my workspace, so she got as good as she gave."

Jac lounged against the counter. Her legs were brown below the worn pair of multi-coloured shorts, Birkenstocks on her feet. Maren had never found the hippie vibe of patterned shorts and Birks appealing, but Jac's brown thighs drew her gaze as if on wires.

"She's not coming tomorrow," Jac continued. "I'm getting quotes for repairs to the BMW. That will take up the morning, and in the afternoon I have a half-day city tour booked."

"Is that mainly where you take people?"

Jac lifted a shoulder. "Half and half. Overseas visitors usually want the city highlights: the Harbour Bridge, the Opera House, Bondi Beach. Aussies are more likely to want to see the national parks and the quieter beaches. I take a lot of people south to the Illawarra." She shuffled her feet. "I don't mean to be rude, but my dinner's ready—and there's not enough for two. You're welcome to have a beer and sit and watch me eat—"

"Thank you." Maren shot up. "But I'll get out of your way. My dinner's likely ready, too. Thanks for letting me know how the day went."

"You're welcome." Jac's lazy smile sent a trickle of warmth down her spine as she held Maren's gaze. "Maybe next time we can sit and have that beer."

"I'd like that." Maren realised she was staring.

Jac broke the connection by taking a bowl from a rack and spooning rice into it.

"I'll see you around." Maren turned and left down the hall.

Once back on her own deck, she pressed her palms to her cheeks. *How awkward.* Eighteen years with Marcus, and she'd never once strayed. She'd pushed her attraction to women down, burying it under a warm and pleasant marriage to her best friend. Even once Marcus and she had split, and he'd moved in with Rick, there'd been Orli to consider.

And there still was.

An inconvenient attraction to her new next-door neighbour was not something she could indulge in.

CHAPTER 14
THE DOWNSIDE OF BUSINESS

TWO DAYS LATER, JAC HUMMED as she readied the Honda Goldwing for the afternoon's booking. A scuffle in the doorway made her look up.

Orli stood there, dressed in old jeans and a T-shirt and her Docs. "Hi. You didn't tell me when I should come back, but I heard you out here."

Jac pushed back her hair and glanced at the T-shirt. The faded old shirt had the name of a punk band on the front. Definitely not Maren's. "I have a booking this afternoon. I'm leaving in an hour."

Orli sucked her lower lip. "I could help? I could pack those panniers for you, or something." She shrugged. "Or not. I don't care."

Jac glanced up at the slight tremble in Orli's voice. "It's a bit of an art packing panniers. The balance has to be equal; you don't want stuff dislodging on a corner."

"S'okay, then. I'll go home."

The vulnerability in Orli's voice made her hesitate. "How about we do it together? I can show you the best way, then maybe next time, you can do it."

A shrug. "Sure."

Jac gathered waterproof clothing, water bottles, and the rest of the gear, and showed Orli where it went. "Everything in its place. Then I immediately know if something is missing."

"Not like your workshop, then." A glimmer of a smile.

"No one's perfect. Certainly not me."

"Or me." Another half-smile.

When the panniers were packed, she handed Orli some chrome polish and a cloth. "Can you give it a final shine while I go change?"

When she returned, dressed top to toe in her leathers, Orli was still shining the chrome. "You're doing a great job. I'm off now, but I could use a hand tomorrow. I want to sort my spare parts."

A nod.

Jac straddled the Goldwing and started the engine. As the Goldwing rumbled out of the shed, she glanced across at Orli. Her hands were shoved in the front pocket of her jeans, but her eyes... They swept over the smooth lines of the Goldwing in an almost caressing gaze.

If she never had a client like that one again, it would be too soon. The overseas tourist had looked her up and down when she'd greeted him. "Sure you can handle this big bike, honey? Want me to drive?"

"I've been riding this bike for over three years; I can manage." She'd softened it with a chuckle, even as her fingers had twitched with the urge to wipe the cocky grin off his face.

It had gone downhill from there, with the man demanding she go faster—never mind the speed limit—and downing two beers at lunchtime, despite having signed the conditions which limited passengers to one alcoholic drink during the day.

"Maybe you girls can't handle your liquor, but I can."

"It's for safety reasons," Jac said. "If you have any more, I'll be forced to cancel the rest of the ride and you can take a taxi back to your hotel."

She was mostly silent during the rest of the ride, pointing out the tourist attractions and little else. She posed for a photo with him and the bike, as so many people wanted, but shrugged off his hand when it strayed downward from her back, and refused his suggestion they go for a beer.

Her teeth ached from clenching her jaw, and she wanted nothing more than a beer, but she'd ride the Goldwing into Sydney Harbour before she went with that prick.

She pulled into her driveway thirty minutes later, and stopped, letting the bike idle. The workshop door stood wide open. *That bloody kid didn't close up.* She rode up to the shed and stopped. The concrete in front was swept clean of leaves, and what she could see inside the workshop looked different. More organised. The pile of rags was gone, the jumble of occy straps sorted by length and hung on the wall hooks—where they were supposed to be stored but seldom were.

Orli appeared from the back of the shed.

Jac killed the engine and took off her helmet, then shook out her flattened hair. "You've been busy."

"Yeah." Another shrug. The kid could shrug for Australia. "Nothing to do at home, so I thought I'd do something here."

"Thanks." She went inside and looked around. The area around the sink was clean, the helmets arranged in size order on the bench—which was now free of random screws and hand tools—and when she pulled open the fridge to grab a soft drink, the cans were all arranged by brand. She pulled out a Solo. "Want something?"

"Coke, please, but not that diet shit."

They took their drinks out to the bench outside. The late afternoon sun slanted over them, and cicadas shrilled an intermittent chorus.

Jac took a long slug of her lemon drink. "You must be really bored at home if coming here was better."

"Mum took my laptop and phone. I'm only allowed them for an hour in the evening. Supervised, as if I were six. She took it after I crashed your bike. So, I paint the walls in my room. Janelle is teaching me how to cook, and I come here."

"Doesn't your mum do things with you?"

"She tries. Said it would be fun to learn to kitesurf or something. Suggests shopping trips, or that we go for a drive somewhere."

"That doesn't sound too bad." What was she missing? Maren had said she wanted to spend more time with Orli. It sounded as if she was trying.

"Yeah, I'd do them with friends. But with Mum? Not cool."

"Sounds like she wants to spend more time with you. What's wrong with that?"

"She does—now." Orli turned the can in her hands. "She didn't before. In Melbourne. Too busy being 'Australia's favourite news-reader'." She made air quotes with her fingers. "I had friends in Melbs. I don't here."

"You'll make them. But in the meantime, why not hang out with your mum a bit? She doesn't know anyone here either."

"I'm not desperate. I just want to go back to Melbs. To my friends."

The friends Maren had mentioned. "What did you do with them?"

"Hang out mainly. Smoke weed." A sideways glance. "Sometimes we'd steal cars. Or just have sex."

What the hell do I say to that?

"Got no answer? Not going to tell me I'm too young to fuck, and I shouldn't steal cars? Gonna stop me coming around now you know what I do?" She crushed the empty can and stared at Jac.

"No. I guessed you smoked weed—the seedlings you planted— and your mum told me about the joyriding. Before you have a go at her, it's only fair I knew what you were like before I agreed to have you here."

"Oh." Orli deflated, chewing her lower lip. "But you let me come, anyway."

"I did. But you fuck with my property or bikes and I'm going straight to the police. That's the deal. I'm not joking." Jac folded her arms and stared back.

Orli was the first to drop her eyes. "Why did you let me come in the first place?"

"Truth?" At Orli's nod, she continued, "Because you liked my bikes. You touched them in a way that made me think you imagined what it was like to ride. Because you asked if I'd take you out. Because you seemed to care about them—and everyone needs something to care about. And people, too. Like your mum."

"Yeah, right." She aimed the Coke can at the bin. It bounced off the rim and rolled onto the grass. Orli rose and retrieved it. "Guess I'll keep coming, though. If it's okay with you."

"Sure it is. Unless you fuck up. Then it's not."

"Guess I better not fuck up." Orli's second attempt at binning the can went home. "Thanks for the drink. See you tomorrow." She ambled off down the drive.

Maren picked up her phone at the ding of an incoming text.

Orli great today. No worries, no dramas.

Well, that was good. She'd heard Orli come home about twenty minutes ago and go straight to her room.

Janelle was out with her friend again, and the large house had a hollow, echoey feel. No talk, no laughter, just her alone with a ticking clock.

That's great. Thank you. She hesitated. That text seemed so sterile, as if she was confirming a hotel reservation. But what else could she say? Earlier, she'd seen Jac go down the drive on the armchair-like bike, looking relaxed, as if riding was the most wonderful thing she could be doing. Jac had stopped at the gate, flipped down her visor, and fiddled with one of the controls. The black leather gear had hugged her figure, showing lean legs and a trim upper body. Maren hadn't been able to look away.

Her mobile screen had gone black as she daydreamed. She reactivated it.

How was the ride today? She pressed *send*.

Not great, to be honest. Customer was a condescending, sexist pig, who tried to grope my arse when he took a selfie and then asked me out for a drink.

Right. Maren knew all about that. Celebrities weren't immune, either, even middling ones like her. It was as if having a well-known face made them public property.

Not cool. I hope you bent his fingers back, but I'm guessing that would be bad for business.

She waited, and in a minute, the reply came.

Exactly. Bad reviews hang around longer than good ones, and no one questions if they're fair or even genuine.

Maren rose and went to look out of the side window. Jac's house was in darkness except for a single light burning in what she now knew to be the kitchen. Jac must be cooking dinner. But what if she was staring into the fridge and wondering what to cook?

I'm about to order takeaway for me and Orli. Want to join us? Although Orli will probably take hers into her room. It's amazing she doesn't have mice in there.

Was that a step too far, inviting Jac? They barely knew each other, after all, and after a morning with Orli, she probably wanted to sit and veg with some comfort food. The minutes stretched with no reply.

Thanks, but I'm meeting friends at the pub. It's our beer, chat, and pool night. I'd invite you along, but Kyra would probably embarrass herself and drool all over you, then try to hit on you. Don't want to make you uncomfortable.

Right. As if being hit on by a woman would faze her. But the unknown Kyra wasn't Jac. A jolt made her tense. *It would be nice if Jac hit on me.*

I'll pass tonight, thanks. Janelle's out, and I'm reluctant to leave Orli alone. Another time would be fun, though.

Jac responded with a thumbs up.

Maren threw the phone on the couch and went to see if Orli wanted Thai, pizza, sushi, or something else entirely.

CHAPTER 15

NOT TEN-BUCK MERLOT

JAC LIFTED A CHAIN GUARD and added it to the pile of BMW parts. Next to her, Orli turned a gearbox sprocket over in her hands. "Which bike is this for?"

"The Norton. I have the most parts for that bike, as it's the oldest. It does the least, but gets the most repairs."

"Why keep it then?" Orli put it with the rest of the Norton parts.

"It's a classic, and enthusiasts love them. And I love it too. It was my bike before I started City and Coast Motorbike Tours. It's the one I take if I'm going for a ride by myself."

"I love it, too." Orli looked across at the black paintwork, partly covered by a dust sheet. "That's the one I'd ride, if I could." She tilted her head. "Will you take me out on it one day? I'll pay you."

Jac considered. In the two weeks Orli had been helping her she'd done a lot of grunt work, mostly without complaint. She'd fixed the grass and gatepost she'd wrecked, and followed instructions—albeit with a bit of smack chat. She'd probably be sensible on a bike.

"I do take people at sixteen, but you'll need parental permission. If your mum says it's okay, then yeah, I'll take you."

The leap of enthusiasm in Orli's eyes and the grin that flashed on her face made Jac smile in response. Then Orli turned away. "She'll never agree."

"She might. If you put it sensibly. Don't make it sound like a mad sprint around the city, because that's exactly what it's not."

"Will you ask her for me?"

"No. You need to ask. But if she asks me what I think, I'll back you up."

"Thanks." For a second, it seemed as if Orli would hug her, but she thrust her hands in her pockets and hunched her shoulders. "I'll ask her tonight."

Jac's phone dinged with a text message.

Would it be okay if I came around for a few minutes? Would like to talk with you, but don't want O to overhear.

Jac could guess what it was about. But if Maren at least wanted to talk about it, maybe there was a chance she'd agree.

Sure. Come around. I have beer and chips.

A couple of minutes later, Maren called a "hello" from the front door. She lifted a bottle of wine. "I'm already intruding without drinking your beer as well, so I brought this."

The label was a vintage shiraz that Jac had seen in the bottle shop but dismissed as being above her price bracket. "You needn't have, but I won't turn down that bottle. Take a seat on the deck; I'll get glasses."

The fine wine demanded more than chips, so she put some crackers and cheese on a board. When she returned to the deck, Maren had shed her sandals and was relaxing in one of the canvas chairs.

Jac poured wine and handed her a glass before sitting in the chair next to Maren's. She buried her nose in the glass and sniffed, letting the aromas tantalise her nose before she took a sip, closing her eyes as the wine rolled over her tongue.

"You seem to be enjoying that," Maren said. "A full-on sensual experience."

The purr in Maren's voice jolted Jac's eyes open. "I guess it is. Honestly, I buy ten-buck merlot—nothing as good as this."

"I like fine wine." Maren glanced at the glass cradled in her hands, then across at Jac. "Wine is a rare pleasure in life."

"I'd have thought you'd have many pleasures." Jac shook her head. "Uh, sorry, that sounded weird. I meant you have your career, you're famous, have a lovely house."

"Please, Jac." Maren set down her glass and reached out a hand to touch Jac's arm. "I'm not some major celebrity. I just read the news. Or I did. Not this year. It means I can afford decent gin, and a large house, but that's it. I have my battles. You're witnessing one of them—with Orli."

Jac cut herself a piece of cheese. "Do you watch the news? Your program?"

"Ex-program. But sure I do. Luka and I are friends. I helped make him a part of the team."

"You had good chemistry." Was it more than on-screen banter and shared smiles? Maybe Luka was Maren's boyfriend. He'd joined the team after Maren had split from her husband, after all.

"The chemistry is real—we're close friends. And I've read the gossip mags, implying it's more. It's not."

A flicker of pleasure flared in Jac's chest. So, the handsome Luka wasn't involved with Maren. Not that it was any of her business, but the knowledge gave her a warm glow.

Rather than analyse her reaction, she said, "Zoey seems to fit in well. It must be strange to watch someone else in your spot. My mate, Kyra, says she doesn't have the natural delivery you do."

A flash of a smile. "Please thank Kyra for me."

Kyra was gunning to meet Maren, but Jac didn't want to mention that. It sounded a bit stalkerish, and she didn't want to put Maren off.

"But no, it's not too strange. Most newsreaders are fairly anony-mous. I'm sure many people haven't even noticed there's been a change. Zoey is…ambitious. I'm sure she'll go far." She took a sip of wine.

Ambitious. Was that a polite way of saying Maren was concerned about her job? Surely not. Despite her self-deprecating words, Jac would bet she couldn't go to the supermarket without being recognised, without getting requests for selfies in front of the organic tomatoes.

"Maybe I should ask you for a selfie." Jac widened her eyes and fluttered her lashes. "Post it on my webpage. It would be good for business."

"You're welcome to the selfie if you want to show Kyra. But please don't post it on your webpage. My contract limits my endorsements."

"I was joking about posting it. But a selfie would be good, if you don't mind. If it doesn't sound too creepy. Kyra would love it."

"Sure. Where do you want to stand?"

Jac pulled out her phone. "Maybe by my front door. Kyra'll be so excited. I might even get a beer from her!"

"Let's do it." Maren uncrossed her long legs and rose to walk over to the front door.

Jac stood next to her and extended her arm, holding the phone. She shuffled closer. "Got to get us both on the screen and show the house."

The heat from Maren's body radiated into Jac's arm.

"How about this?" Maren slung an arm around Jac's waist and tugged her close, so they touched from shoulder to hip. "Can you get us in now?"

"Yes." Jac forced the word out. Maren's closeness had stolen her power of speech. She clicked the camera.

"Another," Maren said. She turned her face and pressed her lips to Jac's cheek, holding the pose with a side-eye to the camera.

Jac stopped breathing. Maren's lips were soft on her skin, warm, and, her body angled toward Jac, pressed her breast into Jac's shoulder. Liquid heat spread from the contact into her own chest. Her nipples hardened against her bra. Her breath returned in a rush, and she clicked the camera three times in quick succession.

Maren moved away and sat again.

Wow. Jac was sure she had a stunned look on her face. She covered it with a brief smile and cut herself another piece of cheese.

"What do they look like?" Maren flicked Jac a glance from under her ridiculously long lashes.

Jac shifted her chair closer so they could both look. The first one had a stiff and stilted look about it. The second had caught Jac's wide-eyed surprise, but the third... Maren's lips rested on Jac's cheek with the edge of a smile. It reached her eyes, which were looking sideways at the camera. Jac, too, had relaxed into the pose and her eyes were looking across at Maren. It was the pose of close friends. *Very* close friends.

"Nice. You should show Kyra the third one." Maren sat back.

"You, uh, don't mind? It makes us look a lot closer than we are."

A tiny, wicked smile. "Like we're 'special friends'?" Those air quotes again.

"Well, yes. And Kyra's gay...all of my pool-playing mates are." If Maren didn't know Jac loved women, she surely did now.

"That's fine. I love teasing people. You'll have to tell me Kyra's reaction. But, uh, best not to post that one on your socials, either."

"I won't. I don't have personal socials. Business only." Did that mean Maren didn't want people to think she was gay? She knew very little about her personal life. Only her marriage to Marcus was public knowledge.

"It's not that I care if people assume I'm gay." Maren must be reading her mind. "Far from it." She stared Jac directly in the face.

For the second time, Maren's clear gaze stole Jac's breath. *Is she implying what I think she is? Or am I projecting?*

"But I have Orli to consider. She had a hard time when Marcus and I divorced. Harder still when he and Rick moved in together. We think today's teens don't care about people's sexualities—but when it's another way of being cruel, well, it comes out."

Marcus lives with a boyfriend? The media had kept that quiet—or maybe she was just out of touch. "I didn't know your ex had a partner." What an inane thing to say.

"Yes. He and Rick got together after our divorce. Marcus and I were best friends before we married, and we still are. He's very happy with Rick."

Jac sank lower in the chair and took another sip of the excellent wine. Still so much better than her ten-buck merlot. Maren was raising more questions than she was answering. And the biggest one hung in glowing letters of fire above her head: was she queer and in the closet? Had her marriage been a sham, or had it been real? Jac shoved those questions aside.

"But I didn't come here to talk about me." Maren's lashes flicked downwards, and again that smile peeped. "I actually want to talk about Orli. My daughter, who I'm on the verge of putting up for adoption." She took another sip of wine. "That's untrue, of course. She's my life. She said you'd agreed to take her out on the bike, but you needed my permission."

"That's right. Or yours and Marcus's…I don't know the arrangement you have."

"I'd love to say yes. I haven't seen Orli as excited about anything since we moved here. Which means she actually mentioned it, and asked if she could go. That's excitement for a sixteen-year-old. But I don't think I can let her. I'm sure you're a very safe rider—you have to be, given your business—and I'm sure you have all the safety gear and well-maintained motorbikes…but she's barely ridden a pushbike. And you've seen firsthand how she's not the most obedient kid on the block. What if she disregards your instructions?"

"If she's a danger to herself, me, or others, I stop the ride immediately. I'd tell an adult to take a taxi back. For Orli, I'd call you to come and collect her and wait with her until you arrived."

"Has that happened often?"

"A few times. Mainly young males, first-time riders. Trying to be cool. It nearly happened to that rider I told you about the other day. It's natural for people to get excited first time on a bike, and that euphoria affects everyone differently. Usually, I pull over somewhere safe and explain why what they're doing is dangerous, and that if they don't stop, they'll be calling a taxi. Most apologise and that's the end of it."

Maren heaved a breath. "I trust you, Jac. It's other road users I worry about—and Orli herself."

"There's risk in everything we do in life. She could get hit by a car crossing Pitt Street. Especially if she has her hoodie up. You need focus and a clear head to ride a bike—maybe it would be a good thing for her."

"Maybe. I guess because I've never ridden, I'm more concerned."

"That's natural. Many people are nervous their first time. First times for anything can be like that—I was terrified my first time on a plane. It was a school trip to Tasmania, and I shook for the entire flight and then thew up on landing. My mate Steph doesn't let me forget it—it was her I thew up on."

"What if Orli's like that? She thinks she'll love it, but it could be all bravado."

"I do a loop of the block first, check in with my passenger. If they don't want to go any further, I refund fifty per cent of their payment and go home." She tilted her head and regarded Maren. "I'm happy to take you out first, if you want. A half-day trip. See how you feel at the end. You can decide then if it's something Orli can do."

The spontaneous offer suddenly took on more importance. Jac subdued the butterflies in her stomach. Maren behind her on the bike, hands on Jac's waist, or wrapped around her and pressed close. Even if Maren wanted to ride the Goldwing, they would still be in close quarters—or could be.

Maren's gaze flew to Jac, her eyes wide. "Really? I'm not sure. I don't know if that's my thing."

"There's only one way to find out. We'll do a sedate circuit of Suttons Bay first, and you can leave it at that. Or we'll head south, through the Royal National Park and over the Sea Cliff Bridge and down to Wollongong. It's a lovely ride, and there's plenty of beaches and cafés to stop at."

Maren sucked her lip, her eyes meeting Jac's then sliding away. "Is that where you'd take Orli?"

"Yes. City traffic can be a bit unnerving for a first timer."

A quick nod. "Let's do it. When are you free?"

"You act quickly when you decide, don't you?" Jac grinned. "I could pretend to consult my diary—however, I have no bookings tomorrow. But with the BMW in for repairs, that gives you the choice of the Goldwing or the Norton, which is a smaller bike. You can decide tomorrow. Or if that doesn't suit, I can do next Monday."

"Tomorrow. I hope I don't regret this. What should I wear?"

93

"Your sturdiest boots and thick socks—I have a selection of clean socks and leather boots in most sizes if you have nothing suitable—and thin leggings, ideally cotton, and a thin long-sleeve T-shirt. I supply protective over-pants, jacket, helmet, and gloves. If you come in the morning, I'm sure Orli would show you around."

"Tomorrow morning it is."

Jac poured more wine. "Here's to your new obsession, starting tomorrow."

Maren's eyes shot sparks over the rim of her wineglass. "The bike?"

Maren was flirting. Jac was sure of it. Not overtly so, but subtly, telegraphing her interest. The possibilities of that made the butterflies in her stomach turn into fireflies, sending whirls of heat throughout her body.

"Of course. What else could I possibly mean?" Her lashes lowered.

Right. No doubt she was reading this wrong. But in case she wasn't, tomorrow could be a very interesting day.

CHAPTER 16
DARING TO TRY

"THIS IS A HONDA GOLDWING." Orli flung out her arm to indicate the bike. "It's built for touring, camping with all the panniers and luggage space, and it's super comfy for both rider and passenger."

"You sound like a Honda salesperson," Maren said. "You know your stuff." She bit back the remark that "knowing stuff" was never Orli's problem. The girl was whip-smart and guzzled knowledge like an echidna slurping termites.

The shiny paintwork, chrome exhausts, and leather seats looked reassuringly solid. Indeed, the seats wouldn't have looked out of place in a modern living area. "Is that your favourite?" she asked Orli.

"Nah, the Norton is. That's the one I want Jac to take me on." Orli pointed to a smaller black and chrome bike in the corner. It was old style, possibly even vintage, and it looked small and unsafe compared to the bulky Honda. The pillion appeared so small that any passenger could go tumbling off the back if the bike accelerated too quick. She looked back at the Goldwing.

"It's your choice," Jac said quietly.

She lifted her chin, pushing down the nerves twirling in her stomach. "The Norton."

"Yeah, Mum. Good choice." The approval on Orli's face was worth the surge of apprehension.

"Can I wheel it out?" Orli asked Jac.

Jac's hesitation was barely enough to notice. "Sure."

Orli's shoulders lifted from their usual hunch. She went over to the Norton and rolled it forward off the stand, wheeling it out to the front of the shed before rocking it backward onto the centre stand again.

Jac led Maren over to a rack of protective gear and selected pants and a jacket. "These should fit. Your boots look fine, but if you want something sturdier, take your pick." She indicated the rack of calf-height leather boots.

Once Maren was dressed, they went back to the bike. Jac took her through the basics of pillion riding. "It will feel strange at first, but I'm sure you've seen bikers on the road leaning into the curves. While we won't be as fast or extreme as many of them, that's what you need to do. The easiest way to learn is to sit close behind me, wrap your arms around my waist, and mimic my body movements as closely as possible. If you're not comfortable with your arms around me, you can grip my waist instead, but you still need to sit close. Lean forward, rather than backward. Don't let your feet dangle—keep them on the pegs. Our helmets have built in Bluetooth headsets, so if you're feeling in any way unsafe, uncomfortable, or want to stop for a bit, you only have to say."

Maren glanced at Orli, who was listening intently. "I understand."

"You're lucky it's a dry day. No rain forecast at all. It makes it a lot more pleasant."

Jac straddled the bike and gestured for Maren to mount. The seat was narrower than she'd expected and there seemed to be little behind her.

She swallowed hard. "I wish there was a back support or something."

"There is. Orli, can you grab the backrest for the Norton? It's on the—"

"I know where it is." Orli turned and hurried into the depths of the shed, before returning in moments with a sturdy low support.

They both dismounted, and Jac fitted the rest behind the seat.

"Thanks." Maren touched Jac's shoulder when they were both astride again. "This feels much safer."

"Great," Jac said. "Are you okay for a short circuit of Suttons Bay?" Her voice echoed through the headset.

"I'm ready," she said in her confident newsreader voice. If she wasn't gripping the sides of the seat so hard, she was sure her knees would tremble. She clasped Jac's waist.

Jac gave a thumbs up to Orli and eased the clutch. The bike rumbled into motion.

Maren gripped Jac's waist harder. They were going maybe ten kilometres per hour, not much faster than a brisk walk, but the ground seemed very close.

"You can wave to Orli," Jac said. "I won't change direction until you're holding on again.

Daringly, she lifted a hand and waved, but didn't dare turn her head to see if she responded.

"She's waving back," Jac said. "Hang tight again, we're turning left onto the road. No need to lean at this slow speed."

Maren grabbed Jac's waist once more, wishing she could slip her hands underneath her jacket. If she could feel the play of Jac's muscles, the flexing of her body as she blended with the bike's movements, she might feel safer.

Once on the street, Jac sped up. "We're doing fifty kilometres per hour—the speed limit. How do you feel?"

The tarmac seemed close, the white lines rushing past, and a slight whistle of air creeping into the helmet added to the feeling of speed. "Okay."

"I'm going to pull over so you can adjust your position." She drew to a halt by the side of the road. "If you're comfortable doing so, move a little closer to me," Jac said. "Tuck your thighs into the backs of mine and lean forward a little so your body is at the same angle as mine. You might feel more secure if you wrap your arms around my waist."

Maren inched forward, and when she was ready, Jac drew away from the kerb. Instantly, the wind noise eased and her body, now that it was no longer rigidly upright, felt more relaxed. Her breathing steadied.

"Turning left," Jac said. "Copy my body movement."

She did, and her lips twitched. Not quite a relaxed smile, not yet, but the seed was there. *I can do this.*

Five minutes later, Jac pulled to the side of the road. "How was that? Do you need to stretch your legs?"

"No, I'm fine, thanks."

"You're doing great. You're a lot less stiff. The bike is easier to handle now you're more at ease."

"I feel it too. You're very reassuring."

Jac flipped up the visor of her helmet. "Want to do the full tour? We'll be gone three to four hours."

Did she? With a nervous thrill, the answer blazed in her mind: *Hell, yeah!* If it felt this good cruising suburban streets at fifty kilometres an hour, what would it feel like at one hundred on the open road? Or winding along the coast south of Sydney? And the Sea Cliff Bridge, its wide curves soaring above the ocean? That would be incredible.

"Yes, please. Just let me call Orli to let her know."

Jac nodded.

"And of course, I'll pay your usual rate."

Jac was shaking her head before the sentence had finished. "There's no need for that. Not for you. If Orli rides, you can pay for her. But for you, it's a good neighbour thing."

"You took Mrs Armstrong, who owned the house before me, on the bike? Right before she went off to the aged care home?"

Jac huffed a laugh. "No. I took her on the Goldwing about two years ago."

Oh. She hadn't expected that.

"She loved it. Kept badgering me to take her on the Norton, but her orthopaedic surgeon forbade it. Something about her knee replacement not being able to bend sufficiently. Millie was very upset—but she came out on the Goldwing a couple more times."

"Well, anything Millie can do, I'm sure I can, too." She fished her phone from inside her jacket and called Orli. "Don't wait at Jac's, honey. Go home to Janelle."

The reply was indistinct.

"I promise I'll call you the second I'm back so you can hear all about it. Love you. Bye."

She put the phone away. "Let's go!"

CHAPTER 17
TWENTY YEARS

THE MEANDER THROUGH ROYAL NATIONAL Park was peaceful and beautiful. From the bike, the trees seemed taller, more immediate. The nature closer. And although she couldn't hear the birdsong, the quiet purr of the bike's engine wasn't too intrusive. It was a long way from the revving dirt bikes that had ripped up tracks in the state forests when she was growing up.

But if the national park was peace and beauty, the ride over the Sea Cliff Bridge was pure exhilaration. Although they weren't going fast, the onshore wind buffeted the bike, and riding the swooping curves felt like flying. Far below them, the waves rolled in, and the ocean was the clearest blue.

Jac stopped in the carpark at the ocean pools at Austinmer and cut the engine. "Want to stretch your legs?"

Maren dismounted and took off her helmet, shaking out her hair. "Yes, please." She looked around at the waves rolling over the flat rocks and filling the pools. "I used to come here as a kid. Swim in the baths, get flattened when the enormous waves broke over the top. Get frightened when seaweed wrapped around my leg, or I touched the occasional fish that got washed in."

"I still swim here sometimes—it's nicer than the sea baths around Cronulla, even though they're closer."

"I'm not a strong swimmer, and the possibility of sharks makes me too nervous to swim in the ocean, so these are perfect. So far, Orli hasn't taken up my suggestion that we learn to surf together. Have to say, I'm quite relieved about that."

Jac locked the helmets to the bike. "Fancy a short walk? We can go around the pools and then there's a quiet beach just around the headland."

"Sure."

"If you'd like to dump the protective gear, we can lock it in the panniers." As Jac spoke, she unzipped her jacket and shucked it, leaving a thin, long-sleeve T-shirt underneath. A clinging T-shirt.

Maren forced her gaze away and unzipped her own jacket, sighing in pleasure as the sea breeze cooled her skin through her own T-shirt. She shed her boots and socks and then wiggled out of the tight leather trousers. When she looked up again, Jac had her back to her and was working the trousers down her legs. Her taut backside encased in patterned leggings faced Maren. She let her gaze caress the long length of Jac's thighs and the curve of her buttocks.

Jac locked the clothing away, and then they walked barefoot down to the ocean pools. The tide was out, and the water was calm. A few people swam laps, while some teens jumped from the rock wall. The tang of salt and seaweed filled the air.

They picked their way over the flat rocks and around the headland. The cove on the far side was nearly deserted. At the far end, a woman threw a stick into the sea for a golden retriever who plunged after it with excited barks.

"It's amazing to think we're only an hour from Australia's largest city." Maren shaded her eyes and peered out to sea where tankers lined up, waiting to go into port. "These beaches are still some of the best I know. Better than Melbourne beaches. They're very tame."

"There's the beach pavilion a short distance further on," Jac said. "That's often my lunch stop on the full-day tour."

"How did you end up running your business?" Maren turned to look at her.

Jac was close enough to see the warmth of her brown eyes, the fine lines that radiated out from the corners when she smiled.

"I was a nursing aide before this. The job was fine, but I knew I didn't want to do it forever. Then my gran got pancreatic cancer. There was no way my parents could nurse her—they both worked full time and had a mortgage, and my youngest brother was at home. I lived in a rented studio apartment near Parramatta. So, I moved in to take care of Gran until she died. Pancreatic cancer is a bitch; she lasted less than a year. She left me the house and some money—enough to buy the Goldwing. I already had the Norton. That was the start."

"It's just you in the business?"

"Mostly. Liz does casual work for me when I have more than one booking. I also teach safe riding courses a few times each year. I don't earn a fortune, but I manage. And I'm doing what I love."

"I can see that." Jac's passion shone out of her when she talked about her bikes, when she ran a hand over a gleaming fuel tank, when she leaned into a curve, moving so fluidly with the bike it was as if she were welded to the machine.

"What about you? Do you love what you do?"

They had ambled half the length to the next headland. Maren stopped and faced the ocean. "Mostly, yes. I don't love the time in makeup or having to dress a certain way. The hours are long, too." She sighed. "I think that's half the problem with Orli. I was away from the house too much. Marcus says I shouldn't blame myself...but even so. I can't help but."

Jac faced her and her hand found its way to Maren's, clasping it and squeezing gently. "It's not only the woman's job to manage a family's emotional needs. Marcus obviously realises that. He wasn't there, either."

"True. But now I've moved up here, and for the next year, Orli is my focus."

"Just Orli?" Jac's fingers slipped from Maren's.

She missed her touch.

"What about friends, your parents, other family? Do you date now that you're a free woman? What will you do when Orli is living her life?"

"You make me sound very dull." Maren wrapped her arms around her waist. "I've got no close friends around here except Marcus and Rick, and my parents moved away a long time ago. I'm getting the house in order. Organising tradespeople for changes to the kitchen, and a new bathroom for Orli. Janelle and I are trying our hand at painting walls. But when Orli starts school in February, I won't be tied down as much. I'll have more time to look up old friends. And I know people from the industry based in Sydney."

"But still..." Jac tilted her head. "Do you date?" She shook her head. "I'm sorry; don't answer if that's too nosy. You're an interesting woman, Maren. I'm curious about you."

"I haven't dated since Marcus and I split. Orli—"

"Yes, you said." Jac resumed walking. "Maybe I should find you a date."

"Please don't." The words slipped out. For a second, a montage of Jac filled her mind. Her thighs in the leggings when she'd removed the leather pants. The feel of her body pressed against her own as the Norton roared around the curves on the coast road. Jac's strong fingers, tanned and weatherbeaten, with short, clipped nails. The silver ring she wore on her thumb. She didn't want a date with a random stranger.

But she would like to date Jac.

The golden retriever bounded up to them, coat wet with seawater, tongue hanging out. Maren bent to pat it, but it bounded away and shook itself. She laughed. "Lucky it didn't do that near us."

"Sorry." The dog's owner walked up. "Molly thinks everyone is her friend."

"No worries," Jac said.

The woman continued on, following the line where wet sand met dry.

Jac resumed walking. "So, no dates then. What do you do when Orli's in her room, or hanging around my workshop?" A mischievous sideways glance.

Maren hunched her shoulders. Was Jac inviting confidences? The answer was not much. She read, talked with Janelle, sugar-soaped walls, went shopping. After her hectic life in Melbourne, the unstructured time was a gift. But still...there were too many times when she sat on the deck with her thoughts, waiting for Orli to need her. Jac's questions were too close to reality. She needed a life. Maybe she didn't need a partner yet, but she needed something. Someone. A friend, or...

She stopped, toes digging into the wet sand. Jac halted, too, and she was close, near enough that the flecks in her brown eyes made them seem dark and alluring. A seagull shrieked overhead, and it echoed the pulse in Maren's mind. No more overthinking. She reached and took Jac's hand in her own, curling her fingers around her palm.

Jac looked down at their entwined hands. Her eyebrow arched, but she said nothing.

Maren tugged, and when Jac didn't move, she closed the gap that separated them. Her free hand wrapped around Jac's neck. For a second, she caught the look of surprise that widened Jac's eyes, then she tilted forward and pressed her lips to Jac's, slanting a hot kiss across her unresisting lips. One kiss, then a breath, and a second kiss.

Her head and heart pounded the same beat, and the crash of waves on the shore obliterated any other thought. What had started as a distraction kiss, as a way of showing Jac she wasn't a colourless woman waiting for her daughter to remember she was there, lit and caught fire between them.

After the first beat of hesitation, Jac turned fully toward her, ran her hands from Maren's shoulder to her waist, and then linked them behind her back. The kiss escalated, lips, tongues, breath, all joined in the small space where their mouths met.

A white-hot blaze engulfed Maren's mind. Jac's lips, Jac's mouth, Jac's kiss...they consumed her, and blew all other thoughts from her head.

She lifted her mouth, changed direction, and slanted another kiss over Jac's lips.

Her own lips tingled, and a trickle of flame wound its way down into her chest, dividing into two so her nipples peaked and pressed against the fabric. Surely Jac could feel them pressing into her.

Jac eased away until there was space between them. Her hands were still around Maren's waist, and she took a deep, shuddering breath. "That was unexpected."

"Unwelcome?" She had to ask, even though she was sure of the answer.

"No, not at all. But I'm surprised."

"Because?" Her lips pulsed hot, and already she missed Jac's kiss.

Jac dropped her hands and took a step away, facing out to sea. "Was this an experiment, Maren? Did you try kissing a woman to see if you like it? It's okay with me if it is…many people are bi-curious." In profile, the corner of her mouth lifted. "I wish more people would act on that curiosity, to be honest. Maybe they wouldn't go back."

"I've kissed women—I had a girlfriend before Marcus."

"I didn't know." A shoulder lifted. "Guess I should follow more celebrity gossip."

"I'm not out." She, too, took a pace away. "Most of twenty years ago, Marcus's ex-boyfriend threatened to out him. I agreed to marry Marcus to silence the rumours. Back then, a gay pro-rugby player would have been shunned. The sport is the most macho of macho now. Back then, it was even worse. He was—still is—my best friend."

"What about you?"

"I thought I was a lesbian. And, although I doubt I'd have lost my job over it, our marriage was a cover for me as well. Marcus and I… didn't have a normal marriage. We tried at one point…that's how Orli came about…but while I was willing to make our marriage more real, Marcus is gay, not bisexual. He couldn't continue it in the end. I don't hold any animosity toward him for that. We are what we are."

"Did you have girlfriends during that marriage?"

"No, we agreed not to have other partners. It was difficult, but we felt it was the only way we could make it work for us. But two years ago, Marcus had retired from playing professionally and had been coaching and commentating for a few years. He wanted the freedom to be who he was, so we agreed on an amicable split. He met Rick, his boyfriend, after we parted."

"But you didn't give yourself that same freedom?" Jac's voice was neutral, no censure, or avid curiosity. It was as if she was trying to get the information so she could decide what to do.

"Purely because of Orli. She had a lot of questions once Marcus got together with Rick. Oh, she's fine with it, and she loves Rick. But two gay parents…I think that would be too much for her right now. Especially now, when things are difficult. I think it would raise questions I don't want to answer." She lifted a shoulder. "She doesn't need another excuse to go off the rails."

Jac turned and resumed walking back to the bike.

Maren watched her profile against the background of the ocean. A pulse pounded in her head. Maybe she'd done the wrong thing, telling Jac about her marriage, but her gut told her Jac wouldn't race off to sell the story. Hadn't she already said she didn't read the gossip mags?

Jac turned to her. "I'm not sure where you're going with this, Maren. Why you're telling me this? We kissed. What now?"

"You thought I'd never been with a woman—I wanted to let you know how it is. As for us—we can do this again if we both want. Or not."

Jac laughed. "I guess I can't imagine going that long without kissing a woman. No worries, Maren. This won't be awkward on my part."

Maren touched Jac's arm to stop her, then stepped in front. "I never said I'd go another twenty years." She lunged forward, suddenly desperate to feel Jac's lips again.

The gap between them closed instantly. Maren wasn't sure who moved first, but then they were in each other's arms. Jac's hands roamed around her back as she pressed her lips to Maren's. The kiss was wild, hot, a dance of duelling tongues that left them both gasping. Jac's hands pressed into Maren's buttocks, bringing her closer so their bodies touched: breasts, hips, thighs.

They eased apart.

"Not even twenty minutes," Maren said. She took a breath, willing her knees to stop trembling, her pulse to slow, and the world to stop spinning.

Jac bent and picked up a shell, then handed it to Maren.

She ran a finger over its fluted edge, turning it over in her fingers.

"To remind you of your first kiss with a woman in twenty years." She grinned. "And while I'd like to make that twenty kisses, we need to get back."

Hand in hand, they walked back around the headland to the Norton.

CHAPTER 18
CELEBRITIES PLAY POOL, TOO

"WELL?" ORLI DEMANDED.

Maren dismounted. Her legs wobbled, as if she'd just disembarked a yacht. "Well, what? Well, are we having madras curry for dinner? Well, can you raise my allowance? It's no to that one, by the way." She reached out a hand to twitch Orli's hoodie, but she ducked away.

"How was the ride? Was it awesome? Where did you go? How fast did you go? Were you scared? Are you going again? When can I go?"

"Oh, those 'wells'." Maren removed her helmet and gloves and set them on the ground. "The ride was awesome. We went down to Thirroul via the national park and the lookout at Stanwell Tops. We kept to the speed limit, although it felt much faster. I'd like to go again."

"And?" Orli demanded.

"I need to speak with Jac first before I can decide. Although"—she put her hands on her hips and glared at her daughter—"weren't you told to go home and not hang around Jac's property?"

"I was at home." Orli glared back. "Ask Janelle if you don't believe me—which you obviously don't. I heard the bike come down the street and ran over."

"I believe you." Maren smiled at Orli. "But I need to talk to Jac before I can decide. Alone," she added, when it seemed Orli would stay. "Go home, honey. I'll be over in a few minutes."

Orli slouched off. Maren waited until she was out of earshot before turning to Jac.

"That really was awesome. Although the most amazing part actually had nothing to do with motorbikes."

Jac grinned. "Glad you thought so."

Maren itched to move closer and taste those grinning, cocky lips once more. "About Orli. Honestly, that ride was incredible. I loved it—and I'd like to go again sometime. But Orli... Were you serious when you said you were happy to take her? That you'd ensure she obeyed you absolutely? And you'd call me if there were any problems, and certainly before you stranded her in Wollongong for disobeying?"

"I promise." The grin had disappeared from Jac's face. "I take this seriously. Everyone who rides with me is basically in my care."

"Then I'll let her go. But I'd rather she went for a shorter ride first. Say just around the national park. That way, you can assess how she goes, and if all's good, she can go down to the Illawarra next time. Is that okay?"

"It is." Jac nodded. "I'm busy in the lead up to Christmas, but I'll take her as soon as I can. Will that work?"

"I'll let her know. I think she's going to be ecstatic." Maren hesitated. An invitation was hammering in her brain...but was it one she should issue? The reasons she should thank Jac and walk away scrolled through her mind like a newsreader's teletext. The reasons she should ask Jac came down to one: because she wanted to.

Jac reached for her hand and ran her thumb over Maren's knuckles. "And what about the other part of your amazing morning? Would you like to have dinner with me one night?"

Had Jac just read her mind? The "yes" hovered on her lips, but she bit it back.

Jac's eyes hooded. "No pressure, Maren. You can say no without me taking offence."

"I want to say yes...but there's Orli. I just can't... I wouldn't know what to say to her."

"How about coming to the pub then, with me and my friends tomorrow night? We drink beer, have a pub feed, play pool, and chat.

You'll have to deal with Kyra mooning over you, but maybe you'd like that...now you've broken your drought."

The unknown Kyra couldn't possibly compete with the woman in front of her. "Are your friends discreet? I don't want photos of me sold to news outlets. And...no talk of our kiss. I can't, because—"

"Of Orli." Jac's lips thinned. "You've made that very clear, Maren. My friends are discreet—if you ask them to be."

"Then I'd like that. What time?"

"Do you want to go on the bike? I only have one light beer if I'm riding." At Maren's nod, she said, "Then come over here at 6:30. It's only a few kilometres away. Wear jeans, sturdy shoes, and a jacket."

"Okay." Maren looked down at their hands, Jac still idly caressing the back. "I'll look forward to it."

Jac licked her lips and leaned toward her.

She took a step back. "Not here. Sorry."

"Then I'll stop somewhere on the way back from the pub tomorrow."

"Now I'm really looking forward to it." She went over to the rack and shrugged out of the jacket, hanging it with the others, then wiggled out of the tight pants and boots. After retrieving her shoes from where she'd left them, with a last glance at Jac, she went home to tell Orli the good news.

"Oh my god!" Kyra's booted feet hit the floor with a thump followed by her jaw. "Jac, you total shit. Why didn't you tell me who you were bringing?"

Jac smothered a grin. "Because I wanted to see your reaction. My friend, you never disappoint. Try to behave yourself." She turned to Maren. "These are Liz, Caitlin, and Kyra. Watch Kyra; she may drool on your boots."

"I will not. I assumed you were bringing a pick-up from—" Pink stained her cheeks. "That is...I'm assuming...Maren isn't."

Jac rolled her eyes. "You can shut up any time you like, Kyra, before you need a ladder to get out of that hole you're digging. Maren is a friend."

Liz shook her hand. "Nice to meet you, Maren. I'm a big fan. I'm glad you're getting on with Jac."

"Jac's been good enough to take my daughter and her newfound passion for motorbikes under her wing. I went out with Jac yesterday, and now Orli can't wait to go, too."

"Bikes have that effect on people," Liz said. "I nearly shit myself the first time Jac took me out, over ten years ago. Now I have my own bike."

Kyra smoothed back her hair with both palms and put on her best butch swagger as she went over to Maren. "Let me buy you a drink to welcome you to Suttons Bay. What would you like?"

"Just a light beer, please. I came with Jac on the bike, and I'm still not used to it."

"No worries."

"Do you play pool?" Caitlin asked.

"Badly. And not for a long time."

"We'll take it in turns," Caitlin said.

"I'll sit out this evening." Jac said. "Maren can take my place."

Maren's newsreader smile was glued in place, and she clutched the beer Kyra handed her. "I hope it's not a serious competition." Her eyes crinkled as she glanced at Jac. "I wouldn't want to wreck your standing in the group."

"You've raised it just by coming along this evening. But no, it's not serious. The losing pair buys the winning pair a drink."

"I better get my wallet out now." She moved away to inspect the cues.

Jac's gaze drifted up and down Maren's rear view. Her palms tingled as she remembered how Maren's butt had felt under her palms, right before Maren had pulled her close. Right before the kiss that blew her mind into shrapnel and turned her legs to jelly.

She sipped her beer as Maren picked a cue and gave a polite smile when Kyra claimed her as her pool partner. It was a very different smile to the unrestrained grin she'd worn during the bike ride, or the affectionate ones she gave Orli.

Caitlin sidled up to Jac as Kyra broke and pocketed a stripe. Maren's high-five made Kyra blush.

"So," Caitlin said. "You've got a celebrity as a neighbour, and she's slumming it enough to drink beer and play pool with us. That doesn't fit with the celebrity gossip. Is there anything you want to tell me?"

Across the room, Liz took her shot and missed, and Maren stepped up. She lined the cue up with careful precision, nodding at Kyra when she suggested a slight change.

"I'm just being neighbourly. She's not long moved here and doesn't know anyone." Their kiss flashed through her mind again. Would it always be there, on repeat, playing out in front of her eyes every time she thought of Maren? She didn't kiss her other neighbours. Between everything, she and Maren were already more than neighbours.

"Still. She's a celebrity. And you're...not." Caitlin went over to the table to take her shot.

Jac took another mouthful of beer. At this rate, her single beer for the night would be gone in five minutes. She set the beer down and sauntered over to the table to be the cheer squad.

The night ended by ten with the usual hugs and kisses all around, including Maren. Jac's lips twitched in amusement as Kyra hugged for longer and kissed Maren's cheek. When she stepped back, Kyra's cheeks were as rosy as her scarlet shirt.

The other three drove off, leaving Maren and Jac alone in the car park. Jac unlocked the helmets and handed Maren's to her. Their fingers brushed and her blood thrummed.

"That was a fun evening," Maren said. "Your friends are lovely."

"I hope Kyra didn't make you uncomfortable. You've been her celebrity crush for years."

"She was fine. Didn't cross any boundaries. I'm sure if we do this again, she'll realise I'm just a normal person, and she'll treat me as your neighbour who was on TV once."

"Is that how I should treat you?" Jac stepped closer, the urge to press her lips to Maren's once more a jagged beat in her head.

"I think we're working that out as we go."

"Home?" Jac asked.

"That's a question. What else is on offer?" The slight, upward curl of Maren's lips started a drumbeat of desire in Jac's belly. *What is she suggesting?*

"It's a clear night. If you'd like, we can ride down to Cronulla Beach, take a walk. It will probably be quiet there."

Maren's eyes shone like silver. "I'd like that. As long as I'm home by eleven, it will be fine. Janelle won't go to bed before I get back, so she'll check on Orli."

"That gives us nearly an hour. Time for a short stroll."

They straddled the Norton. Maren pressed up close to Jac's back as she rode through the quiet streets of Suttons Bay down to the busier area around Cronulla. People were spilling out of pubs, and there was more traffic. She found a parking spot at one end of the beach, away from the busy areas, and they dismounted, then locked their helmets to the bike.

"I'm glad I wore jeans tonight," Maren said. "There's no way I'd have been able to bend over the pool table in bike pants."

"Your rear view is better in jeans. Everyone's is, but particularly yours." Jac turned and walked along the path above the beach, heading toward the shadowy end where the light was less. Her heart thumped, and the last time they'd been on a beach together spooled through her mind. Would they kiss again? They would, if she had anything to do with it. If Maren wanted the same.

Their hands swung close together. Jac captured Maren's with her own and linked their fingers. "Is this okay?"

Maren glanced around, then tightened her grip. "No one's paying us any attention. It's not as if I get much, anyway. Aussies are very laid back with celebrity—and for a minor one like me, there's even less attention. That's not to say there isn't unwanted attention at times. The paps followed me around for a while after Marcus and I divorced. I think they were trying to see if I was dating anyone. I stuck to my female friends." She lifted their linked hands. "If only they knew my preferences."

"The great bisexual invisibility. Any woman who has ever dated a man is presumed heterosexual until proven otherwise."

"Exactly." Maren steered them to the steps that led to the sand.

The sand gave under Jac's feet, and they walked down to where the tide had washed the beach flat, the sand packed hard. The moonlight tipped the waves with silver as they rose, hung, and rolled into shore before breaking.

"This is glorious." Maren walked closer to the water, then stopped and faced the ocean. The reach of the tide came within a couple of metres of their feet.

Jac glanced around. They were as alone as it was possible to be on a popular city beach. Just a couple strolling, someone breaking the no-dog rule and letting their cocker spaniel gambol around. Jac tightened her hand on Maren's and turned to face her.

The breeze blew strands of hair across her face, and Jac brushed them back with gentle fingers. "I'm glad you enjoyed the evening."

"I did. Thank you for including me."

"Anytime." Jac rested a hand on Maren's hip and took a small step closer. "I hope this will be a good end to the evening." She leaned in.

Maren's eyes glittered, and her breath hitched.

In anticipation? Jac hoped so.

And then they were kissing, a kiss that went from zero to one hundred in mere moments. Their mouths met, clung, opened, explored. Jac's thoughts blurred into a haze of feeling, a pulsing urgency driving her on. Maren tasted faintly of lime and bitters from the soft drink she'd switched to after her beer. Her tongue danced around Jac's mouth with no hesitation.

They broke apart.

"Is that why you brought me down here?" Maren asked.

"Maybe that was an ulterior motive. But mainly, I thought you'd enjoy the ride."

"I did. I do. But if we're comparing, your kiss was a bigger thrill."

Jac ran a hand around her hip and down over her backside. "For me too." She sighed. "But if you want to get back by eleven, we better stop now."

A nod, and without breaking their clasp, they strolled back to the bike.

CHAPTER 19
SOMEONE SHINING BRIGHTLY

"How was your evening?" Janelle asked the next morning. She put a mug of coffee down in front of Maren and picked up her own, coming to sit next to her at the counter.

"Great. Jac's friends are a relaxed bunch. Welcoming. Thank you for keeping an eye on Orli."

"There wasn't much to do. We watched a couple of episodes of *Dark Matter*, talked a bit. She seems very taken with Jac, and she won't stop talking about her upcoming bike ride."

Maren sighed. "I hope I haven't unleashed a monster."

"You doubtless have. She's already talking about getting her learner rider licence and she hasn't even been out on a bike yet."

"I'll meet that when it comes to it. Hopefully, going to Marcus and Rick's for Christmas this week will give her something else to focus on." She looked at Janelle. "How are your preparations for the cruise going?"

Janelle's lined face lit up. "Good. Cheri and I are having a massive planning session over Christmas. After all, a cruise of several weeks and different climate zones takes a lot of organisation. And, although we've got a suite, I don't think we can take huge amounts of baggage."

"Not long to go."

"Three weeks," Janelle said. "I'll miss you and Orli."

"For five minutes, you will. Then you'll be drinking Bloody Marys and watching the sunset, going to all those shows, and meeting new people who are a lot more exciting than us."

"I doubt that. Cheri wants us to learn bridge. That doesn't sound exciting, but she's pulling older-sister rank."

"You'll be learning." Maren sniggered. "Good luck getting out of that."

Her mobile rang, and she glanced at the screen. Her eyebrows rose. "It's Ethan. I'd better take this."

Janelle stood and went toward the bathroom.

"Hi, Ethan. What makes you call at eight in the morning?"

"Best time of day." Her producer—or was that ex-producer now?—grunted. "Actually, it's the only time I have free. I'm just checking in on you. After all, you're still a member of my team."

With a guilty start, she realised she hadn't given Ethan or anyone at Channel 12 a thought in weeks. What did that say about her? She hadn't watched the news in days. "It seems the program's doing well."

"It is. Zoey's settled in well. Ratings are still down from when you were anchor, but they're creeping back up."

"That's good." Was it? Was it churlish of her to hope that Zoey couldn't command the viewers that she could?

"The public is fickle. And that's why I'm calling. I know you're on a year's break—"

"It's only been a couple of months, Ethan."

"Yes, yes. But I'm wondering if you could do a couple of fill-in spots. You could work from the Sydney studios."

Oh! She hadn't expected that. "I'll need to think about it. Orli still needs my attention. I'm not sure that resuming work will send the right message to her."

"I'll be candid. Zoey's doing well, and I expect the ratings for Luka and her will soon equal those of Luka and you. Maybe even exceed them. But talking as your friend, Maren, I suggest you consider an earlier return date. Zoey's ambitious as hell and it's no secret that she wants your spot permanently."

"I'm aware. I knew that before I took this break."

"Then you'll also know that upon your return, while you're still entitled to the same or similar job as the one you left, there's no guarantee of the same position. There's talk higher-up of cementing Zoey in the role."

She bit her lip. Was this break going to be career suicide? The end of everything she'd built so painstakingly over her years in television? Newsreaders were expendable—unless you were one of the golden few that the public loved. That had been her, and she'd hoped to continue again after the break. But if Zoey was shining so brightly... Ethan was right. She should return, at least in some way, before a year was up.

"I'm not suggesting you come back full time. That would mean moving back to Melbourne. I'm suggesting you commit to the Sydney desk at least twice a week."

"I really appreciate you telling me this, but I need to think it through. I promised Orli this year would be for us, and I'm not sure I can go back on that promise." *Even if Orli doesn't seem to want to spend time with me.* "She's doing better, but she's still fragile, and I can't let her backslide now."

"I understand," Ethan said. "Maren, there'll be some role here for you, even if you take the full year out, but to be brutal, I think you'll find it a much reduced one if you leave it much longer."

"Zoey's nearly twenty years younger than me. Who'd have thought that forty-six would be considered over the hill?"

"It's more difficult in television," Ethan said. "The camera is unforgiving."

She nodded. "And the silver foxes are all male."

A beat of silence. "It's changing, but slowly. Maren, I've got to go. Meeting. You know how it is. At least consider my suggestion?"

"I will. I'll get back to you. Thanks, Ethan."

"Take care, Maren, and I hope you have a good Christmas and New Year." The call ended.

Maren stood and paced to the front balcony. Outside, overnight rain had soaked the grass, drops beading on the plants. The air smelled fresh, newborn. Magpies patrolled the lawn, darting on insects.

Ethan was right. She should return, even if only part time. But to do so would negate the message she was sending to Orli—that she was the centre of Maren's universe; that she would do whatever was necessary to ensure she was okay. That she loved her.

Even if Orli didn't seem to want that.

CHAPTER 20

DREAMS OF FLYING

"So, when can I go on the bike?" Orli asked. "It's been, like, ages since you took Mum. She's cool with it. So, when?"

"Christmas is my busiest time. I had bookings every day except Christmas Day, and even I get a day off," Jac said. "Wait your turn."

"When?" Orli drew out the word to a whine. "It could be my Christmas present. You didn't give me one."

"Figured you had enough stuff. Besides, you didn't get me anything, either."

"Adults give kids the presents, not the other way around. And isn't my sparkling company enough?"

Jac rolled her eyes and tipped Orli's baseball cap over her eyes. "Well, your company is better than it was."

Orli huffed a laugh. She was sitting on the floor of the shed, legs spread around the front wheel of the Norton, polishing the chrome at half speed. Her short hair flopped over her eyes, and she wore a grunge band T-shirt and denim overalls that would probably fit her beefy father. "So, when will you take me?"

"Do you never give up? Okay, soon. When I have a couple of hours free."

"A couple of *hours*? You took Mum for a whole afternoon. You could practically have gone to Melbourne in that time."

"It's a motorbike, not a rocket. There's no wormhole to Melbourne."

"What are you talking about?" Orli gave her a blank stare.

The generation gap had never been wider. Every kid in Jac's day knew about *Star Trek*. "We weren't on the bike all the time. With new riders, it's best to take frequent breaks." Her mind fizzled. For kisses, in Maren's case. She flicked a glance at the house next door. She hadn't seen Maren since the pool night. A quick wave from the front balcony yesterday, and that was it. No evening chats. No Christmas drinks on the deck. Not even a request for an update on how Orli was doing. Jac had expected *something* after the pool evening. You didn't just kiss someone and vanish from their lives. She sucked her lip. Well, that wasn't true; she did that with her occasional hook-ups, but Maren was a neighbour. Jac was putting up with her daughter a few times each week. And there had been more than one kiss.

Jac wanted more.

"Well?" Orli asked. "Or are you gonna keep putting me off?"

"I'm not," Jac said. "But with the BMW out of action, I have only the Goldwing and the Norton to keep my business going, so I have to work harder—not everyone wants to ride those bikes. The Beemer suits most everyone."

A wash of red stole up Orli's neck. "Sorry. I didn't, like, think of that when I took your bike."

"I doubt you thought of much at all after half a bottle of bourbon."

Orli's cheeks were now fiery red. "Yeah, well, there is that." She was silent for a moment. "Can I ask you something?"

Alarm bells clanged in Jac's head. Had Orli somehow divined that Jac was attracted to Maren? Not that she cared, but Maren might. "Sure."

"You're queer, right?"

"Yes." She would never hide that one. Never hide who she was. Never again.

"Figured." Orli went back to rubbing tiny circles with her polishing rag. "I mean the bikes, the leather gear. Your hair, just...your attitude, I guess."

What the hell? Orli was right in some ways, but so wrong in others. "You're stereotyping. Not all women who ride motorbikes are queer. The rest of it, too."

"Dykes on Bikes." Orli nodded. "I've seen them leading the Sydney Mardi Gras Parade. They're rad. And I know what you're saying. It's different for my generation, though. We don't have to present a certain way or whatever. We can just *be*."

"Everyone can. But you're right, in that previously, there were expectations…and more people had to hide who they were." *And don't I know all about that.* "Some still have to. It's good that people you know are free to be."

"My friend Raz is pansexual. No one cares."

"That's good."

"Yeah." Orli's mouth opened as if she was going to say more.

Jac waited. If Orli wanted to confide in her about something, well, she'd listen.

"So, when can I come on the bike?"

Jac huffed a laugh. "You're more persistent than a magpie stealing a sandwich."

"Don't want you to forget."

"No chance of that."

"So, when?"

Jac threw up her hands. "I have a client this afternoon, but if your mum agrees, we can go for a quick ride at lunchtime today. If that goes okay, if you want, you can also come with me to Sydney tomorrow. The BMW is fixed, and we could ride home from there. But we'll have to go into Sydney on the train and then there's a bit of a walk to the repair place."

"That's sick! Thank you." Orli jumped up, all arms and legs, and threw her arms around Jac's neck. "I'll go ask Mum now."

She disappeared in a blur of T-shirt and denim.

Jac went to check the Norton. It was ready to go, and she was certain that any second Orli would come streaking back saying it was fine and could they—

"Mum said yes. And she'll drive us to the repair place tomorrow so we'll have longer to ride home. And it's gone eleven now, and that's nearly lunchtime, so can we go now?"

She suppressed a grin. So exactly what she'd thought.

"Okay then. But I'll need Maren to sign the paperwork for you. It's a onetime thing."

"She said that. She'll come over in a minute. I've already picked out my helmet and gear. I'll get dressed while we're waiting for her."

Maren was coming over. Jac looked down at herself: workshop overalls, oil under her fingernails. Not the sort of look to impress Maren McEvoy. Not the sort of image to entice Maren to come out with her again. To kiss her again. To do more than kiss. She'd change when Orli was ready, but at least she could scrub clean. She went over to the sink and used the degreaser on her hands, scrubbing her short nails with the brush.

"Hi. I'm here to sign Orli's life away."

Maren stood silhouetted against the light. She wore close-fitting jeans and a short-sleeve linen shirt in an olive green. A pair of sunglasses perched on top of her head.

"Hi, yourself." Jac's pulse sped up. Maren looked delectable, and the small, curled smile she offered Jac unfurled a shoot of heat in her belly.

"Give me a minute, and I'll get the paperwork." Jac dried her hands on the towel and went to the desk on one side of the workshop.

Maren followed her over. "Is it the same as what I signed?"

"Basically. Except there's a section for a parent or guardian, making you aware that if the minor behaves recklessly, the ride will stop, and I will wait until you come and collect them. If I have to wait longer than the booked ride time, there's an extra charge."

"No worries. We agreed I'd pay for Orli's ride."

"For today, yes. Tomorrow, though, she's just coming along when I collect the bike, so there's no charge for that. Especially as I hear you're going to drop us there."

"Sure. Wherever 'there' is."

"Parramatta. So, it won't be a scenic ride home. I'll take the freeway."

"I think you could ride through a tunnel and Orli wouldn't care, as long as she was riding."

"That's quite prophetic—the tunnel is the quickest and safest way to go."

"Am I okay?" Orli returned. She'd picked black pants and jacket and the helmet was under her arm. Her usual Docs were on her feet.

"You'll need a hi-vis vest, but the rest is fine. Put the helmet on so I can check the fit."

Maren's stare burned a hole in the back of Jac's neck as she checked Orli's helmet. She cleared her throat. "Okay, Orli, I'm agreeing to this, but your part of the deal is you listen to Jac, and you do exactly as she says with no arguments. I don't want to come out and collect you from the side of the road."

"Mu-um, I *said* I would."

Maren signed the pages with a flourish. "Make sure you do."

Her pale neck was revealed as her hair fell to one side. Jac dragged her eyes away from the exposed skin and imagined kissing that sweet curve, working her way down, pushing aside the T-shirt to kiss her shoulder. She mentally blanked that out. Right now, she had a ride to take.

"You did good." In the hour and a half of the ride, Orli had behaved perfectly. Better than that, she'd got the feel of the bike. She'd clung to Jac's waist, and quickly learned to lean into the curves. "You're a natural." Jac dismounted, took off her helmet and shook out her curly hair.

Orli did the same. Her eyes were shining. "I loved it. I freakin' loved it! I know we were only riding around Suttons Bay and through the national park. I know we didn't go fast, but it was rad. Thank you, Jac. I can't wait for tomorrow. If we're taking the freeway, we'll go faster, right?"

"If traffic is light, we'll do the speed limit. One hundred kilometres per hour in some places."

"I think it will feel like flying."

"You'd be right."

Orli set down her helmet and put the bike on the stand as Jac had shown her.

"I'm going to grab some lunch now," Jac said. "I've only got thirty minutes until I have to leave."

"I can come back after lunch and tidy up for you."

"Sure. Thank you." They'd come a long way. Orli was proving herself trustworthy to be left alone in the workshop. She was very different from the rebellious teen of a few weeks ago.

Orli hasn't stopped talking about her ride. Are you free for a few minutes? I'd like to hear your version.

Jac stared at Maren's text. She could easily have heard about it on the drive to Parramatta the next day. Maybe the text meant Maren was keen to see Jac for other reasons. Kissing reasons.

Sure. Come over if you want.

Footsteps sounded on the steps a few minutes later, then Maren appeared, wearing the same jeans and shirt as earlier.

"Want a beer?" Jac offered. "I was just about to have one."

"Please." Maren followed her into the kitchen.

Jac pulled two beers from the fridge and handed one to her. Up close, Maren's eyes glowed silver. She took a step closer to Jac and trailed her fingers down her arm.

Each fingertip touch shot sparks into Jac's chest. She tilted her head. "Did you really want to know about the bike ride?"

That wicked, tilted smile shone on Maren's face. "I heard about it endlessly from Orli, who apparently knows what life is all about now, and was a perfect angel with you."

"She was. She's a natural."

"Better than me?"

"Definitely. You were good. Orli is instinctive."

Maren's fingers walked up Jac's arm again. "I have other talents." Her fingers pushed Jac's hair back from her face. "Wait."

She broke away, and Jac waited. Maren went and turned off the light, so the kitchen was only lit by the last glow of sunset.

"That's better." She walked up close to Jac and wrapped her arms around her shoulders. "Now I can do this without feeling as if I'm in a fishbowl." Her lips claimed Jac's with an assurance that made her gasp. A few kisses and Maren's confidence in what she was doing—knowing that Jac wanted this—had soared. Instantly her lips parted, and Maren's tongue swept around her mouth. The kiss was hot, intense.

Jac's nipples tightened, pressing against her bra, and licks of heat trailed down into her belly. Maren kissed like a cyclone, a whirl of fierce intensity around her calm centre.

They parted, drew breath, and returned at another angle.

Jac slid her hands down to Maren's backside and pulled her closer, pushing her thigh between Maren's.

Maren moaned into her mouth, and then she ground down, riding Jac's thigh as if it were the Norton, pressing, sliding. She gripped either side of Jac's face and deepened the kiss.

Jac's head spun. There was only one place this should go. She worked a hand between their bodies, found the button of Maren's jeans and flicked it open, then lowered the zip, tracing her fingers down to the top of her undies.

She broke the kiss. "Bedroom?"

Maren froze, her body tightening. "Oh god." She eased away from Jac's leg so that Jac's fingers fell away. "I can't. Orli's expecting me to return and tell her what you said."

Right. She closed her eyes, but the sound of the zip being done up told her what Maren was doing. "Of course."

"I'm sorry." A touch of fingers on her cheek. "I didn't mean to lead you on...but I can't do this."

"Can't do this now because of Orli, or can't do this at all?"

A beat. "I want to say can't do this now, but I can't promise anything. But I want... I'd like..." A quick, passionate kiss. "Can we put this on hold for now?"

Jac heaved a breath and swallowed away her disappointment. "Sure."

What else could she say?

CHAPTER 21
DEEP DOWN DIVE

It shouldn't have made any difference. Orli was sixteen. She knew about sex... Hell, if she'd told the truth in Melbourne, she was already sexually active. So why had Maren pulled back from Jac?

Maren stared at the ceiling in the dark bedroom.

She'd wanted nothing more than an insanely hot quickie with Jac, and Orli be damned. If Orli could accept Marcus and Rick, she surely would have no problem with Maren and Jac. But Marcus and Rick were a loving, established couple. She and Jac? Well, who knows, but they would probably never be more than hot sex and friendship. But it was more than that holding Maren back.

This time was for Orli. To be there for her, help her settle into a new life, one that kept her out of jail. How could she take on an extra distraction?

Janelle was leaving at the end of the week, and Orli was already upset about that. She loved Janelle—they both did—but Janelle had already put her life on hold for them once, delaying her retirement cruise by six weeks to help them settle into Suttons Bay. There was no way she'd ask Janelle to delay a second time.

Maren turned on her side. So many demands on her time. She still hadn't got back to Ethan about working from the Sydney studio. There wasn't really anyone she could talk to about that. Certainly not Luka, who seemed to get on well with Zoey. Maybe Marcus and Rick. And while she'd had plenty of people she was friendly with in

Melbourne, most were colleagues, and she didn't want to trust them with this. There was no one she could ask for advice, no one who had her back—except Marcus.

How sad was that?

Orli was visiting Marcus and Rick on the weekend—maybe Maren would take up their offer to stay over Friday night after dropping Orli off. "Dinner, delightful wine, stimulating conversation, and a comfortable bed," Marcus had said. "It's been a long time since we had a proper catch up."

Yes, that's what she'd do.

Maren pulled the car into Marcus and Rick's drive. There was barely enough room to park it in front of the double garage and for the security gates to close. Space in inner Sydney was at a premium— Marcus and Rick were lucky to have parking at all.

Orli bounded out of the car the second it stopped and reached the front door as it opened. A fluffy, toffee-coloured goldendoodle bounced around Orli with a series of excited barks.

"Maple!" Orli dropped to her knees and let Maple cover her with kisses. "I've missed you."

Marcus stood in the doorway, arms extended. He encompassed Maren in a hug, dropping a kiss on the top of her head. "We've missed you. It seems like forever since we've had you for an entire evening."

"Family dinner." Maren turned to Rick, where he stood next to Marcus and kissed him on the cheek, receiving a squeeze in return.

"About that." Rick glanced at Marcus, then shot a look at Orli, still cuddling Maple. He took Maren's arm and led her into the hall. "Please say no if it's not what you want, but my company promotes Mia Raines, the indie singer. I know she's one of Orli's favourites, and she's playing an all-ages gig at the Hordern Pavilion tonight. I've got two tickets. If you're okay with it, I can see if Orli would like to come with me. That leaves you and Marcus to have a catch up. I'll see you when we get back—or at breakfast."

"Orli would love that—but it's up to her. If she wants to go, that's fine with me. More to the point, are you okay for an entire evening of screaming teens?"

"I like Mia Raines, actually, so I'll probably be screaming along with them. Marcus doesn't want to go, before you ask." He went back outside and called to Orli.

"Is this a setup?" Maren asked Marcus.

He raised a shoulder. "You and I haven't had a heart-to-heart in months. And you sounded a little lost when we spoke on the phone. I thought you might want to talk without Orli around."

She sighed. "You're right. Thank you for suggesting it. I hope Rick's not going to hate me in the morning after a night of teen angst."

"He'll be fine. If Orli agrees, Rick is going to suggest burgers on the way to the gig. So, you and I can do whatever we want for dinner. We can go out, or order in. The chef in this house has a date with our daughter."

"Let's order in. If anyone sees the two of us having an intimate dinner, rumours will start."

"We could go to McDonald's. That's the least intimate place in Sydney."

She tapped his biceps. "I have standards. And I'd like sushi."

Unsurprisingly, Orli was ecstatic at the idea of the Mia Raines gig, and she and Rick went off in an Uber.

An hour later, Maren and Marcus were sitting at the breakfast bar. The counter was littered with takeaway containers, and Marcus had opened a bottle of pinot grigio.

Maren snagged a piece of seared salmon nigiri with her chopsticks and wiped it through the wasabi and soy sauce. "I need to find a sushi place as good as this near Suttons Bay. This is fantastic."

"It is." Marcus popped an edamame bean into his mouth and regarded her. "But you don't want to talk about raw fish, do you?"

Maren set down the chopsticks. "No. But I have a dilemma." She outlined Ethan's suggestion that she return two days per week at the Sydney studio.

"You don't want that?"

"I don't know. Maybe. But I committed to this year off because of Orli. What message does it send if I renege on that?"

"Take Orli out of it for a moment. Would you want to return then?" Marcus swiped a finger through the soy sauce and sucked it.

"If Orli did that, I'd tell her off for being disgusting."

"It's just you and me here, and we've shared a lot more than a bit of saliva. Don't avoid the question."

"I wouldn't have taken a break at all. But since I have, if not for Orli, yes, I'd consider it. I worked hard to get where I did—but at the end of the year, I'll have to start again. There's no way I'll get Zoey out of my job. I hate to say it, but she's getting better all the time. She and Luka are good together on screen." She compressed her lips. "And they're closer in age."

"That shouldn't matter." Marcus shuffled his stool nearer and slung an arm around her shoulders.

"But it does. Newsreaders aren't as badly off as actors in that regard, but think of the number of middle-aged male newsreaders compared to female. It's about four to one."

"Google 'Australia's favourite newsreader'," Marcus said. "You're still number one."

"That will change."

"It will. But, Maren, if you want it badly enough, Orli will have to understand. She seems a lot more settled these past few weeks. Maybe when she goes back to school, you could resume work?"

Maren chewed her lip. "Maybe. But what if she runs off the rails again? It's just her and me—"

"And me and Rick. We're only forty minutes away. She can stay with us more often." He tapped her hand where it fiddled with the chopsticks. "I know you're blaming yourself for what happened with her in Melbourne, but that's not right. You could blame me for leaving. Blame me and Rick for getting together. For moving to Sydney and being less available for Orli. What you shouldn't do is take all the blame and shame for this."

She stared at him. "Thank you. Logical me knows you're right, but emotional me thinks it still comes down to the mother."

"You're wrong." His voice sharpened. "I'm sorry, Maren, but that's complete and utter bullshit. It's not 1970 anymore. Parents are equally responsible. You and I share responsibility. Rick, too, by extension. He loves Orli. At times, I wonder why, but he does."

"Right now, he's probably having his eardrums shattered by thousands of screaming teenagers. He may not love her tomorrow."

"He will."

"He'll always love you, I think," Maren said. "You got lucky, Marcus Coffey."

He slid off the stool and came closer, pulling her into a hug. "I did. Starting with you."

She rested her head on his chest, comforted and warmed. Tears pricked at the back of her eyes.

He squeezed again then released her, turning back to the counter to rummage through the empty sushi containers. "I thought we had some scallops left." His voice was gruff.

For a moment, Maren watched him. His thickset body, kind face with an off-kilter nose from his rugby days, one that had defied the plastic surgeons to straighten. Now forty-six—the same as her—he was still an attractive man. She'd loved him enough as a friend that she'd been prepared to have a real try at their marriage—they both had—but it hadn't been enough.

Marcus found a single piece of scallop sashimi hiding in the corner of a container and ate it. "What about you?"

"What about me?"

"Is there anyone in your life? Not just your friends in Melbourne, or Janelle, who's probably boarding the cruise ship in Sydney harbour as we speak, or Orli. A romantic prospect."

"You make it sound like marketing a new brand."

"You know what I mean. Are you getting any?" He nudged her.

An image of Jac flashed into her head, standing in her leathers, eyes serious as she checked the fit of Orli's helmet. A kind person. And eyes flashing fire in the moment before she kissed Maren. Before Maren had kissed her back. Before Maren had become incandescent with the heat twisting in her belly.

"Not yet. But maybe."

He laughed. "You're not sure if someone is attracted to you? Half of Australia is."

"Was. Zoey's the one they write fan letters to now."

"Choices, Maren. How important is it to you to keep that slot open?"

"I don't know," she admitted. "Strangely, it seems less important than it was."

Marcus went to the fridge to retrieve the wine and topped up their glasses. "When I retired from professional rugby, I thought that was it. That I was finished, and nothing would ever enthral me like that again. I was forty: old to stop playing professionally, even if it was in the minor leagues by then."

"I remember," she murmured. It wasn't just Marcus's angst about giving up something he loved that she remembered. It was also the creeping feeling that now he was out of the macho world of rugby, he'd rethink their comfortable marriage.

"It took me a while to find something that worked for me." He clasped her hand. "I'll always love you for that alone. You supported me, encouraged me to take however long I needed. It took me a while to become comfortable as a commentator, with writing my sports column, with a life that wasn't flying over the mud. But I'm there now."

"You're there now," she echoed.

"What I'm saying is, you'll find something that works for you, too, if you want it. Something that isn't news reading. That might free you from the belief you have to somehow be younger, more attractive, because that's what the public wants." He squeezed her hand. "You're more attractive the older you get, Maren. Your life is on your face, and it's a good life, a loving one. But"—he leaned closer, scanning her face from forehead to chin—"still no Botox?"

"I won't do that. Maybe I should—"

"No, don't. It's right for some, not for you, I think." He sat back. "If it's money—"

"It's not. I'm doing well. The financial advisor you put me on to is terrific. I don't need to worry about money for a few years."

"Good. But if it ever becomes a worry, you come to me and Rick first, okay?"

"I will."

"Rick loves you, too, you know. He's always been grateful that you didn't make it hard for him. And you could have. You could have sold your story: 'Australia's favourite newsreader jilted by gay husband.' You could have been difficult about the divorce, about custody of Orli, or frozen Rick out of your life."

"Rick is wonderful, and he's very good with you. Why would I do that? We both knew what we were getting into twenty years ago. Our mutual arrangement—"

"Our marriage."

"Yes, our marriage, well, we probably never expected it to last as long as it did. Or give us Orli."

"Things have changed. And I know you mainly did it for me. A gay rugby player? The shock, the outrage, the pearl-clutching that would have happened, even in the noughties. It would have been easier for you, in your industry. After all, there was Ellen DeGeneres and others."

Tears sprang to her eyes, and she glanced away, willing them not to fall. Marcus had always been her best friend. Their marriage had added another layer of love to that friendship. "And it turned out we were both at least a little bit bisexual. Pansexual, maybe. For me, it was always about you, not just any man."

"Can you be a little bit pansexual? Isn't it like saying you're a little bit pregnant?"

She laughed. "Probably."

He was silent for a moment. "So, now you're free to date again. Any gender you want…the reasons for our marriage don't exist any-more—at least for most Australians. Rick and I barely had a mention when we got together. So, who is this 'maybe' person for you?"

Jac sprang into her head, and her hot, deep, luscious kisses. The feel of her springy hair. Her lean body, and how it swayed to the rhythm of the bike.

She'd been silent too long.

"Well?" Marcus asked.

"My…neighbour." She moistened her lips. The words felt dangerous, as if telling Marcus made them more real. Set a path in motion.

"Jac?"

Maren's eyes widened. "How do you know?"

"Orli mentions her constantly. Oh, not in relation to you. She seems obsessed with the motorbikes."

"Yes, Jac. Such a cliché. A sexy woman in black leather."

"Something large and throbbing between her thighs."

She thumped his shoulder. "That is such a dick thing to say."

"Sorry, I couldn't resist."

"Resist away. Particularly when Orli's around. After that pregnancy scare, I'd be happy if she doesn't think of anything remotely sexual for the next ten years. That should be long enough for her to leave home."

"So, Jac then," Marcus said. "What's the skinny?"

"I like her. She's been exceptionally kind to Orli when she could have called the cops."

"And?"

"And she kisses like a demon. She makes me melt. She makes me want to drag her by the belt into the house and not come up for air for days."

"Is it more than lust?"

"Just because you fell in love with Rick over a week doesn't mean it happens to everyone like that."

"Rick kisses like that." Marcus's gaze drifted to the ceiling. "And he fell in love with me, too." He refocussed on Maren. "So, what's holding you back?"

She raised her eyebrows. "Several things. There's an age gap, for one. Eleven years. And don't you chatter about the fifteen-year gap between you and Rick. I think it matters between me and Jac."

Marcus made a rude sound with his lips. "I don't buy that. What else is stopping you?"

"Do you really need to ask me that?"

"Apparently I do, as I can't see any reason you shouldn't jump her bones."

She took a sip of wine and licked her lips again. "Please don't take this the wrong way, but one of Orli's parents has already come out and is in a same-sex relationship. She's fine with that. She loves Rick, loves the two of you together. But if both parents are? She's already thrown at me that given you're gay—her words—how come she exists? If I'm in a relationship with a woman, she's going to question everything she's known about us. Everything will be upended for her. I don't know what she thinks right now—but I'm sure she assumes I'm straight."

"With respect, Maren, that's flawed reasoning. Orli's generation is the one most likely to accept non-traditional families and evolving sexualities without question. Straight, gay, non-binary, trans... People are people to Orli and her friends. I'm not saying that's the same for every kid her age. There are definitely ones battling prejudice, discrimination, non-acceptance, parents...but it *is* getting better all the time. Orli's the lucky one compared to you and me."

"You're right of course, but it hasn't been easy for her. I feel I'm treading on glass, hoping nothing upsets her equilibrium again. Jac didn't report her to the police. Another time, she might not be so lucky. If she thinks our entire marriage was a farce, it takes away the foundations of her life."

"Other kids deal with far worse situations than that."

"You're right, but why risk it when I don't have to? Orli holds things close to her chest. She never told me she was struggling in Melbourne; she just ran off the rails. And I didn't notice until it was too late. What would happen this time if I didn't notice?"

Marcus took the glass from her hand and unclenched her fist, one finger at a time. "You're doing it again: blaming yourself. You were alone in Melbourne. Here, you have me and Rick. And you've said yourself—Orli seems more settled. She's taking an interest in the bikes."

"It seems a fragile truce."

"How long are you going to put your life on hold for her? When are you going to reclaim *your* life?"

"Maybe soon, when she's in her new school, hopefully making new friends, then. Maybe."

"She's not around all the time. She's with me and Rick tomorrow night. You don't have to announce to her you want to date, that you have a first date. You can have a life beyond that of a parent, Maren. It's allowed."

It's allowed. The words echoed in her mind. Maybe she could have something for herself. Something that wasn't a career or trying to nurture a child. Something for her, as a woman.

Maybe.

CHAPTER 22

WHO'S HUNGRY ANYWAY?

JAC'S MOBILE CHIRPED WITH A message, and she glanced at the screen. *Maren.* Angling her body away from Kyra, she opened the message.

> *Would you like to have dinner tonight at my place? Orli is with her father, and I feel like adult company.*

Adult company? Did Maren just mean someone older than sixteen, or was adult company a euphemism for adult pastimes that went beyond kissing?

"Is that a message from a debt collector?" Kyra waved a hand in front of Jac's face. "You've got a stunned-mullet look about you, as if you've got unexpected news."

She was right about that.

"No, just a text from a friend." She slipped the phone in her pocket. "I'll answer later." She increased her pace. "Reckon we can walk to the café by the breakwater? I fancy a slice of their lemon-and-ginger cheesecake."

Maren glanced at her mobile again. Still no response from Jac. Maybe she'd misread the whole situation, and Jac was even now out on a date with another woman. She stood and went over to the window.

She'd been so confident of Jac's acceptance that she'd stopped on the way home from Marcus's to buy prawns from the expensive market on the north shore. Oh well, she could always freeze them, although that seemed a waste.

Her phone pinged, and she snatched it up, heart thumping. A text from Jac. Fingers fumbling over the screen lock, she opened it.

Sorry, was out for a walk with Kyra. That sounds great. What time? And what can I bring?

She dashed off a reply. Seven was now only a couple of hours away.

When the doorbell rang at ten-past seven, Maren was twitchy with anticipation. What was it about this evening? She'd hosted dinner parties all the time in Melbourne, had intimate dinners with people, and kept things friendly and light. But somehow, between the kisses they'd shared and Marcus's words, she'd reached…not a decision, that was too final, but a mood of go-with-the-flow. Although what that flow was right now, she didn't know. She looked down at her dark-purple silk blouse and loose black pants. Was she overdressed? Probably. But just because she'd only ever seen Jac in bike leathers, jeans, or shorts and a T-shirt didn't mean she didn't dress up at all. Although, most likely, Jac wouldn't dress up for a casual dinner with a neighbour.

She flung the door wide. "Welcome, it's good—" Her words caught in her throat as she took in Jac.

She was wearing steel-grey tapered pants paired with a white, button-down shirt, and oh my god, a waistcoat fastened across her flat stomach with a gold chain. She'd slicked her hair back, and she held a posy of native flowers.

Maren cleared her throat. "I was about to say it's good to see you, but I take it back. It's fantastic to see you. You look incredible."

Jac ran a hand over her hair. "I wondered if it was too much, but I see I read the occasion right." Her gaze roamed over Maren from face to feet, lingering on the vee in her blouse.

Maren's nipples tightened, and she resisted the urge to glance down to check if they were visible.

Jac stepped inside and handed her the flowers with a flourish. "May I kiss you?"

The drumbeat in her chest was almost painful. In answer, she set the flowers on the hall table and wrapped her arms around Jac's neck, pulling her close.

Their mouths met, softly at first, then with increasing urgency. Lips melded, tongues danced. Maren fell into the kiss, gasping as Jac's hands palmed her buttocks, pulling her closer. When they broke apart, she was panting.

"The occasion," Jac said in a husky voice, "is the seduction of Maren McEvoy."

The words shot sparks deep into her body that danced along her nerve pathways. To hear Jac say those words so confidently, knowing it was what they both wanted, had her as incandescent as the sun.

"What about the fucking of Jacinta Fowler?"

Jac's mouth stretched into a lazy grin. "I like your dirty talk." Another swift, hard kiss. She took another pace into the hall and closed the door behind her with a foot. Pressing her hands to Maren's shoulders, she walked her back until she collided with the wall with a soft thump. Jac ran her hands down Maren's arms and lifted them above her head, holding them there with one hand.

The posture thrust Maren's breasts forward. The sparks in her body were now an inferno, one she couldn't control—and didn't want to.

Jac's eyes glittered, and she ran her free hand over Maren's cheek, pressing her thumb to the corner of her mouth.

Maren opened her lips, and Jac's thumb pressed inside before withdrawing to run over Maren's bottom lip, tender, swollen from Jac's kisses.

Jac's hand drifted down Maren's neck and she rested her fingers on the pulse point. "Your heart is pounding, like you're anticipating something. I wonder what that is?" She leaned forward and her lips settled on that same pulse in a wet, open-mouthed kiss.

"No marks," Maren managed, and felt Jac nod as she kissed, then tickled the spot with the point of her tongue.

What would that feel like between her legs? The flickering tongue, such pin-point accuracy? She bit her lip as Jac released her pinned hands and meandered her way down Maren's body. Her lips settled in the hollow of Maren's throat, then her tongue trailed over a collarbone, and her hands drifted down, brushing the sides of Maren's breasts. Just a light touch, no more than a wardrobe supervisor would do, adjusting Maren's clothes before going on camera.

But this was different, so different. No wardrobe supervisor had made her instantly wet, had made her breath come in shallow pants, had made her legs quiver as if they wouldn't support her anymore.

Jac straightened, and her eyes met Maren's, one eyebrow raised in question as her fingers toyed with the top button of her blouse.

She nodded.

Jac flicked the button open and followed the line of them down until the blouse hung open. Jac bent and sucked each nipple through the thin material of her bra.

"You're beautiful," Jac said with an outgoing breath. "You're making me so wet. I want to be inside you. Feel you clench around my fingers when you come."

Her knees jerked and her clit throbbed. "Then do it."

Jac shot her a wicked glance, an upward flick of her eyelashes. It was at once so mischievous, so sexy, promising a very happy end to the evening.

And they were only just beginning.

Jac bent and kissed her way down Maren's belly to the waist of her pants. She grabbed a cushion from the hall chair, positioned it in front of Maren, and dropped to her knees.

"I'll be here for a while. I may as well be comfortable." Her voice dripped with promise.

Jac's fingers undid the button of Maren's pants, lowered the zip, then she hooked her fingers into the material and dragged them and Maren's undies down to her knees in one quick movement.

Maren fumbled the pants down and off, happy she was barefoot. And then there was no time to think, no time to think of anything other than Jac's hand on her hip, branding her with its heat, the other delving between her thighs. She leaned back against the wall again, thighs spread, helpless to do anything other than push her hands into Jac's hair and urge her on. Her chest felt as if it would split open, her heart was beating so hard.

For a long moment, Jac kneeled there, staring at her sex. Was she wishing Maren waxed or trimmed, maybe a landing strip, anything neater than her ungroomed pubes?

"I love that you're natural," Jac said in a husky voice. "I can smell your scent, and it's intoxicating." She ran her fingers lightly up the inside of Maren's thigh, coming to rest just below her sex. "Your thighs are damp. You must be so wet."

And then her fingers moved up, touched Maren's lips, and brushed back and forth.

The anticipation had her trembling. Her nipples were painfully hard against her bra, and between her thighs throbbed with an urgent intensity. "Please," she said.

"Please what?" Jac looked up along her body through slitted eyes. "Please touch you?" Her fingers moved along her lips once more. "Kiss you?" And the world stopped spinning as Jac pressed an open-mouthed kiss between her legs, her tongue dragging along the slit, then delving between her lips to pass over her clit, soft enough to make her shudder, hard enough to make her cry out and tremble.

"You're so wet," Jac said when she pulled away. "I'm drowning down here. You're wet enough to be fucked. Do you want that?"

Maren nodded, then barely had time to gasp as Jac spread her lips and pushed what seemed like two fingers inside. Her pussy twitched, her clit throbbed in time, and her hips arched off the wall.

Jac waited a second, then started thrusting, her thumb pressing on Maren's clit with every upstroke.

She closed her eyes, gripped Jac's hair and concentrated on the spiralling feelings radiating out from her clit. *This is just so damn good.* She was on the edge, at the point of no return, when Jac's hard strokes softened, slowed, until they were a leisurely glide in and out.

Maren pushed her hips forward. "More. Harder."

"Impatient." A smile shimmered in Jac's voice. "Not yet."

"I want to come. I'm close."

"Oh, you'll come all right. I promise that. More than once."

The confidence in Jac's voice rippled through Maren's body, and she tightened around Jac's fingers. "Please."

Jac increased her rhythm again. "Do you want more fingers inside?"

It was hard to concentrate on the words through the haze of lust in her mind. "One more."

And then she was filled, the ache of fullness, and she clenched around Jac's fingers. It was nearly too much. The fullness inside, the insistent press of Jac's thumb on her clit, and the feel of Jac's curly hair under her hands.

Just when she thought she couldn't take any more pleasure, Jac leaned forward again, and her tongue—*oh my god, her tongue*—slid between her lips and ran around her entrance, around where Jac's fingers were still buried. Then that same accurate tongue pressed on one side of her clit, brushing over the tip, then the rolling over the other side. When it returned to flicker on the tip of her clit, it was too much. Maren's hips jerked, her head flung back, hitting the wall with a thump, but she didn't care. Her orgasm crashed over her in a gasping, leg-jerking howl of sensation, as she clenched around Jac's fingers, riding the waves.

Jac eased her face back, leaving her fingers in place. She looked up at Maren. "Okay?"

Maren pushed her limp, sweaty hair from her face. "More than okay."

Jac's fingers moved softly inside Maren. "Good," she said, then she leaned in again, parted Maren's lower lips with her fingers, pressed her mouth to Maren's clit and sucked.

Oh my god, oh my god. If she'd thought it was incredible before, the second time was intense. In only seconds, she was coming harder than she thought possible against Jac's mouth, clenching and releasing on her fingers, her hips pushed forward in a spasm of need, a rush of liquid, and the world turned white behind her closed eyes.

She hadn't realised she was crying until Jac slowly slid out of her, and rose to take her in her arms, kissing her softly on the lips, then on each cheek.

"Are you okay?"

She swiped at her cheeks with shaking fingers. "Yes. More than okay. That was..."

"Intense? You're incredible, Maren. So responsive. So utterly abandoned. You're beautiful when you come." Jac kissed her mouth again, deeper this time, so she tasted herself on Jac's tongue.

"You're the incredible one." She heaved a breath, her body spiralling down from the high. "I've never come like that. With anyone."

"Not Marcus? Not any previous girlfriend?"

"No." She wanted to tell Jac about Marcus, but now was not the time. Instead, she straightened and ran shaking hands over her hips.

Jac took a pace back, pushed her hands into the pockets of her tapered pants.

Jac.

Maren moved closer, kissing Jac's sticky lips. "I'm nearly naked and you're fully dressed."

"This is true." Jac stood there without making a move.

"You have a choice. I can either take you into the bedroom and fuck you until you're as wet as I am, until you scream as loud as a banshee, until you come on my fingers, my mouth...on my toys. Or I can get dressed, wash my hands, and we can eat dinner."

"And after dinner?" Jac asked.

"After dinner, I will do whatever you want until you beg me to stop. Slow and sensual. Hard and fast. I could go down on you until you've come as many times as you can. And then, in the morning..."

Jac's lips twitched. "It seems a pity to waste your dinner preparation. And I am rather hungry. And I like the idea of a long night with you and what we can do together."

Maren kissed her long and deep and her hand ran down Jac's body to rub between her legs. "That's a promise."

Jac's eyes glittered in the overhead light. "Then let's eat."

CHAPTER 23

BETTER THAN DINNER

MAREN HAD PREPARED A PLATTER of tiger prawns with a chilli-lime mayonnaise. It was delicious, as was the accompanying salad, the scallops with sage and brown butter they'd had for a starter, and the light and creamy lemon cheesecake, although Maren said that had come from a bakery in the city. But dinner could have been a greasy burger from a freeway fuel stop for all Jac cared.

Maren also hadn't redressed properly for dinner. She'd discarded her bra, and only partially re-buttoned her blouse, leaving enough of a gap that the shape of her breasts was clearly visible through the thin material, and her cleavage beckoned to Jac's lips.

Jac had wondered if the night's invitation had come with more—and it had. But the suddenness and intensity of that more had left her gasping. Who would have thought that the cool and self-possessed Maren McEvoy would be so abandoned when it came to sex? Maren's cries still echoed in her ears, and Jac's mouth tasted not only the succulent meal, but the memory of Maren's orgasm on her tongue.

After dinner, they lounged on the couch together, Maren's head on Jac's shoulder.

"Did you know this would happen tonight?" Jac asked. "You can be honest."

"I hoped," Maren replied. "I didn't presume. What about you?"

"I didn't know," Jac said. "I thought you were feeling your way into this. Some light flirting, kisses. I didn't dare dream I'd be inside you ten minutes after I stepped in the door."

Maren lifted her head from Jac's shoulder. "Expect the unexpected." Her fingers trailed circles on Jac's thigh through the pants. "Do you want more wine?"

"No, thanks,"

"How about a brandy? More cheesecake? A glass of water?"

"None of those."

"Then what do you want?" The smile in her voice made Jac's clit throb. She'd kept herself in check over dinner, but now there was no need. With a twist of her body, she flipped their positions so that Maren lay beneath her on the couch.

"You. I want you. And I want to come from what you do to me."

Maren's lips tilted upward. "That can be arranged. But I think we'll be more comfortable in bed."

Jac rolled off the couch and stood. "No arguments from me."

Maren's bedroom was enormous, with a king bed and glass doors that opened out onto the veranda that ran around the side of the house. She opened the curtains and sliding door, leaving only the fly screen closed.

"Aren't you afraid the neighbour will see?" Jac glanced around, seeing the fresh paint, and tasteful furnishings. Maren had obviously redecorated.

"I happen to know the neighbour is away tonight." Maren winked.

"All night?" The urgency that she'd tamped down during dinner flared anew.

"I hope so. Orli isn't home for a couple of days."

Jac sucked a breath. So, Maren didn't want Orli to know what they were doing. Okay, she could live with that...for now. But if things developed more between them... She pushed that aside. Maren wasn't Talia. She focussed on Maren, standing in front of her, blouse unbuttoned. When had she done that? She reached out and ran a finger around the top of Maren's breasts.

"You looked like you were a million kilometres away for a moment," Maren said. "Got your focus back now?"

"Oh, yes."

"I've been wondering what you look like under all that leather. It's totally hot, of course, but I'm sure you know that. It must be a magnet for sapphic women."

Her lips twitched. "I've had my share of offers from clients."

"Do you ever take them up?" Maren's voice held curiosity, not jealousy.

"Sometimes. Not too often. I don't rate a mention in the tourist guides as something to do in southern Sydney."

"You're not a thing, Jac. You're a warm and lovely woman."

"I was joking, but thank you. And you're not just Australia's favourite newsreader. You're a very beautiful and kind woman."

"All this mutual admiration is distracting us from why we're here." Maren's fingers plucked at the button on Jac's waistcoat. "As androgynous and sexy as this is, I can't see your breasts." She worked her way down the front, unhooking the gold chain and letting it fall.

Jac stood still, letting her do all the work. Her nipples tightened, and her clit pulsed hard enough she thought she might combust. When Maren reached there, if she used fingers, if she used her tongue, it would take maybe ten seconds for her to come. Her nipples tingled at the thought.

The shirt she'd meticulously ironed earlier that evening was now rumpled, but Maren didn't seem to care. She disposed of it quickly.

Her eyebrow arched. "No bra." Her voice hummed.

"I barely need one."

"Your breasts are perfect." Maren covered them with her palms.

Jac's nipples hardened almost to the point of pain from the light friction.

When Maren bent to kiss one, to lave it with the flat of her tongue, sparks shot deep into Jac's belly. When Maren sucked the nipple into her hot, wet mouth, Jac's clit jumped to attention, and she thought she might come from the feel of Maren's mouth on her nipples alone. It seemed there was a lot to be said for delaying the gratification.

"Maren... Please. Don't make me wait..."

Maren looked up and arched an eyebrow. "I have every intention of making you wait." She straightened, and without breaking eye contact with Jac, removed her blouse, shimmied out of her pants and undies, and stood naked in front of her.

Jac's breath came in fast, hard pants and her hands curled by her sides. This was torture of the most exquisite kind, and she wasn't sure if she could stand it. Her fingers moved to the waist of her own pants.

"Stop." Maren's voice cracked like a whip. "I'll do that."

Jac froze. She was used to being the assertive one, the one directing the dance of passion. To lead and cajole, then to share together. And given Maren had been married to a man for so long, she hadn't expected this. Had expected her to be slower to adjust to passion between women.

So not so.

Maren's fingers replaced Jac's at the waistband of her pants, flicking the button, and lowering the zip, before pushing the pants down. The tapered pants bunched rather than pooled.

"Let me take them off before I fall flat on my face," Jac said. "It would wreck your plans for this evening if I'm at the hospital with a broken nose."

"And I thought you were a tough woman." Maren gestured to the bed. "Be my guest."

Jac shuffled to the bed, sat, then removed her shoes, socks, and pants. She was tempted to remove her undies, too, but Maren shook her head.

"I'll do that."

Was this assertiveness a normal part of Maren? Or was she role playing for the evening? Whichever it was, it was melting Jac faster than ice cream in a hot car. She wanted Maren on top of her, she wanted her to kiss her nipples again...and other places. *Oh god, I want her to go down on me. I want her to fuck me.*

Maren approached, hooked her fingers in the top of Jac's undies and tugged. "I should do this with my teeth, but that's so overrated and corny."

"You're doing just fine," she managed through dry lips.

She lay back, lifted her hips, and Maren dragged her undies down her legs, the elastic a sweet friction on her overheated skin. And then she was naked, the light breeze from the ceiling fan cooling her over-heated body, chill on the damp curls between her thighs.

Maren straddled her legs, her slight body resting lightly. She leaned forward and kissed Jac. It was long and slow, a leisurely exploration of her mouth, gentle even. The drumbeat between Jac's legs subsided to a soft tattoo. She raised her arms, wrapped them around Maren's shoulders, and relaxed into the kiss.

And then Maren took her lower lip between her teeth and bit gently.

Jac arched up, the abruptness of it shocking her clit back to pounding alertness.

Maren broke the kiss. "Don't want you getting complacent." She shuffled back until she could bend and kiss Jac's nipples. Back further again, and she trailed her lips lower, down over Jac's belly. Lower still until she pushed Jac's thighs apart with both hands, wide enough that her inner thighs and hips ached for a moment. Moving lower again, and she settled on the bed between Jac's legs.

"Prepare to come."

"Is that an order?" Jac could hardly form the words over the red mist in her head. Every nerve-ending in her skin lit, instantly charged by Maren's words.

"Oh, yes." Maren's fingers stroked Jac's lips, dipping inside with every stroke. Further, deeper, more forceful, until, with a long, gliding stroke, she was inside.

Jac gasped and her legs came together, thighs gripping Maren's shoulders, hips arching helplessly.

One thrust. Two.

"I'm going to—"

And then there were no words as Maren's mouth joined her fingers between Jac's thighs, and her tongue circled her clit. A gentle, suck-ing pressure, and Jac's world exploded into pure feeling as her orgasm engulfed her, and all she could do was cry out and ride the waves until completion.

She sank into the bed as if her bones had dissolved.

With a last kiss to the top of her mound, Maren shuffled up the bed until she lay alongside Jac. She took her hand. "Thank you."

"Seems I should be the one thanking you." She waited a beat. "Dinner was wonderful."

Maren snorted a laugh. "I've never heard it called that before."

Jac laughed as well. "You need to get out more."

"I do. Seriously, Jac, this isn't something I do all the time. Or much at all."

Jac waited. Maren's voice had a confessional quality to it. Was she going to say it was her first time with a woman? She'd said she'd had a girlfriend before her marriage, but equally, she'd been married to Marcus for a long time. Being bisexual didn't depend on actual experience. She'd known she was a lesbian long before she'd even kissed a girl.

Maren ran featherlight fingers down Jac's arm to the engraved silver ring on her thumb. She traced the circle. "Marcus and I were married for eighteen years. I already told you we both were faithful during that time. I realised during that time I was bisexual—or maybe pansexual. And we both wanted a child, so Orli happened. And apart from that…we tried to make our marriage a sexual one. With varying degrees of success."

"How old were you when you got married?"

"Twenty-five. I'll save you the maths. I'm forty-six now."

An eleven-year age gap. Jac wouldn't have thought it was that much. But Maren's pale skin, seemingly untouched by Australia's harsh climate, gave her a younger appearance.

"Before Marcus, I'd had a long-term girlfriend and a couple of flings before I married Marcus," Maren continued. "So, no. You're not the first woman I've slept with, if that's what you're wondering."

Jac linked her fingers with Maren's and shuffled closer so she could press against Maren's body. So maybe she was the first for Maren since her marriage had ended?

"Was it strange to be back with a woman after so long?"

Maren turned and pressed her face against Jac's shoulder. "You want the truth?"

"Always."

"After Marcus and I split, he was lucky enough to meet Rick shortly after, and they didn't hide their relationship. We both considered our marriage to be deep and genuine, so if I'd immediately started dating women, you can imagine what the press would have made of that. Marcus was establishing his career as a sports journalist and commentator. I didn't want to undermine his credibility, make it seem as if he'd been living a lie for eighteen years."

"You could have dated men."

"None I wanted to date," Maren said. "And there's Orli. To her, suddenly having two gay parents would undermine her sense of self. Which is wrong, but, as you know, she's in a rocky place already. Although it's been more stable lately, thanks to you."

Jac processed that. A red flag was poking over the parapet, but she ignored it for the moment. Now was not the time.

"You're the second woman I've slept with since Marcus and I split," Maren said. "The first was a high-class escort whose clients are all women. It had been so long, and despite Marcus and I splitting amicably, I was still raw. I remembered this woman, as we'd done a story about her a couple of years back and her approach was very sympathetic. She has a long-term partner who is accepting of her work. She's from Sydney. One time, when Orli went to stay with Marcus and Rick for a few days, I paid for her to fly to Melbourne for the weekend." She raised her head and looked Jac in the eyes. "Shocked?"

"No. Surprised, but not shocked. You did what was best for you. Was it good?"

Maren laid her head on Jac's shoulder. "Incredible. She was so kind, caring almost. It was cathartic. She focussed on me entirely the first time, and I cried afterwards. I hadn't felt repressed during my marriage with Marcus, but with her... It was freeing. I felt lighter, more truly myself. The second time, I focussed on her, and she came, and I felt so unbelievably powerful."

"Have you seen her since you've been in Sydney?" A curl of something stirred in Jac's belly. Was it jealousy that she wasn't Maren's first since her marriage? No, it wasn't; that was nothing to do with her. What she was feeling was the need to prove herself, to be as good as this unknown escort.

"No. She was lovely, but it was an emotional time for me, and, well, I didn't want to form an attachment. She warned me about that, actually. I left it as an amazing weekend with a wonderful woman."

"And what's this?" Jac raised their linked hands. "Are we two women having an amazing weekend?"

"So far, so good." Maren's smile was positively wicked as she raised up on one elbow. "But I think I need to check the evidence. See if we've surpassed 'amazing' and moved to 'incredible'. Are you up for more research?"

Jac pressed her sticky thighs together as her clit throbbed. "I think that would be very scientific of us." She reared up and fitted her lips to Maren's, sinking into the kiss.

She would take these days for what they were.

CHAPTER 24
ONCE MORE AND IT'S A HABIT

"I don't want to, but I need to leave this bed to do more than pee and drink water," Jac said.

The sun streamed in through the window, illuminating Maren's naked body as she lay on top of the quilt.

"Breakfast would be good. Or is it brunch time?"

"Not yet—it's only eight." Jac leaned over to kiss Maren, who wrapped her arms around Jac's neck and pulled her down to lie on top of her. "You are insatiable."

Maren smirked. "I have twenty years to make up for."

Jac allowed the kiss for a minute, then eased back. "I'm sorry, but I really have to go. I have a booking tomorrow using the BMW and need to refit the panniers and check it over properly. I haven't done that since it returned from the repair shop."

"Did they do a good job?"

"It looks fantastic, better than ever, but I want to be one hundred per cent sure everything's fine. You know, with the bike back, I figure Orli's paid her debt to me. She's been fabulous, actually, a real help."

"I'm not sure I can keep her away. She talks about you non-stop, and lives for the next time you'll take her out on the bike. Is she in your way? There's still another month before she starts her new school. There won't be much time for her to pester you then."

"If she wants, she's welcome to keep coming. I'll take her out again—she loves the Norton."

"Then that makes two of us who can't stay away from you." Maren kissed Jac's shoulder. "When do you have to go?"

Jac hesitated, desire and duty warring inside her. "Maybe another twenty minutes. I'll be taking the BMW for a ride later, if you want to come."

Maren ran her hands down to Jac's buttocks. "I'd love that. But right now, I'll work quickly."

"This is three times now. Once more, and it's a habit. You'll have to buy your own helmet." Jac handed the maroon helmet to Maren.

"Helmet and protective gear… What bike should I buy?" Maren asked.

"I suggest more rides before you commit to that." Jac patted the tank of the BMW. "I got this baby from someone who'd been out three times with their son and thought buying a bike would be a great way to keep the connection going. He passed his test, but then Sydney had its wettest spring in twenty years. He soon realised there was little pleasure in getting drowned every time he went for a ride, and sold the bike. Apparently, he and his son continued their connection attending St George Illawarra Dragons games."

"I'll wait a while then." Maren pulled on her helmet and gloves. "It's early days yet."

Jac's fingers stilled on the tank. Was she talking about the bike or about them? She shrugged that thought away. One amazing night was just that. Just a night of fantastic sex with a new woman. Nothing more. Except…

She pushed away the thought that tickled in the back of her mind: that sex last night had been more than that. That they were already doing things together that went beyond the casual sex connection. Dinner. Pool with Jac's friends. Orli. Tension rippled down Jac's spine, tightening her shoulders. They were neighbours. Of course they did things together. The sex shouldn't affect that.

She shook away her thoughts and turned to Maren. "Ready?" she said through the helmet headset.

"Sure thing."

Jac straddled the bike and waited while Maren settled behind her, shuffling forward so her breasts pressed against Jac's back. Then she let out the throttle and the bike purred forward.

Jac didn't hurry. The day was bright, warm without being a scorcher, the roads dry, the traffic light. Really, a perfect day for riding. She took Maren through Royal National Park again and down through Stanwell Park and over the Sea Cliff Bridge. Despite the lower speed limit, the bike swooped around the curves. Maren's hands tightened on Jac's waist, and as the bike straightened after the final bend, her whoop was full of joy.

"I want to hold my arms out and feel the air," she said over the headset. "The wind, the power, the freedom. Are we flying? It feels like it."

Jac grinned. Like her daughter, Maren got it. The joy of riding a bike, not just as transport, but for the thrill of it. "Sometimes I dream I'm flying, but when I wake up, I realise I was dreaming about riding the Norton."

"Sometimes we fly." Maren sighed, and her grip loosened on Jac's waist as if she was going to spread her wings.

Jac turned into the carpark of the Scarborough Hotel and cut the engine. "Are you hungry? This is a good place for lunch, if you are."

"Starving." Maren dismounted and nudged Jac in the ribs. "I must have burned a few calories last night."

"Then this is the place to replenish them."

Leaving their helmets locked to the bike, they walked through the hotel and down to the tables out the back. From the clifftop, the view stretched to the horizon, the sea a clear denim blue. A smudge of grey on the horizon hinted at rain, and a catamaran bucketed over the waves.

Jac handed the laminated menu to Maren, who scanned through. "Prawn and mango salad."

"Healthy, but delicious."

"With a side of chips. Which I'm sure you'll help me eat." Maren set down the menu.

"Not necessarily. They have great fresh fish here, so I'm going with the beer-battered fish and chips. With a side of salad. Which I'm sure you'll help me eat."

Maren laughed. "We can share."

They were halfway through their meal when Jac noticed the couple standing off to one side, staring at them and talking in whispers.

"I think you've been recognised," she said to Maren in a low voice. "Over to your left. Woman in a pink dress with the bald man."

Maren flashed them a glance. "Possibly."

"Does that happen often?"

"Not as much as it used to. Now that I'm not on TV anymore, a lot less. Celebrity is so fleeting. The press have mostly forgotten about me, although the gossip mags are pushier."

"Excuse me." The woman in the pink dress had approached their table. "Are you Maren McEvoy?"

Maren's polished smile flashed, and she was instantly all practiced charm. "That's me."

The woman melted, her cheeks a fiery red. "You're my favourite newsreader. I miss seeing you—your stand-in is good, but it's not the same without you."

"Thank you. Zoey's doing a fine job."

"When will you be back?"

"I don't have a set date yet. I'm enjoying the break."

Pink-Dress flicked a glance at Jac—probably to see if she, too, was someone famous. Her attention focused back on Maren. "Would you mind if my husband took a photo of us?"

Dismissed. Jac stifled a smile. That was fine with her. She ate a chip.

"Sure," Maren said. "A quick one so we can get back to our lunch."

Pink-Dress's cheeks grew even redder. "I'm so sorry...I didn't notice."

"That's okay. This won't take a minute." Maren flashed her TV smile again, stood and took Pink-Dress's elbow, then walked a few paces so they had the sea behind them. "How about this?"

They posed together, shoulders touching, before Maren nodded, smiled, and returned to Jac, leaving Pink-Dress scrolling through the photos with her husband.

Maren sat back down and grabbed a couple of chips. "Funny how no one ever realises they're interrupting until I point it out. Lucky I ordered a salad."

Jac crunched the batter of her fish. "It was a bit rude. They could have waited until you'd finished eating."

"I doubt she even registered that. But she was polite. Brushing off selfie seekers is a sure-fire way to get negative press. The Australian tall-poppy syndrome. It brings out the who-does-she-think-she-is brigade. It's better to be pleasant, allow a photo, and end the interaction. That way, everyone's happy."

"So, you're not sure when you're returning to work? Must be nice to have that freedom."

Some of the light went out of Maren's eyes. "Yes, but it's a bit more complicated than that. Zoey is gunning for my job. My boss has suggested I make myself available more, at least on a part-time basis."

"Are you going to do that?"

"I don't know. I guess I'll see how Orli goes at her new school. After all, this year is about her. We're going on a shopping trip through the factory outlets in a couple of days."

Jac dipped her last chip into the aioli. Obligations. Commitments. Other people's lives were full of them. Hers, not so much. Just her business and her friends, who understood if she dropped out from time to time. She gave a mental shake. Maren's problems were not hers.

After lunch, they meandered on down the coast, through the older suburbs of Thirroul and Austinmer, through the city of Wollongong, and out to Shellharbour. Jac stopped the bike at a quiet beach, backed by a line of dunes.

"Fancy a short walk? Stretch out after the bike?"

"Sure."

They walked along the path above the beach, avoiding the soft sand. A woman walked a dog, and an older couple ate sandwiches and drank tea from a Thermos at one of the picnic tables.

"I lived near the beach in Melbourne," Maren said. "But it was a lot busier than this. Closer to the city."

"Wollongong's considered a city. I think I'm lucky to live in Sydney but still have some space. I still thank my gran every day for leaving me the house."

They reached the end, and Jac left the path to walk down the steps to the beach. The tide was out, leaving a gleaming expanse of wet sand and rock pools. She headed for a sheltered spot in the dunes where a driftwood log made a comfortable seat. It was a squash for two, but she didn't care. With her arm over Maren's shoulders and Maren nestled against her side, they stared out to sea.

Closer to the water, a man stood, hands in pockets, facing out to sea, but other than that, there was no one around.

"You picked this place deliberately, didn't you?" Maren asked. Her hand settled on Jac's thigh, curving over the leather, running up the inner side to the junction of Jac's legs. "I wanted to touch you at lunch. But it wouldn't have been a good idea."

Jac ran fingers up and down Maren's arm. "Because you're famous? Because of Marcus?" Her fingers stilled. "Or because I'm a woman?"

"Not Marcus. The first, yes. And because you're a woman?" She bit her lip. "I haven't come out publicly, Jac. And I don't know that I need to."

A chill stole over Jac's chest. Another closeted woman. It was Talia all over again—although her ex's reasons for remaining closeted were very different to Maren's. But still... After Talia, she'd sworn not to get involved with someone who couldn't be out. She bit her lip. But so far, she wasn't involved. So far, it was one night of fabulous sex and a growing friendship. She was getting ahead of herself.

"So, if you were with a woman"—she made her voice light and as breezy as the wind coming off the ocean—"you'd hide her away?"

Maren shifted her shoulders. "I didn't say that. It would depend on a few things: the stage of my career for one. Orli for another."

Orli again. She wouldn't go there now. "Why would it affect your career?"

"It shouldn't. Not now. But it's hard enough for older women in TV without adding another complication into the mix. I don't want that sort of publicity."

"We've already kissed on the beach." Jac pushed aside her disquiet and turned to face Maren. "What if someone had seen us?"

"No one would—that beach was as quiet as this one. But I wouldn't kiss anyone—of any gender—in a crowded street. I haven't done that since I started in TV." She side-eyed Jac. "No one will see us now." Maren gestured to the deserted beach in front of them. There was only the same man, still intent on the ocean. No kids playing, no dog walkers, no rock-pool paddlers.

"Is that a hint?"

"It could be."

Her heart somersaulted in her chest. Leaning forward, she took Maren's face between her palms and kissed her. Instantly, the kiss sprang to life, no tender press, no gentle explorations. It went from zero to one hundred in a second, a hot merging of mouths and tongues. Fully formed, heated. Jac's nipples tingled against the confines of her leathers, and her clit pulsed.

Surely last night had been enough. One night with a new woman usually was. Once she'd enjoyed the night, taken a late-night or morning good-bye kiss, she'd move on. But this…this kiss was like starting all over again. Like a first kiss, full of anticipation.

There'd been no one since Talia who'd tempted her to make it more. Until now. Until Maren.

Maren pushed her hands into Jac's hair, flattened by the helmet. She pulled her even closer as the kiss deepened and grew to an incendiary level. A quick breath, and then Jac returned. Her heart pounded along with her clit, and trickles of heat coalesced between her legs.

Maren broke the kiss. "I thought bike leathers were sexy. But right now, I wish you weren't wearing them. I wish you weren't wearing anything."

"That could be arranged. Later."

Maren's eyes hooded. "Later. How fast does this bike go?"

Jac broke the embrace and stood, taking deep breaths. "If we take the motorway and do the speed limit, we'll be home in under an hour."

Maren's smile spread like sunshine. "Then take me home."

CHAPTER 25
NOT LIKE PORNHUB

THE FREEDOM. THE ANONYMITY. THE speed. It was all so thrilling.

Maren pressed into Jac's back, moving with her and the bike. The bike was almost a living thing, throbbing between her legs, the roar of the engine, the way it leaned and weaved. Almost a sexual thing.

Jac reached the M1, and once out of the sixty-kilometre limit, the bike accelerated to one hundred kilometres per hour. Maren moved with Jac and laughed aloud.

"I love hearing your joy," Jac said into the headset.

Maren's body followed the lean of the bike as Jac overtook a slow-moving van. "I love this."

"I can tell." Jac was smiling; Maren could hear it in her voice, even over the tinny communicator.

The physical excitement of the bike heightened the anticipation of what was to come.

Jac turned into her drive and idled up to her shed. "I need to put the bike away."

Her heated eyes promised the wait would be worth it. Maren stripped off her protective gear, hung it on the rack, and slipped into her shoes she'd left there earlier. When they were both in leggings and T-shirts, the BMW back in the shed, they faced each other.

"My place?" Jac asked. "It's not as swish as yours, but I have a big, firm bed and a decent bottle of wine."

"No food?" Maren teased.

"You need it?"

"Not yet. Later. After."

"Lucky someone invented Uber Eats."

Inside the house, Jac took Maren's hand, leading her along the hall, nudging open the door to the bedroom.

Maren glanced around, but the details of the room hardly registered over the pounding of desire. There was indeed a king bed made up with a patterned doona turned down invitingly, crisp, white sheets beckoning.

Jac switched on the fan so cool air wafted over them, then turned back to Maren. Without breaking eye contact, she hooked her fingers into the top of her leggings, and pushed them and her undies down over her hips.

Maren's gaze followed their descent. The softer, pale skin on Jac's belly, that seldom saw the sun. The flat plane leading down to a clipped patch of hair, and the slight hollows by her hip bones. Her lean, strong thighs.

Maren's sex tightened at the thought of lying between those thighs, tasting her. How Jac's legs would tighten around her as she bucked her way into orgasm.

"Sex isn't a spectator sport," Jac said.

"Guess you don't watch Pornhub." Maren tilted her head and tugged her own leggings down.

They matched each other, stripping off their own clothes until they both stood naked.

"Nothing on Pornhub can match what I see now," Jac murmured. "Plus, the lesbian sex is just so…"

"Unreal? I think most of it's aimed at straight men."

"A man has no place in my bedroom." Jac ran a finger down from Maren's chin, down between her breasts, to come to a stop at the top of her pubes. "You, however…"

She shuddered as the heat from Jac's seeking finger trickled lower. She moistened her suddenly dry lips. "I want…" She closed her eyes as Jac's finger feathered over her hair, down to rest lower, where her clit pulsed.

Jac walked her back until her legs bumped the bed, and she sat. Jac leaned over her, taking her lips in another kiss that was even hotter than the ones on the beach, as now, they didn't have to stop.

They lay together, lips, fingers, skin, all fused in a glorious explosion of sensation. Jac's fingers circled Maren's nipples, then her tongue traced the same path. Maren's belly tightened. The kisses on the beach, the wild freedom of the bike ride, Jac's body against her own—it had all been foreplay. When Jac touched her between her legs, the sensations were so immediate, so intense, she thought she'd come in that moment.

She breathed into it, tightening her inner muscles, until her orgasm crashed over her in waves of pleasure, and she cried aloud into the dim room.

When she'd got her breath back, she pushed Jac onto her back and kissed her way down her body, tonguing each nipple, breathing kisses over Jac's belly until she reached the juncture of her thighs. She pushed her legs apart and settled between them and her mouth covered Jac's sex, her tongue circling her clit. It was as good as she remembered. Better. Now she knew what Jac liked, and so in moments, Jac, too, was bucking her way through her orgasm.

For moments, they lay together, arms around each other, hands gliding over skin. Then, with a wicked smile, Jac flipped over so that she was on top of Maren, grinding onto her thigh as she leaned to kiss her. Maren had thought the first orgasm was intense, but when Jac moved down the bed and fucked her hard with three fingers, her mind shattered into a kaleidoscope of colours as she came hard for a second time, and then for a third time in a quake of aftershocks.

Afterwards, they lay together, letting the waft of air from the fan cool their bodies.

Maren relaxed into the bed, her fingers playing with the patch of hair between Jac's legs, then smoothing over her thigh. Her mind swam in a hazy lethargy.

Jac ran a leisurely hand down Maren's side, from shoulder to hip. "Food? Or shower?"

"Let's order food, then shower while it's coming."

"Coming." Jac sniggered. "There's been enough coming in this room for a while."

Heat leaped back into Maren's body, jerking her back to alertness. "Me yes. But you…I think we can improve on your score."

"Sex is definitely not a spectator sport with you," Jac said.

Maren was happy to prove her right.

Later, showered and dressed in a pair of Jac's shorts and T-shirt, Maren topped up their wine glasses. The ruins of Malaysian noodles lay on the counter between them, and the bottle was nearly empty.

"Will you stay over tonight?" Jac asked.

She nodded. "I'd like that."

"I have bookings tomorrow, but not too early."

"Marcus is bringing Orli home in the afternoon. He's taking her shopping in the morning for school stuff. She won't be happy. I get to take her for the fun shopping the day after."

"Depending when she gets home, she could come for a quick ride with me. Just for an hour."

"She'd love that. If you don't mind." Maren hesitated. She'd offered to pay for Orli's rides, and Jac had agreed, but so far, Jac hadn't mentioned payment. It seemed wrong to assume there was now no need because they were… Were what? She didn't know. "Don't forget to let me know what I owe you for Orli's rides."

Jac heaved a breath. "I intended billing you. I didn't want Orli there at all, at first, but she's been fine. She's an okay kid." A quick grin. "Now she is, now she's stopped destroying my property. She's made amends, Maren. She's worked hard, and she's genuinely helped me. You paid for the BMW to be fixed. There's nothing owing."

"Are you sure? That wasn't what we agreed."

"I'm sure. And if Orli wants to continue helping, I think I should pay her. Limited hours, of course, around school, but if this is doing her good, then I'm happy with that."

"Thank you. She'll be thrilled." Her heart expanded a little more. Jac was a decent person and even seemed to enjoy Orli's company. That meant a lot.

CHAPTER 26
FEELING THE WAY

"You look very sharp." Maren set down her coffee and looked Orli over as she showed Maren her new school uniform. "The dark green suits you."

"It's shit," Orli said. "It's outdated. Uniforms are an antiquated form of bonding—"

"But you have to wear it. At least this year."

Orli's mouth turned down. "At least there's a pants option.

For which Maren was very thankful. It had been hard enough persuading Orli she had to wear the uniform at all; if a skirt was part of it, there was no way she would have agreed. Her daughter, the tomboy.

She held up a fry pan. "Fried eggs and baked beans as a hearty first-day breakfast?"

Orli's mouth twitched. "Yeah, thanks."

"On it." Maren turned on the gas and bustled around, pulling a carton of eggs from the fridge.

Orli poured herself a cup of coffee and sat at the counter. She picked up the pepper grinder and twisted it so that ground pepper spilled onto the counter.

Maren held her tongue and waited.

Orli put the grinder down, took a mouthful of coffee, set it down, added three sugars. "What if no one talks to me? What if they're all stuck-up bitches?"

"Someone will talk to you." Maren refrained from mentioning that as a new girl, Orli would have a classmate assigned to look after her. "And I'm sure an entire class won't be bitches."

"Still. You know what I mean."

"I think you'll be fine. Aren't you interesting and kind and likeable?"

Orli's mouth turned down. "This isn't a 1950s school story."

"And you went to see Mia Raines, and you ride motorbikes."

"Yeah." Orli nearly cracked a smile. "There is that." She bent her head and stared at the counter. "But you want me to like school so you can go back to work. Back to news reading. That's what you want."

Maren's smile froze on her face. Is that what Orli really thought? That Maren had just been marking time until she could return to work? She opened her mouth to refute that, but one glance at Orli's messy hair and haphazard parting closed it again. Now wasn't the time for that. "I think you'll be fine, Orli. Because you are brave and brilliant, and funny."

She put down a full plate in front of Orli. "Eat this. Can't show your brilliance on an empty stomach."

Orli picked up her cutlery and moved one egg to the other side of the plate.

"I didn't cook it for you to play with it," Maren said.

Orli bent her head and picked at her breakfast. "Can Jac pick me up from school on the Norton?"

It was like a knife to her heart. "Not the first day. I'll be there."

"My famous mother, waiting for me at the gates," Orli said. "I'm not sure if that's rad or total cringe."

Maren leaned across and opened the passenger door for Orli. She threw her bag in the back and dropped into the seat.

Maren waited until she'd pulled away and traffic was crawling before she asked, "How was your day?"

"Okay, I guess." Orli slouched lower and stretched out her legs, staring at her school shoes. "These shoes are ugly. I can't wait to change."

"How was school?" Maren prompted.

"I got paired with Mackenzie to show me around. She was okay. She surfs and volunteers at a cool place in western Sydney. Some sort of farm for kids."

"She sounds nice."

Orli shrugged. "So far. Can I go see Jac when we get home?"

"If she's at the shed you can, but don't disturb her otherwise." Heat bloomed in her chest as she thought of disturbing Jac in other ways. But there couldn't be any of that with Orli around.

"At least it's only a two-day week," Orli said. "Then the weekend with Dad in the city."

And that left Maren free on the weekend. Her stomach twisted in anticipation.

Maren's bed was sinfully large, luxuriously comfortable with sheets as soft as butter. Jac lay on her back, watching Maren kiss her way down Jac's body before settling between her thighs. All thoughts of Egyptian cotton fled her head at the first touch of Maren's tongue, and then the only thing she thought about was how good it felt, and the white, hot shout of orgasm.

Later, when Jac had brought Maren to her own peak, they lay in bed together, the moonlight streaming through the window and turning their bodies to silver.

"Are you doing anything tomorrow night?" Maren asked. "Orli won't be back until Sunday afternoon."

"I'm helping Kyra move apartment in the arvo, but the evening is free." She raised up on one elbow. "Want to go on a date? A planned evening, just the two of us. A moonlit bike ride, dinner at a restaurant, then home to bed?" She waggled her eyebrows. "I know which part I'm looking forward to the most."

"You're asking me out?" Maren traced a circle around Jac's nipple. "Bit late for that, isn't it?"

"If you don't want to, just say so." Jac pretended affront, but her palm smoothed over Maren's belly. "I'll have pizza with Kyra instead."

"Of course I want. But I pick the restaurant, and that part will be my treat. How smart can you dress on the bike?"

"If you want smart, we better take an Uber. I was thinking of a casual Turkish place I know about an hour away. Bike gear would be fine there."

"Another time. I'll drive this time. I want to see you in those tapered pants and that waistcoat again." Maren wiggled her eyebrows.

"I can't compete with you as the best-dressed woman around town."

"The restaurant I'm thinking of is very private. Discreet service, so I won't need to worry that people might realise we're on a date."

Jac's hand stilled. "Is it still important to you that no one see us together?"

Maren made a left-right movement with her mouth. "Of course not. We've already been seen together, but we could be just friends. A romantic dinner...well, that's different."

"You still don't want anyone to know you date women?" Jac tried to keep her voice neutral, but a flinty edge crept in that she couldn't control.

Maren was silent. "There are so many things I have to consider right now. Orli for one."

"Who has no problem that her father is gay and lives with a man."

"But if she has a second gay parent? She'll question her own place with us. How she came about. Whether she was a wanted baby."

"With respect, Maren, that doesn't make sense. There are many gay couples with kids. No one questions how those babies came about. And Orli must know very well she's wanted and loved. Surely she doesn't know every last thing about your relationship with Marcus. Do you intend never telling her about any relationships you have?"

"In time, if I have a girlfriend, I'll tell her."

So she wasn't girlfriend material. Jac pushed down the pang of hurt. "In time? When she's left home? On her fortieth birthday? And what about the public? Do you plan on coming out? It doesn't seem to have hurt Marcus any."

"That was Marcus's decision." Maren removed her hand. "But for what it's worth, I believe that a person's sexuality is no one's business but their own. Yes, celebrities come out. And good on them, if they do. But there's many, many more in the closet. Others live a quiet life with their same-sex partner and no announcement. No one expects a heterosexual person to announce they're straight."

Jac bit her lip. "Coming out is a personal decision. I'm not trying to force you to do so. But I am asking if it's something you'd ever do." Memories forced their way to the front of her mind. Talia, saying she could never come out, that it was against her religion, that her parents would disown her. That the *church* would ostracise her. The way she told it made it sound as if that was the worse of the two.

"I don't know, Jac." Maren looked her in the face, grey eyes troubled. "But it's not going to happen right now. It's not just Orli. My career—"

"Really? There are many, many gay celebrities, and people mostly don't care."

Maren lay back, so there was a space between their bodies.

Jac's fingers tingled with the need to touch her skin, but she resisted.

"The Channel 12 audience is an older demographic. We're not a conservative channel, but we're certainly not progressive either. They always have a male-female anchor team, and it's expected that the newsreaders show a certain chemistry. Not flirty, but…there's an edge to it. The scripted banter plays up to this. We want our middle-aged mums and dads to feel the wholesome, professional newsreader also has a human side. An attractive *heterosexual* human side that shows up in the banter. My contract has clauses about makeup, dress, and how I appear in public. Even now, while I'm on a year's break, I'm still on contract. I can't go down to the supermarket in a tatty T-shirt, shorts, and a pair of thongs, for example. Professional…but still be attractive to a male viewpoint. I have a clause about Botox. If the station thinks I need it, I have to get it. So far, I've escaped that one."

"That's ridiculous. They can't demand you undergo a procedure because they say so."

"It's in my contract. If I didn't sign it, that would have been the end of my position with them. And before you ask, Luka and the other male newsreaders have the same clause."

"None of that means you can't date a woman. Or is that explicitly banned, too?"

"No, that would be discrimination. But it's strongly implied. I have to appeal to your average middle-aged Aussie male. I'm forty-six, Jac. My use-by date is fast approaching. So, while I'm still with Channel 12, I have to be careful and play their game."

Jac was silent. It seemed unrealistic and restrictive to her, but what did she know about branding and TV channels and audience appeal. Nothing. "What about bike gear? Are you breaching your contract by not being feminine enough?" She couldn't quite keep the sarcasm from her voice.

"No clothing is barred; I'm just expected to keep a neat, well-dressed appearance in public."

"So, as long as we're together, we should act like friends?" *Exactly like Talia.* Acid burned in her throat.

"Is that a problem?"

"I'm uncomfortable with that, Maren." Jac took a deep breath. "Some years ago, I was going out with Talia. Her parents came to Australia as refugees—and while they were happy to be here, they tried hard to hold on to the customs of their country of origin. Food, family, traditions, religion. They were strict with their kids and tried to make them live as if they were still in the old country. Their religion and traditions consider homosexuality a sin. I would call it a cult, but Talia accepted it as the way things had to be. We were together for nearly a year."

Jac sat up and leaned against the headboard. "Talia was conflicted. She loved me but couldn't ever see a way we could be together. So, we snuck around, seldom being seen together in public. She'd come to my place, but always leave to go home for her curfew—she couldn't stay overnight with anyone of any gender. She couldn't play sport, couldn't go swimming, had to live her life in preparation for being a wife and mother.

"At first, it was okay. Exciting even. Breaking the rules. And I loved her. But it didn't take long for me to hate it. Hate the restrictions on her, but also on me. I wanted the freedom for the simple things: to walk down the street holding her hand. To go to the beach together. Kiss her in public."

"What happened?" Maren asked. Her eyes never left Jac's face.

She shrugged. "Exactly what you'd think. I couldn't take sneaking around any longer, so I gave her an ultimatum: be more open together, be seen, and let whatever happened happen. Or else we were over. She chose her family and the life she knew. She married a man who shares her background, and they have a kid. I saw her by chance not long ago, and she seemed happy. I'm glad if she is, but it made me feel second-best. Like she never loved me."

She dragged in a huge breath. "And because of Talia, and how her situation made me feel, I've always said I'll be open about who I am. And while I wouldn't expect anyone else to follow that if they didn't want to, I'm reluctant to hide away again."

A dog barking outside broke the silence in the room.

"Are you giving me an ultimatum?" Maren asked. "Because it sure feels like it."

"No." Jac sighed again, even as she steeled herself for Maren's rejection. "What we have is light-years from my relationship with Talia. I'm not sure what you and I have, Maren. I don't have a name for it, and I don't presume to tell you what to do. I'm just saying how it is for me."

"But if we were to keep going with…this"—Maren waved a hand over their bodies, the rumpled bed—"you're saying, you'd want me to be out?

"It's different. I don't know. But I know I don't want that feeling of not being true to myself." She forced a smile. "Well, I've killed the mood now." She picked up her phone from the bedside table and glanced at the time. "Do you want me to go home?"

"Not unless you want to."

Jac hesitated. "I don't want to," she said in a low voice. "I'd like to kiss you, try to get back to how we were ten minutes ago."

"And our date tomorrow?" Maren wore an inscrutable look. "Because nothing's changed for me, although I wish it had. I'd still like to go to that quiet restaurant, where we won't be seen. Then come back here with you."

Jac closed her eyes. Was she digging herself in too deep? Talia's face as she told Jac it was over, that she was getting married, shoved front and centre in her mind. Talia had broken her heart—the only person who had.

But no. She and Maren were not girlfriends. Not in a relationship. There were no feelings involved past liking and friendship and a huge amount of sexual attraction. She'd told Maren where she stood. They would move on past this and see what happened. She'd enjoy Maren's company, and the sex.

She nodded, and forced a smile. "Let's go to that restaurant."

Maren wasn't Talia. This was different.

She hoped.

CHAPTER 27
NOT ALL ABOUT YOU

"Nice pants." Jac nodded at Orli's canvas pants. They had three pockets on each leg, plus padded knees.

"Mum got them for me," Orli said. "She said if I'm working properly with you, I should have, like, more appropriate clothes. These came from the tradie shop—the men's section."

"They're great. I should get some."

"You should, if you don't mind wearing men's clothes."

Jac laughed. "Have you ever actually looked at how I dress? Most of my clothes are androgynous."

"I like androgynous stuff," Orli said. "Makes me feel more myself." She busied herself with the oil filter on the Goldwing, tightening it carefully.

She was now reliable enough that Jac had shown her how to do basic mechanics on the bikes: grease points, oil change, checking tyre pressures. Jac still oversaw her work, but seldom was there anything to correct.

"How's the new school going?" Jac glanced away, in case the question was too intrusive. But in the couple of weeks since Orli had started school, Maren said she seemed more settled.

"Okay, I guess. Mackenzie is kinda cool. When I was at Dad's on the weekend, we went to the farm she volunteers at. Banksia Farm. It's for city kids, so they can ride ponies and look after animals. It's rad."

"What does Mackenzie do there?" It sounded cool. Maybe she could suggest they ride there on the bike one time.

"Leads ponies for the little kids, works in the veggie garden. Other stuff. Hangs out with the other volunteers. Some are our age, some are, like, real old." She shrugged. "I had fun."

"Maybe you could volunteer with her?"

"Maybe." Orli wiped her hands on a rag. "Dunno if they'd want me."

Jac's heart cracked at the small voice. "They're idiots, if they don't." She tipped Orli's cap over her eyes. "Aren't you the best oil-changer and pillion-rider in south Sydney?"

Orli laughed. "So, tell Mum to let me get my L-plates. I'll be old enough in three months. Sixteen years and nine months, right?"

"Right." Jac thought. "If your mum agrees, though, I can give you a couple of lessons on a private road safety course I know. It will give you a bit of a head start."

Orli said nothing, but she bowed her head and her shoulders tensed.

Jac froze. She'd expected the girl to be ecstatic at the offer... What had she said wrong? She went around to Orli and her hand hovered over her shoulder. "Orli? You okay?"

A sniff. "Yeah." Another. Then Orli looked up at her. "I'm just... Yeah. Thanks. That would be rad. I'm just feeling bad. I was such a shit to you at first—the whole breaking-in thing—but you've always been nice. And now this. The lessons. And you paying me. You didn't have to do any of that." Her head ducked again. "But I'm glad you are. It means I pay Mum back quicker for the car I wrecked in Melbourne."

Jac gave her a grin. Now was not the time for sentimentality. So, the hug, the words reinforcing how great she was...they would wait. If indeed Orli would accept a hug. "No point having an assistant who can't ride a bike, is there?"

Orli laughed and turned back to the Goldwing.

"Have you seen today's celebrity gossip?" Ethan's voice echoed down the phone line.

Maren groaned. "At seven in the morning? I don't care who's supposedly doing what to who."

Ethan didn't laugh. "You'll want to know this. I'll wait while you search your name."

Her name? Maren's pulse juddered. Had the press found something out about Orli? She opened the browser on her phone and typed her name.

Australia's favourite newsreader caught in sizzling, same-sex kiss. Her heart seemed to stop beating for a moment and her fingertips were instantly icy despite the warm room.

> It seems queerness runs in the family. Nearly two years after Maren McEvoy's ex-husband Marcus Coffey came out, Maren is following in his footsteps. Since Maren's move to Sydney, the newsreader has kept a low profile. With Zoey Hammond filling her prime-time slot, Australia has seen less of Maren, but this photo, taken on an Illawarra beach, may account for that. Maren was seen strolling along the beach, hand in hand with the mystery woman, before sharing a sizzling kiss. Afterwards, the pair donned motorbike gear and rode off together, Maren on the pillion.

Shit! Maren closed her eyes. The accompanying photo showed her and Jac on Shellharbour beach—what they'd thought was a secluded beach. They were sitting in the dunes, pressed close together, kissing. Oblivious to everything. A second, grainy photo, obviously taken with a telephoto lens, showed them walking hand in hand along the beach. Maren frowned. The photos were taken most of six weeks ago. Why the mystery photographer had waited until now to release them was beyond her. She flung her mind back to that day. There'd been a couple of people on the beach that day. Maybe it wasn't a paparazzo, but an opportunistic member of the public. Or maybe someone who hadn't realised who she was until now.

Whatever the reason, whoever the photographer, the damage was done. The question now was: what was she going to do about it?

"Maren?" Ethan's voice came through the speaker again.

She'd forgotten he was still on the line.

"While this is news to me, I can't say it's entirely unexpected. The question is, how do you want to handle this?"

"I can't answer that now." She pressed her fingers to her cheeks. "I need to talk to Orli first."

"Of course."

"Does this affect anything with Channel 12?"

Ethan was silent for a moment. "Officially, of course not. Channel 12 welcomes diversity. Unofficially, however... You might want to consider returning a couple of days each week to the Sydney studio. Those sidelines are long, and there's a lot of wannabes lining them."

"I'll think about it." And she would. Ethan was probably right; she should work a couple of days a week. But how would Orli handle that? Not only that her mum was seeing a woman, but that it was *Jac*. Orli's friend and mentor.

Her breath shuddered. Forget the station, the public, any backlash that may or may not happen—Orli was her primary reason for remaining in the closet. She set her phone down and listened. No sound from Orli's room. But any moment now, her daughter would get up for school. Even if she left it to her customary last-minute wake up, she couldn't let her go off to school without knowing.

"I'll get back to you on this," she said to Ethan. "I have to check on Orli right now."

He nodded. "We'll talk soon, Maren."

She got out of bed and threw on yesterday's clothes, then went to the kitchen to start the coffee machine. For a moment, she wished Janelle was there. Her solid, stable presence had a way of defusing the worst of Orli's surliness.

Orli entered the kitchen a few moments later, drawn out by the smell of coffee.

Maren shunted a cup over to her. "You want eggs?"

"Thanks. Yeah." Orli buried her face in the mug.

Maren pulled the eggs from the fridge and faced the stove to compose herself. "There's something we need to talk about." She turned back to Orli.

"I'll tidy my room when I get home, okay? Don't nag."

"It's not that." Her chest was tight, and she dragged a deep breath. "I've been seeing someone. A woman. It's not a relationship, not yet, but she's important to me." She glanced at her daughter.

Orli gaped at her for a second before her face morphed into the blank, non-reactive one she'd grown to dread seeing. She wrapped her fingers around her own coffee mug to ease the cold.

"Why are you telling me now?"

She could barely draw breath against the bands around her chest. "Because the press saw us out together. Took a photo of us kissing. And because it's someone you know." She activated her mobile and handed it to Orli.

"That's Jac." Orli set the phone down, the screen face-up showing the picture of her with Jac on the beach.

"Yes."

"That's you with Jac. Kissing."

"It looks like it."

Orli huffed a breath. "I'm not an idiot. If someone manipulated the photo, why would they pick on Jac? You're wearing the leggings you wear under the bike gear. That's the beach south of Wollongong." She got up and went to the cupboard, pulling out the cereal.

"I thought you wanted eggs."

Orli gave her a long look. "I've changed my mind." She found a bowl and filled it with Crunchy Clusters.

"I wanted you to see this before you went to school. In case other kids mention it."

"Right. Because it's always all about you." She pulled the carton of milk from the fridge and poured it on her cereal. Some of it splashed on the counter.

Maren held her tongue. Now was not the time for the small stuff. "Do you want to talk about this?"

"What is there to talk about?" Orli levelled a glare at her. "I made a friend, and you had to butt in, make it all about you. Just as you did in Melbourne with your *career*."

"It's not all about me. And Jac is still your friend."

"My friend, but your girlfriend? Was she being nice to me just to get to you? Because it sure looks like it from here."

"I didn't allow those photos."

"I'm sure you didn't. I didn't know you liked women that way. You and dad, both queer. How the fuck did I ever happen? Was it all a fake those years? Dad had his boyfriends, you had girlfriends?"

"No. It was real, in our way. You happened the normal way, and you were very much wanted. And your dad and I respected our marriage vows."

"You got married in a park. With no vows. Just the legal stuff. That's what you always told me."

"That's true. But we respected each other. Loved each other. We still do. Just not—"

"Not romantically." Orli spooned cereal at a fast rate. She pushed her bowl aside. "I've gotta go to school. Are you gonna drive me, or should I ask your girlfriend?"

"Jac is our friend, yours and mine. She's not my girlfriend." She swallowed against the knot of words in her throat, words that were more truthful than that denial. But Orli was sixteen—surely not old enough to learn about her mother's sex life. If she ever would. *What else can I possibly say?*

"Could have fooled me. I've never seen you kiss your other friends like that." Orli jammed her hands on her hips.

"Get your bag, and we'll go."

Orli turned the car radio up to a volume that made conversation impossible.

Maren let it go, not lowering the volume until they arrived. "I'll see you later."

Orli's expressionless face stared back at her. "Just remember, Maren, it's not all about you."

Maren. Not Mum. Maren closed her eyes as the word cut into her. She had to talk to Jac.

CHAPTER 28
SO NOT SO

"Hey." Jac looked up as Maren entered her workshop. She rose to her feet and went across to kiss her.

Maren's lips were strangely immobile under her own. "Is everything okay?"

"Depends what you mean by 'okay'. I take it you don't look at gossip sites."

"No. I have better things to do. Most of its incorrect anyway. Who's pregnant? Which member of what royal family is having an affair? Who cares?"

"Which Australian newsreader was caught in a same-sex kiss?" Maren said in a stilted voice. "That would be the same one who's just dropped her furious daughter at school."

Jac pulled back and stared Maren in the face. "You? How did they get a photo of us—I'm assuming it's us and not some other woman you're kissing."

"Of course it's us," Maren snapped. "Some fucking paparazzo was probably strolling the beach. How should I know? But the damage is done. My producer has already called me, and Orli has stomped off to school in a huff, accusing you of befriending her to get to me. Accusing me of making everything about me." She closed her eyes.

Jac's heart twisted at the defeated look on Maren's face. She wrapped her arms around Maren's shoulders. "Hey, it's okay. It seems like the worst thing now, but it will blow over. The gossip always does."

Maren laid her head on Jac's shoulder and snuffled into her T-shirt.

"You think I care about the gossip?" Maren's voice was muffled. "Sure, that's bad. Yes, Ethan pushed even harder for me to return a couple of days each week to solidify my place in the team. But none of that's important compared to Orli. She called me Maren. Not Mum." Her voice cracked at the end.

Jac bit her lip. She had no idea what to say—what would be comforting, what would sound trite. She stroked Maren's hair.

"She's already asked if Marcus's and my marriage was a sham. I told her it was real, that we loved each other. Which, of course, is not a complete answer by a long way, but what else could I tell her?"

"The truth? Tell her how things were for Marcus twenty years ago. For you. She's not oblivious to queer history. She knows I'm a lesbian."

Maren raised her head. "I know my own daughter." Her grey eyes had the chill of early frost. She took a step back out of Jac's arms.

Jac raised her hands. "I'm sorry. That was a stupid thing to say. I'm just trying to ease things for you. Come inside the house, we'll have a coffee and try to figure out a way through this." A little voice in her head was hammering an answer, one she was sure Maren would choose. The ice from Maren's eyes was already seeping into Jac's chest. Slowly, insidiously, surprising her with how it was making her feel.

Maren pressed the heels of her hands to her eyes for a moment. She nodded. "Let's go indoors. Worst-case scenario is I now have the paps stalking me and Orli, trying to find out who you are."

"Me? Why would they want to know about me?"

"Really, Jac, don't be dense. It's not about you; it's about me. They'll think they can get to me through you. They'll think you'll sell your story—"

She gripped Maren's elbows and waited until she met her gaze. "I would never do that. I hope you know that anyway, but I won't do anything that would harm you or Orli." She sucked a quick breath. "You've both become important people in my life."

Maren's eyes searched her face, and then she nodded. "I believe you. You've always done the decent thing, going back to when Orli broke into your shed."

Once inside the house, Jac made two cups of coffee. "I'm guessing you'll want to sit on the back deck, not the front."

"Please."

"Tell me what you want me to do," Jac said. "I can talk to Orli, reassure her she was my friend first, and she still is. If you want to make a statement to the press, I can support you in that."

Maren shook her head. "I'm still not sure you understand. I don't want to remain closeted—"

"Then don't. Make that statement. Talk to Orli." She took a breath, her heart battering against her ribs.

"—but I have to, for now. I'm not sure I can refute this photo, but I can ignore it. I can't come out publicly. Because of my career, yes, but mainly for Orli, until she comes to accept the idea that I'm bisexual. That I might have girlfriends in my life in the future."

Girlfriends. Plural. Jac swallowed hard as a knot of sorrow tightened in her chest. Was Maren ending what they had now, until at some perfect point in the future, she'd tell Orli what she surely already knew if she'd seen the photo—that her mother was queer. Or was this Talia all over again? If they wanted to keep seeing each other, was Jac letting herself in for months of secrecy again, of hiding, playing the friends façade?

"So, what about us?" She rested a hand on Maren's arm. "I thought we were getting on well. Having fun together. Enjoying each other's company."

Maren stared at Jac's hand, as if wondering how it got there. "We are. I don't know, Jac. I'd love for what we have to continue...but I don't know if it can. It depends on so much that's out of my control. On what else is published." She took a breath. "I told Orli you and I are friends, that while we're interested in each other, we aren't girlfriends."

Jac turned away, and her stomach churned enough that acid burned in her throat. She shouldn't feel like this—they weren't girlfriends. *Not yet.* But they were something, and to hear Maren deny it so completely put an icy lump in her chest. "What about me? This should depend on you and me, not on others."

Maren's lips twisted and she hunched in on herself, wrapping her arms around her middle. "I wish it was just us. But it isn't, and it can't be. I'm a public figure, struggling to keep my career. And a mother, trying to do what's best for my daughter."

"Surely, what's best for Orli is showing her you're true to yourself? That you can seize your happiness—especially after you've put yourself second for so many years."

"It's different for you, Jac. You're out. You have nothing to lose in this—and maybe something to gain. Your business would benefit if you're identified as the mystery woman."

"You say that after I've told you I'll never do anything to harm you or Orli? I can't believe you think that." Jac stood and took a pace away, running shaking hands through her hair. "My business is doing just fine. Next, you're going to suggest I arranged the photographer to be there." She swung around to face Maren and jammed her hands on her hips.

"No, I don't think that for a moment." Maren folded in on herself. "I'm sorry, Jac, what I said was uncalled for...and wrong. I'm just scared. Scared Orli will turn on me. Scared I'll be forced into the open about something that should be my decision alone."

Jac's breath shuddered in her lungs. "Can you not embrace the moment? Shrug this off? Go about your life as a woman who loves women? Orli will think more of you for doing so, than hiding—"

"Are you trying to run my life?"

Her cold words sent an Antarctic blast through Jac's head. "No. Of course not. I'm sorry, Maren, but I'm struggling with this." She stared out at the garden, picking and discarding words in her head until the ones that were best presented themselves. "It's just"—she faced Maren again—"I like you, Maren. I like what we have. Rapport. Friendship. Incredible sex. I don't want to lose it."

"Neither do I." Maren's voice was so low Jac had to strain to hear her words. "But I'm not sure that's my choice to make." She turned around and, with a long look at Jac, left via the back steps.

Jac slumped on the couch. What the hell had just happened? Orli, Maren, gossip magazines...and somehow, she was caught in the middle of it. But the thundering, thumping beat of her heart was echoing the refrain in her head: *Talia. It's Talia all over again.*

Later that afternoon, a shuffle of feet alerted Jac that she wasn't alone in the shed. She looked up.

Orli stood there, her face a blank mask. She wasn't wearing her overalls; instead, her old hoodie hung over her face, and her hands balled in the pockets of her baggy jeans.

"Hey." Jac gave her a grin. "How's things?"

Orli's face didn't change. "How do you think things are? Both my parents are gay. I was probably mixed in a test tube and implanted in Maren's uterus like a row of lettuce, and my only friend here used me to get to her. That's you, by the way."

Right. So, things are not good, then.

"I think there's a bit more to it than that," she said. "Do you want to talk?"

Orli's eyes were shiny, and she shook her head. "What I'd like, you probably won't do anymore."

"What's that?"

"Go for a ride."

Jac thought fast. She had the time, and if it smoothed things with Orli, she'd do it. For her, but also for Maren. "If your mum says it's okay, we can go. I've got about three hours."

Orli nodded and shuffled off, pushing her way through the newly planted shrubs on the boundary. She was back in less than five minutes. "She says that's okay."

"Go get dressed then. I'll get the bike out."

"Can we take the Norton?"

"Sure. Where do you want to go?"

Orli sucked her lip. "Somewhere by the beach where we can get fish and chips."

Twenty minutes later, Jac guided the bike onto the freeway and opened it up to the limit. Sadness, upset, the feeling life was falling apart—in her experience, riding fast eased all of those. Behind her, she heard Orli's gasp as the bike flew down the outside lane. "Okay?" she said into the headset.

"I'm good." Already there was an uplift in Orli's voice.

Jac rode past Wollongong, down to Kiama, then stopped the bike. She took in Orli's flushed face and bright eyes. "Fish and chips?" She indicated the kiosk near the beach.

Orli nodded. Together, they left their helmets and found a table overlooking the water.

Jac waited until they both had portions of flake and chips. "Have you talked to your mum?"

Orli broke off a piece of fish and dipped it into her sauce. "She just repeats what she said before: that she and Dad loved each other, and that I was planned. But Dad's gay, and now Mum's…whatever she is."

"That's just it, Orli." Jac pushed her fish around the wrapping paper. "She's whatever she is, and only she can know that unless she tells you, and if she does, then you need to listen."

"My friend Eboni is bisexual. Now she is. Before, she was a lesbian."

"It can take time to figure out who you are."

"Did you know?" Orli fixed wide eyes on Jac's face. "That you were a lesbian?"

"I did, yes. From when I was quite young. But I didn't have the words for it until later." Was this all about Maren, she wondered, or was Orli doing some questioning of her own? "Would it bother you if your mum wanted to date women?"

Orli rolled her eyes. "Duh. D'you think I'm some homophobe? But she's always said… That is, she and Dad, were always…"

Jac waited.

"I don't know." Orli hunched her shoulders. "I just don't know. But it seems that every time something is happening in my life, Mum, like, gets in first with something bigger and better."

"And that's why you're feeling weird now? Because you're working through stuff and now it seems it's all about her?"

"Yeah. I was thinking…and I know…and…" Her jaw moved left and right. "But it doesn't matter. Now it doesn't. Because the internet buzz is all about her and her secret girlfriend. And you're my friend and you didn't tell me."

Jac took a mouthful from her water bottle. "There's nothing to tell, Orli. Your mum and I became friends through you." The word "friends" caught in her throat. It seemed so inadequate for what she and Maren were. So not so. "And I didn't have any idea who my neighbour was when you moved in."

"You're using me to get to her."

Jac laughed. "You broke into my shed. And it was your mum's idea that you work with me. Apart from I didn't pay you wages at first, that doesn't sound like I was using you."

She chewed her lip. "Are you sleeping with her?"

Shit. How was she supposed to answer this? She had no clue what Maren would want her to do. "That's not something for me to answer. You can ask your mum, but she may not answer you either. That information—whatever the answer—is private, unless it's offered to you freely."

"Figured." She was silent for a moment as she ate her chips.

"I know your mum loves you very much," Jac said when the silence had stretched too long. "She's doing all this for you: moving here, pausing her career, letting you work with me."

"Now she is." Bitterness seeped into Orli's voice. "Back in Melbourne she was always working."

"Give her a chance, hey? You both love the bikes. Maybe that will be something you can do together."

"Maybe."

Jac's knee jiggled. The stilted conversation was awkward and uncomfortable. She balled the fish wrapper and chucked it toward the bin. Amazingly, it dropped through the top. "Score!" She flung both arms in the air. "Fowler scores from five paces. Can Coffey equalise?"

A smile twitched on Orli's lips, and she scrunched up her wrapper and tossed it toward the bin. It hit the edge and for a second, it seemed it would fall outside. Then it dropped inside.

"The equaliser." Jac held up her hand for a high five, letting her breath out in relief when Orli matched her. "Shall we have coffee before we head back, or go back the long way instead?"

"The long way." The smile flickered on Orli's face again.

Jac blew out a slow sigh of relief.

CHAPTER 29
RUNS IN THE FAMILY

THE DOORBELL RANG THE NEXT morning, waking Maren. The bedside clock said three minutes to six. She lay for a moment, waiting for Janelle to get it, before remembering Janelle was on her cruise, hopefully sailing calm, blue oceans toward Japan. She had no idea who it could be at stupid o'clock in the morning.

Then feet sounded on the wooden floor, the creak of the front door opening, and Orli's voice said, "Nas Caspian? Come on in. Would you like coffee?"

Maren frowned. Who the hell was Nas Caspian? It sounded as if Orli hadn't met her either, although she seemed to be expecting her. She got out of bed and dressed as fast as she could, then went out to the kitchen.

Orli sat at the bench opposite a young, brown-skinned woman, who was pulling a notepad from her bag. A digital voice recorder sat on the bench, and two mugs steamed in front of them. Maren frowned, her Spidey senses tingling. A journalist.

"What's this about?" Her voice sliced the air. "Who are you?"

The woman slid from the stool and held out her hand. "Nas Caspian from *Out and About*. I'm here to interview Orli. I'm sorry if we woke you."

"I know nothing about this. You're aware my daughter is sixteen? Unless parental permission has been given, you aren't able to interview her alone."

"Mum, butt out. I set this up, and I'm plenty old enough."

Maren jammed her hands on her hips. "And what exactly is the interview about?"

Orli's chin jutted out. "That's my business."

Nas looked from one to the other. "Why don't I wait outside while you sort this out?" Without waiting for an answer, she hitched her bag higher on her shoulder and started for the front door.

Maren glanced at the DVR where the red light was blinking. She picked it up and turned it off. "Take this with you, unless you want me to throw it after you."

Nas flushed red and took it. "I'll be outside," she said to Orli.

Maren waited until the front door had closed behind her then folded her arms. "Talk."

"About what?" Orli matched her posture.

"What's the interview about? Is it about you, or have you sold some fabricated story about me to a gossip mag? If you want to have any chance of me allowing this to go ahead, you need to tell me what's going on."

"Fine." Orli slumped on the stool. "It's not about you. There's enough about you in the world as it is."

Maren tamped down the simmering anger and took a deep breath. "Then what is it about?"

Orli lifted a shoulder. "As it's not about you, why does it matter?"

"Because you're sixteen. Because there are many journalists who will twist your words, make it seem like you said something hateful or unkind. And Nas should have known to contact me or Marcus first."

"I told her I was eighteen," Orli mumbled.

"Then she didn't fact check before she came around. I'll ask you again: what's this about?"

"I told you: me. *Out and About* is a LGBTQ+ magazine and website. I'm coming out as non-binary." She scanned Maren's face. "Shocked? You're not the only one who can hide a queer identity."

"You're non-binary?" Relief coursed through her and she smiled as the tension left her body. "Sweetie, you are who you are. You can be exactly who you want to be, and you can love whoever you want to.

I'm happy for you, and I will love you just as much as I always have." She held out her arms. Would Orli accept her hug?

And then with a stiff step, then another, Orli was in her embrace, her arms wrapping around Maren's waist.

Maren stroked her hair as she had when she was little, and bit by bit, the tension left Orli's body, until she sighed and relaxed into Maren's arms.

"I'm sorry." Orli's words were muffled by Maren's shirt. "I thought you didn't care, that you would love me less. I thought you wouldn't want me if I wasn't your daughter anymore."

"Of course I care. You're my person, and I'll always love you. Nothing you could do could stop that. And you have the courage to be who you are." She put her arms on Orli's shoulders and held her away so she could look at her. "What are your pronouns? And if not as my daughter, how do you want me to refer to you?"

Relief shone in Orli's eyes. "They/them. And maybe you could just call me your teen."

"Got it." She glanced toward the front porch where Nas still waited. "Now, what do you want to do about this journalist? If you want to do the interview, that's fine by me, although I'll be here with you. If I think she's veering into inappropriate territory, I'll shut it down. Is that okay?"

Orli sucked their lip. "But you won't interfere otherwise?"

"Only if she asks about me. This is about you, right?"

A glimmer of a smile flitted across Orli's mouth. "Yeah. Right."

"Then you bring Nas back in; I'll make us all fresh coffee."

So far, Maren couldn't fault the young journalist. Her questions to Orli were sensitive, age-appropriate, and obviously designed to appeal to a young audience.

"Do you have a favourite non-binary or queer person you look up to?" Nas asked.

The red light on the DVR blinked on the bench in front of them.

"G Flip's amazing," Orli said. "I love their music—I saw them play in Melbourne last year. I also love how unapologetically themself they are—the world can take them or leave them."

"Is that how you see yourself?" Nas took a sip of the fresh coffee Maren had made.

"I'd like to. I don't think I'm there yet."

"Is your mother an inspiration? Coming out as she did—"

"Stop right there." Maren held up a hand. "You agreed this wouldn't be about me."

"I'm asking Orli if you've helped them along their path. Two supportive queer parents—"

"Again, this isn't about me. My personal life is private."

"But the photos of you on the beach, kissing a woman. Those photos are everywhere. You can't expect to remain closeted—"

Maren picked up the voice recorder and turned it off. "Nas, you were doing great until a minute ago. This interview is about Orli, and you agreed not to turn this into being about me. If you can't respect that, I will ask you to leave."

Nas's eyes flashed. She turned the recorder back on again. "What about your TV career? Are you going to return to Channel 12?"

"That is irrelevant to Orli." She kept her gaze locked on Nas's face until the reporter flushed and looked away.

"I hear Zoey Hammond has received an offer to remain permanently on the six o'clock news," Nas said.

She has? A flash of irritation shafted through her. Ethan hadn't mentioned that—if, indeed, it was true. Maybe Nas was baiting her. "No comment."

Nas looked at Orli. "How did your mum take your coming out?" She raised an eyebrow and glanced at Maren.

Maren gave a brief nod. That was acceptable—as long as she didn't take it any further.

Orli straightened their shoulders and shot Maren a look, one eyebrow raised.

She nodded once, keeping her face blank. Maybe her daugh— her *teen*—had got this. Maybe this would be the thing that brought them closer together.

"Mum's cool. I came out to her before she agreed I could do this interview, and she supported me all the way."

Warmth trickled through Maren's chest, singing in her blood. "Thanks, hon. I love you, too."

"What Mum does is her business. And Jac's my friend as well as hers."

Maren closed her eyes briefly. *Damn.* There was no way Nas would miss that slip.

"Jac?"

"A friend of ours," Maren said.

Nas turned to Maren. "Is she the woman you were caught kissing?"

"This interview is over." Maren stood. "I hope you've got what you need from Orli. And, Nas…" She waited until Nas met her eyes. "If you print anything about me except in the context of being Orli's mother, you'll be hearing from my lawyer."

"I understand. Orli, if there's anything you'd like to add, you have my e-mail address." She pulled over her canvas bag, brought out business cards and handed one to each of them. "You can get in contact with me if you need to. I apologise for stepping over the line."

"Apology accepted—as long as that's the end of it." She rose to her feet. "Let me show you out."

Once Nas had got into a blue Barina and driven off in a roar of slipping clutch and exhaust smoke, Maren went back inside.

"Sorry." Orli tried a smile. "I didn't mean to mention Jac. I didn't know what to do when she started asking you stuff."

"That's okay. Reporters have a way of needling you into saying something you didn't mean to. It's happened to all of us. You did well, Orli. You were so composed and had thoughtful answers to her questions."

"Thanks. I was nervous, though."

"It didn't show." Maren waited a beat. "But if she e-mails you wanting more information about me—"

"I'll tell her no." They stood tall, their baggy jeans low on their hips showing the band of what looked like boxer briefs.

"I trust you." Maren glanced at the clock on the wall. "You need to get ready for school. Remember, Dad is picking you up tonight."

"I hadn't forgotten. I hope he'll be cool with me being enby and all."

"I'm sure he will be. Do you have plans for the weekend?" She held her breath, hoping she hadn't pushed Orli too far.

"Mackenzie's taking me to the farm she volunteers at—Banksia Farm, for a better look around. Last time was too quick."

"I'm sure you'll have a great time."

Whether she would, this weekend, was another matter.

CHAPTER 30

A CLOSET IS A DEEP, DARK PLACE

JAC STOOD AT HER FRONT-ROOM window staring absently out at the street. She needed to bring her bins in and get rid of the junk mail cluttering the mailbox. As she watched, Maren's sleek car drove slowly into the driveway. For a moment, Maren glanced up, and their eyes met. Maren gave her a quick smile, then she looked forward again, and the car continued up the drive.

Jac returned to the kitchen and slumped on the stool. It had been three days since she and Maren had had—not an argument. More, warning shots fired. They both were in different chapters of their lives, different stages of their coming-out process. Jac was out in the open, Maren was still hiding behind the metaphorical curtains.

She missed her. Missed the sex, yes, undeniably. The need for Maren still thrummed in her blood, a wash of desire that overwhelmed her at the strangest times. She'd been in the supermarket yesterday, and a woman had walked past pushing a trolley, and for a second, Jac had seen Maren in her fine profile, in the swing of dark hair that brushed her jaw. A wave of longing had passed through her body, coating her in lust, until it'd seeped out of her toes. She'd stopped, her hand resting on the avocados, staring after the woman, until a man had brushed past her with a brusque, "excuse me", and grabbed two avos without care for ripeness. Jac had shaken her head and resumed picking out the perfect one.

But it was more than sex. She missed their chats over coffee, over a glass of wine. Missed Maren's gasps of excitement as the bike swooped around the bends in the national park, or the whoop she couldn't contain as they cruised over the Sea Cliff Bridge.

Was Jac overreacting with the whole closeted thing? Maren wasn't Talia, and Maren's reasons for remaining closeted were a lot less major than Talia's. Concern for Orli was a big one, but when it came down to it, Orli would be fine. And her career? That, too, would pass. The beach kiss photo had already outed them. Jac had checked the media since and there was no big, collective gasp of horror from the pearl-clutchers at Channel 12. Indeed, there had been little about it since.

As there should be.

So, Maren's reasons for staying closeted seemed to have an end date. A nebulous point in time when she would be comfortable enough to admit it publicly, or else be seen in public with a girlfriend without a big announcement. Talia's reasons had been harsher, had gone deeper, than that. She'd risked losing her entire family, her church, her community. And in the end, she couldn't do it.

In hindsight, Jac accepted that. If she had her time again, she wouldn't have pushed Talia so hard, wouldn't have given her the ultimatum she did. But she had been younger, and didn't want to live her life in secrecy. She still didn't. But she couldn't push Maren. Coming out—or not—was Maren's decision, as it had been Talia's. And what had it been? A few short weeks, a few nights of sex that made her body and mind hum. Not enough to base a major decision on. Could she give Maren more time? Jac rose and flicked on the kettle, and found a coffee bag for her favourite mug.

Maybe. For now, at least.

She picked up her phone.

Am meeting Kyra, Liz, and Caitlin for pool tonight. Want to come?

There was no immediate answer. She put the phone down and looked around. Even if Maren didn't come out with them this evening, even if she didn't come back to Jac's bed, she should tidy the house.

New sheets on the bed, clean towels in the bathroom. Vacuum. Empty the dishwasher. With a sigh, she went to do just that.

When she passed her phone an hour later, it showed a new message. She picked it up with a racing heart.

That would be good. Orli is at Marcus's for the weekend. But, Jac, I can't be public about us, not yet. If you can accept that, then I'd love to come.

The "not yet" could have been written in ten-foot scarlet letters. Not *yet*. That implied that time would come.

She could live with that.

They took the Goldwing to the pub, pulling in next to Caitlin's hatchback. Jac paused. She'd never mentioned what she and Maren were to each other to her friends, and certainly never asked them for discretion. Maybe they hadn't seen the article.

Yeah, right. Kyra with her crush on Maren would have seen it the second it had hit the internet. The amazing thing was she hadn't called Jac to gush.

Her friends were huddled around one of the small tables when they walked in.

"Hey." Jac put her hand on Kyra's shoulder.

Kyra swung around and pulled her into a hug. "You've been holding out on us," she whispered into Jac's ear. "And of course I'm not jealous at all."

"Please don't say anything," Jac whispered back. "It's...difficult."

A nod into her hair, and then Kyra released her.

When the beers were bought, and the pool partners sorted, they started playing. This time, Maren insisted on playing only every other game so that Jac could play too. Jac looked over from chalking her cue and saw Maren deep in conversation with Liz. From Maren's uneasy expression, they weren't talking about who would win the match.

When her game was over, and Kyra was racking the balls for the next game, Jac went over to where Maren sat, momentarily alone.

"You okay?" she asked. She rested her hand on Maren's arm. "We can leave if you're uncomfortable."

"It's fine," Maren said. "Your friends all recognised you in that photo, of course. I hope they're discreet."

"They should be. And if we ask them specifically, they will be." She glanced around. Her friends were laughing as they swapped cues, trying to find the least warped. "Can you lot come over here for a second?"

When they were all around the table, Jac said, "I guess you all saw the photo, and recognised both of us."

Nods around the table.

"Well, duh, yes," Caitlin said.

"We're both asking that you not spread it around. It's new, and things are tricky right now. Will you do that, for me? For both of us?"

Kyra and Liz nodded. Caitlin hesitated, then nodded as well. "You know what's right for you. But Jac...are you okay with that secrecy?"

Jac caught Maren's glance and forced a smile. "This is different from Talia. Different circumstances, different stakes. A different woman." She longed to find Maren's thigh under the table and give a squeeze of reassurance, but she resisted. She would honour the conditions.

But she hoped they would change soon.

They went for a ride after leaving the pub. It was as if they both needed the wind, the speed, the snap of chill air to clear out the tension between them. Jac stopped the bike at the Bald Hill lookout and dismounted. She unstrapped her helmet and rested it by the front wheel. She waited while Maren did the same, then the two of them walked to a bench overlooking the ocean. The night was calm and almost windless, and the water was a dark and slatey grey. Below them, the ocean whispered against the sand and rock, and out to sea, the lights of container ships pierced the blackness. To the south, the lights of the greater Wollongong area meandered along the shore.

"Do you miss Melbourne?" Jac asked when they were comfortable on the bench, a few centimetres gap between their bodies.

"Not much. Friends, yes, but I worked such long hours that catch-ups with genuine friends—not just work colleagues—were few. I've lost contact with many of them for that reason."

"Is it better here?"

"I have more time, yes. Too much, almost. But I've painted my room and the spare and have quotes for a revamp of Orli's bathroom and the kitchen. Marcus and Rick are close by. And you. You've become a friend, Jac." Her hand groped for Jac's, squeezed and released.

"Just a friend?" Jac said in a low voice.

"Well, there is the sex." The smile shone in Maren's voice.

"There is." Jac longed to pull Maren into an embrace, let her rest her head on Jac's shoulder, run her hand down Maren's leg over her jeans. Kiss her.

"Will you stay with me tonight?" Maren turned toward her. Her face gave nothing away, but her hands twisted together in her lap.

Jac stared out to sea. She should resist. Be true to how she was, rather than falling back into Maren the first time she asked. She closed her eyes and images of Maren naked, her and Maren naked together, scrolled inside her head. "Is that what you want?"

"I wouldn't have asked if I didn't. But if you can't deal with that... with us...then I understand. I'm the one making things awkward."

A knot tightened in Jac's stomach, but she took a deep breath, then another, and it eased. She'd already made her decision. She wasn't entirely happy, but she could wait. "I would like that very much."

Awareness leaped into life in the space between them, alive, strung fine, a shining thing.

"I want to kiss you now," Jac said. She glanced around. There were a couple of parked cars, a couple strolled, and a group of young people occupied the second bench. Would anyone notice? It was dark, they were surely unrecognised.

"Not here," Maren said. "Wait until we get home."

Home. How fast could she get there? In that moment, she regret-ted the leisurely ride they'd taken to reach the lookout. They should have just gone home. Her skin tingled, and her mouth went dry with anticipation.

She rose. "Then let's go."

Maren closed her eyes as Jac kissed her way along her body, her mouth and fingers working magic on her nipples, teasing them simultaneously into hard peaks. It was as if there was a direct line to her clit. Jac's tongue circled, while her fingers squeezed Maren's other nipple. She curved her fingers into the mattress in anticipation, before stroking Jac's naked body from shoulder to hip.

Jac's soft, damp pubes brushed Maren's thigh. Already she could feel her own answering moisture. She clenched in anticipation of the time when Jac would fuck her, filling her with her fingers, stroking in and out in the perfect rhythm, the perfect intensity. Perfect.

Perfect.

Jac's fingers continued meandering along Maren's body until they teased the top of her mound. Dipped lower, stroked softly, one fingertip dipping inside.

"You're so wet. All for me." Jac's voice thrummed with smokiness, and a second finger joined the first.

"All for you," Maren said. She hadn't been this wet for a long time, had put her dryness when she self-pleasured down to age, but with Jac she was as wet as a monsoon, as sex-crazed as a teenager.

She spread her legs wide as Jac shifted so she could fill her better. Jac's thumb brushed her clit as she fucked her slowly, pressing her G-spot with each measured stroke, both deliberate and arousing. She watched Jac through slitted eyes, saw her tongue touch her lips, her eyes darken with lust, her concentration on Maren's pleasure.

When she came, clenching around Jac's fingers, she opened her eyes against the bright white stars behind her eyelids and saw Jac's soft smile, the tiny lines around her eyes crinkling.

And when her orgasm had subsided, when she could breathe in something other than gasps, she pushed Jac over and smoothed her palms over every centimetre of her body, her breasts, her throat, trailed fingers over her cheeks, palmed her breasts, mapped her belly, the curve of her hip, and the valley between her thighs. Oh yes, especially there. Maren slid her fingers inside Jac, watching as her eyes fluttered shut and her teeth worried her lower lip, her hips rising convulsively in time with Maren's thrusts.

How had she gone so long without making love to a woman? She'd pushed down her urges when she was with Marcus, opting for her fingers and a vibrator, as they'd agreed not to have other partners. And the time when they'd tried to make their marriage a sexual arrangement too… Well, it had been fine. Pleasurable. There had been warmth and laughter and shared times, but it wasn't like this. Wasn't as all-encompassing. She'd never felt the urgency she did now with Jac.

Could she continue this? Would Jac?

She didn't know. But she did know she wasn't ready to end it.

CHAPTER 31
DANDELION CLOCK

ORLI CAME HOME SUNDAY EVENING in a whirl of enthusiasm, a pile of dirty laundry, and a cake that they and Rick had baked for Maren.

Marcus and Rick came in with them, followed by Maple, who went off on an exploration of the house.

Maren sliced the cake, put it onto four plates, and hit the button for the coffee machine. "Good weekend?" she asked Orli.

"Yeah. We went to Banksia Farm with Mackenzie, and I tagged around behind her for the morning. I got to brush ponies and collect eggs. Dad and Rick just ate cake in the farm café for a couple of hours. They didn't help with anything."

"I had my Italian leather shoes on." Rick rolled his eyes. "What did you *expect* me to do? Grub around in a farmyard?"

Orli grinned and ate a huge bite of cake. "But he did wheedle the recipe for this cake out of Stella who runs the café. So, he's forgiven."

"If I ever fall out with Orli, I just feed them," Rick said. "Works every time."

"And I came out to Dad, Rick, and Mackenzie." Orli inspected their fingernails. "And they're all cool." Their grin covered their face.

Marcus gave a thumbs up to Maren behind Orli's back. "Of course," he mouthed.

"Mackenzie said school is cool with gender stuff. They respect pronouns."

"That's great. Mackenzie sounds like a good person," Maren said.

"How was your weekend?" Marcus asked.

"Yeah, Mum, how was it? Did you see Jac?"

Maren froze. Would admitting that she had, bring the return of sullen Orli again? "We went to the pub with her friends, played pool, went out on the Goldwing. It's like an armchair compared to the Norton."

"Sweet," Orli said. "Maybe I'll try that next time." They stuffed the rest of their cake into their mouth and disappeared toward their room.

Marcus looked around, no doubt checking they were gone. "So, how is it going with Jac?"

Maren glanced down at her plate to hide her smile. "Good. I hope. I relish her company."

"Just her company?" Rick arched an eyebrow.

She nudged his arm. "Not just her company, since you mention it. See this grin?" She pointed at her own mouth. "That is satisfied-woman smirk."

"Thought so." Rick winked.

Marcus covered her hand with his own. "We saw the photo online, of course. Even if Orli hadn't pointed it out in a huff. Are you going public with this?"

Maren's lips tightened. "That's the only sticking point. Jac's fully out and isn't happy that I'm not. But for now, no, I'm not. I need to sort out what I'm going to do about Channel 12 first. Ethan's pushing me harder. What did Orli say to you?"

"They were huffy at first, still upset that you'd stolen their friend. I think we got them out of that funk though," Marcus said. "They asked if I'd always been gay. I think they thought it came over me like a rain cloud when we divorced."

"More like a sunbeam," Rick said.

"I told them the truth: that I'd always been... Well, I fudged it a little, I said I'd always been bisexual. They asked if you knew that, and I said you did."

"Who'd have thought our placid marriage would cause so much upset now?" Maren sighed. "I know Orli will have no problem, eventually. It's just the present time I worry about. They seem so perilous in life."

"Things are getting better for them," Marcus said. "Moving here was a good decision, I think. They're making friends. Finding interests. We're here to take the pressure off you. I think if things are going that way with Jac, maybe you should do what you want for once. Orli will adapt. Come out or not—that's your choice, and no one else's. Not Orli's, not Jac's, and certainly not Channel 12's."

He was right. Of course he was. But a knot of tightness in her chest kept her silent. For the last twenty years she'd been Marcus's wife, Orli's mother, Australia's favourite newsreader. She'd been Maren, famed for her enjoyable dinner parties, a regular on the Melbourne social scene. And now it was all falling away from her. Marcus, Channel 12, even Orli.

Without those familiar situations, without those loved and comfortable ties, who was she? In Melbourne, her path had seemed assured. Even when she and Marcus had split, she'd still had the well-worn grooves in which her life ran. But now...the future seemed nebulous, like peering into a shifting mist. Orli was sixteen—they might need her now, but they wouldn't for much longer. They'd make their own way, leave school, go to university or get a job, or both. Marcus had found his love. Even Janelle was living the dream on a world cruise. And her? She was clinging on to threads that were blowing away in the wind like a dandelion clock.

Maybe it was time for her to make a leap into the future. See what she, too, could be without the weight of other people's expectations.

Marcus stared at her with a slight smile. His reassuring look. Rick scraped the last of the cake from his plate. Both of them supported her. It seemed Jac would too.

So, what was holding her back? Nothing except her own cowardice.

CHAPTER 32
SAFETY SPEAK

"I was thinking," Jac said over the phone, "that tomorrow would be a good day to give Orli their first bike lesson. The road safety school is officially closed then, but I have the okay to use it. I was also thinking you might like to come too. Let Orli see us together in the friend zone."

Maren walked out onto her front balcony. "Where's the school?"

"Penrith. Not far. Either I ride the Norton with Orli on the back, and you drive, or, alternatively, I could see if Liz is free. She could ride the BMW with you on the back. I thought you might like a lesson as well. You could get your bike licence."

A tingle ran down into Maren's fingers. It was one thing to ride pillion with Jac, another to think of controlling the bike by herself. A frisson of worry ran down her spine. What if she couldn't manage it? Fell off? She paused. Those worries were the ones the old Maren would have had. She would have played safe, stuck to driving a car. But the Maren she was now…the one who was taking control of her life… "I'd love that, if you're okay with it. Orli and I could learn together."

"I'll see if Liz is free," Jac said. "But you'll need to up your game. Orli is likely to find it easier than you!"

Liz was delighted with the idea of taking Maren on the back of the BMW. Jac arranged for her to come over by ten the next morning, and ended the call.

She clattered down the steps to check her mailbox. As she was removing the junk mail, a casually dressed man got out of a nondescript silver sedan parked across the road.

"Hi." The man approached her. "I think you're the person I'm looking for."

"How can I help you?" Jac offered a smile. Her address was on her business cards, and while it rarely happened, occasionally people turned up on spec looking for a tour.

"You're the person who runs the bike tours to the Illawarra?" The man studied Jac through large-framed glasses.

"Among other places, yes. Are you wanting to make a booking?"

"I'm just after information at this stage."

"Sure. If you want to wait a moment, I'll get you a brochure." She went inside and took a couple of brochures from the pile by the door. When she returned, the man was halfway down her drive, looking about.

"Nice area, this," he said. "Peaceful."

"It is, yes." She handed him the brochures.

He took a quick look. "You're Jacinta Fowler?"

"I am." She stuck her hands in the front pocket of her jeans. Something about his intent stare made her uneasy. He was studying her, yet his gaze flickered over her house and yard as well. Was he casing out properties in the area? Would she come home and find her house burgled?

She took a few steps back toward the road. "The most popular options are listed there. Call me if you're interested."

"I saw your photo." His gaze sharpened. "With Maren McEvoy."

Her nerve endings twitched and her stomach clenched. Was he stalking Maren, or just a fan? Or a journalist? She raised an eyebrow but remained silent.

"Is she a regular client of yours?" His chuckle raised her senses to red alert.

"I don't confirm or deny if anyone is my client," she said in a monotone. "Nor do I discuss them with anyone."

"You don't need to." He fished out a business card and held it out to her. "It was Maren and you in the photo. It took a bit to track you down, but now that I have, I'm interested in buying the rights to your story. Local dyke on bike turns Australia's favourite newsreader gay. That sort of thing."

She narrowed her eyes. "You need to work on your headline. There's no story here."

"I think there is, and I'm willing to pay for it. Was Maren always gay? Is that what you're saying? After all, her husband now lives with a man."

"I have nothing to say to you. Please leave my property."

His supercilious face didn't change. "Sure. Are you going to take my card?"

"No."

He shrugged. "Suit yourself. I'll leave it in your mailbox, in case you change your mind."

"Don't hold your breath." Her disbelief at the intrusion was giving way to a steely cold anger. "I've asked you to leave once. This is your final warning." Deliberately, she didn't look at Maren's house. Maren was home, and things would be so much worse if Mr Sleeze found out where she lived.

"Don't get your knickers in a knot. I'm going. I'll wait for your call, Jacinta."

She didn't reply, just folded her arms and stared until he was back out on the road. He went to the car and pulled out a camera, pointing it in her direction.

She spun around so all he would get was a rear view, and went inside, slamming the door, then leaned against it, anger simmering in her blood. Maren would be furious—and worse, it would reinforce her decision to remain closeted. Jac's lips twisted. It would be terrible to have your private life dissected for the nation. To have who you loved flashing up on mobile phones in the morning news, as people ate their Weet-Bix.

But then, wasn't that the price of fame?

"Are you okay riding with Liz?" Jac asked. "I totally trust her."

"Of course." Maren flashed a grin. "And I'd rather Orli ride with you. I'm sure Liz is terrific on a bike, but Orli knows you."

"No worries then." Jac gestured to the clothing rack. "Go get dressed. Although, maybe it's time you both bought your own bike gear."

Orli was already at the rack, pulling out the protective clothing they usually wore.

Maren joined them and hunted for the worn black suit she'd worn previously. "Are you excited?" she said to Orli.

They turned to her, eyes shining. "Mum, I cannot wait. Jac said we'll just be riding slowly, stopping, starting and stuff. In and out of cones. But to ride by myself... This is the best thing I've ever done."

Of course it was. "Better than the tennis lessons, ice skating, and snowboarding lessons we gave you? Better than the jungle walk in Thailand? Better than—"

"Better than all of those." Orli fiddled with the collar of their jacket. "I feel free on the bike. I feel more myself. Like it's how I'm supposed to be." They lifted shining eyes to Maren's. "Seems like you're starting to get it, too."

"I am." Maren bit back the comment about riding safely. "Maybe, once we both have our licences, we can ride together sometimes. Go off on overnight trips."

"Yeah. Maybe. If you behave yourself."

"Brat." Maren laughed and moved to ruffle Orli's hair.

They ducked away, but there was a definite smile on their face, one that Maren hadn't seen too often in the last few months.

Once dressed, they went out to where Jac and Liz waited.

"Last chance to ride the comfortable bike," Jac said to Orli.

"Nah. Mum needs the BMW for her old bones."

"Hey!" Maren lifted her eyebrows. "Not so much with the old." But her heart sang at Orli's teasing. Maybe, just maybe, it would be all right between them. "And I know the BMW is carrying the picnic lunch. So, if anything happens, Liz and I won't starve."

"Nothing will happen," Liz said. She straddled the bike and waited while Maren settled her helmet and pulled on her gloves before mounting.

With a thumbs up from Jac, the two bikes rumbled down the driveway to the road.

It was soon apparent that Liz was nearly as good on the bike as Jac. Maren kept her gaze trained on Jac and Orli. Jac was right—Orli was a natural. Their body moved with Jac's and the bike in a seamless wave of motion. Orli hid Jac from view, but as they went around a corner, Jac's lean, black-clad body came into view. A wave of longing washed over her. She knew how that tight body felt under her hands. Knew how Jac responded to her touch.

"Hey," Liz said over the headset. "Try relaxing a little more. You're stiff behind me, and it's affecting the ride here. Feel how I move with the bike and try to do the same."

"Sorry," Maren said. "I was watching my teen." She concentrated on the ride.

"Just Orli?" The smile shone in Liz's voice. "Because Jac's worth watching, too, and not only for her amazing riding skills."

Maren was silent. How much had Jac told her?

"Sorry if I made you uncomfortable." Liz's voice rang in her ears. "Jac hasn't said anything more than what she did in the pub the other week."

"That's okay." She sighed, and the words she wanted to say, that she should say, caught in her throat. Words that implied her sexuality, even if she couldn't say the words outright. The smallest of coming outs to someone who already knew. "But I was watching Orli. I can't see Jac from here."

For a minute, both were silent. Maren let her body relax into the movement of the bike. The seat between her thighs, her feet on the pegs, the feel of Liz's waist underneath her gloves.

"Jac's different since she met you," Liz said eventually. "Normally, she tells us about her women. She's not a player, but she is picky. Women fall all over her. Partly, it's the bike and the leather gear, and the tough-girl image she presents. But partly, I think, it's because she's genuine. Kind. With you, though, she hasn't said a word, except that you're a neighbour and you're more than friends. And, of course, Orli's working for her. That alone is strange for Jac. She normally doesn't have much to do with kids."

Jac hadn't mentioned the reason, even to her closest friends. Warmth bloomed in Maren's chest. Jac'd held Orli's history close. Protected them, even when her teen had done nothing to deserve that. "Orli fell hard for the bikes. We're both lucky Jac didn't mind them hanging around."

"You, though," Liz said. "Tell me to shut up if you want. Jac's very closed mouthed about you and her. Maybe you've asked her to be, given that you're famous, but she's not one to give a stuff about things like that. What she is, though, is loyal. And when she falls, she falls hard."

"Has that happened much in the past?" She tightened her grip on Liz's waist as she waited for the answer.

"No," Liz said. "She told you about Talia?"

"She has." *Talia*—someone who had been important to Jac. Who had meant the world to her, enough that she had suppressed her true self to be with her.

Liz rode onto the slip road for the motorway and increased speed. Jac's bike surged ahead.

Maren could imagine Orli's delighted whoop.

"Well, Talia was Jac's person. And she pressed her to come out, but Talia…couldn't. Her community isn't accepting of same-sex relationships. I felt for Talia, to be honest. She loved Jac, but for her to be what Jac wanted would have meant the loss of all she knew."

"Did you think she should have come out?"

"How can anyone make that decision for someone else? Talia made her choice, and it wasn't Jac. And Jac accepted that. She realises, as well, she was too hard on Talia. I'm not telling you what to do, Maren, I'm just giving you a bit of history. Jac's my friend, and I love her, and I want her to be happy. Maybe she could be happy with you."

Maren moistened her dry lips. "You think?"

"I don't know. But my answer's a definite maybe. If it's what you both want enough. There." Liz laughed. "That's a firm answer for you.

I'm sorry for lecturing when you can't do anything but listen. At least you haven't jumped off the bike."

Maren chuckled. "No way. Thanks, Liz. I hear you. And it's complicated. And you're right: Jac is a unique person. Beyond that…I don't know."

"None of us can. Wouldn't life be boring if we did?"

Maren bit her lip. "Ain't that the truth."

"You two had your headsets on private," Jac said, as they walked across to the training course. "Orli and I couldn't talk to you."

"Sorry," Liz said. "I'll make sure we use the wider channel for the return trip."

Orli bounced along next to Jac. "Where are we going?"

"To those sheds. You'll be riding bikes with less engine capacity—that's all you're allowed on learner plates. Once you reach sixteen years and nine months, you can do the official course to get your L plates. You'll have a head start, as what we'll do today is the equivalent of that."

"I wanted to ride the Norton." Orli's shoulders slumped.

"And you will—once you have your full licence. No one learns on my bikes—they're too valuable to me, and things can happen."

They reached the shed and Jac pulled out a key. Inside, red and blue Hondas stood in a row. The bikes were old, and well used. A dinged tank here, a bent peg there. No wonder Jac didn't want them learning on her precious bikes.

Jac walked down the line, selecting two bikes, one red and one blue. "We'll use these two. Do you want a break first?"

Maren shook her head. "I'm good."

"Then let's do it!"

Jac and Liz stood in the middle of the course watching Maren and Orli ride around the cones and the "roadway" stopping and starting at the junctions, navigating the roundabout. Orli leaned toward overconfidence; they were trying to go faster and weren't treating the practice course with the seriousness it deserved.

Maren, though, rode with care, and her head checks at the junctions were steady and deliberate. Jac watched her.

"You're staring." Liz nudged her.

"Of course I am. You are, too. That's what you do with baby riders. You watch them like a hawk."

"Not that sort of staring," Liz said.

Jac gave up the pretend affront. "Well, Maren is worth looking at. Imagine if Kyra were here!"

Liz laughed. "Poor Kyra. She was a bit put out by that photo of you and Maren, although she'd never admit it. Maren's always been her celebrity crush—and you had to meet her first." She nudged Jac. "It good, between you?"

"Yeah..." Jac breathed out slowly. "It good. But, Liz, please don't ask me more. Not yet. And please don't talk about this."

"I haven't. None of us have. You'll tell us more when you're ready."

Jac turned to her and gripped her hand. "I will. And thank you." She switched her attention back to the riders and lifted the walkie-talkie. "Orli, take it slower. You need to give the head checks your full attention. Sure, there's no one coming fast around a blind bend here, but in real life, there might be."

They ate lunch at a picnic table under the shade of a fig tree. Jac had assembled the lunch she took on the tours: sandwich ingredients, crackers, cold meat, cheese slices, chutney, and salad.

"You both did great," Jac said. "Particularly you, Maren. Orli, you need to watch for over confidence. Yes, it's easy, but the testers will fail you if you rush your safety checks."

Orli snagged a piece of ham and built themself a third salad sandwich. "Okay. I was just so excited."

"I get that," Liz said.

"Can I ride back with Liz?" Orli asked. "I want to see what it's like with another rider."

"Fine with me," Liz said, "but it's up to Maren."

Maren nodded. "Sure." She tamped down the surge of excitement that she'd have her body snug to Jac's, to feel the movement as their bodies aligned, in tune with the bike.

"We'll have the channel open on the ride back, so all four of us can talk," Jac said. Her eyes flashed a warning at Maren: *So nothing inappropriate.*

Of course there wouldn't be.

CHAPTER 33

BREAKING WAVES

"I've no tours today," Jac said. "Fancy a swim in the ocean pools? They're public enough that we'll have to wear clothes." She smoothed a hand down Maren's naked skin from shoulder to hip. "Unfortunately."

Maren shivered as Jac's hand roamed around to her breast. "You've skinny dipped there?"

"Of course I have. At midnight, as a teenager, with my first girlfriend. Katie had an old banger of a car, and we'd drive down to Austinmer." She tilted her head and regarded Maren. "Are you saying you want to skinny dip? Maren McEvoy, you are one enormous surprise." Her mind conjured an image of Maren, ethereal and silvered by the moon, stepping carefully over the wet rocks to lower herself into the sea pool.

"I'd love to. But no, not here, even at midnight. Maybe I should put in a pool here. The garden's private enough with all the screening."

"I could see in from my back balcony." Jac waggled her eyebrows. "And I'd be looking."

"You'd be exempt. In fact, I hope you'll always look."

Jac's breath caught. Maren's words implied a future for them, one where she was always welcome to ogle Maren's naked body. Her mind skittered around the implications of that. Did she want that? Would Maren come out? Was that even where they were going? She crashed that mental door shut. Maren was most likely just bantering, teasing

Jac as she liked to do. "Did you have a pool in Melbourne?" she asked instead.

Something bleak flashed across Maren's expression before it cleared. "No. There wasn't really room, and the beach was just over Beaconsfield Parade—"

"All gritty and crowded, with no surf, just those little lapping waves."

"Sounds like Austinmer on the weekend."

"You've never been there in wild weather then, when the surf breaks into the pool." Jac rolled onto her stomach and heaved up, coming down on top of Maren. "A bit like that. I've just imitated the surf. But not as elegant."

"You're plenty elegant enough for me." Maren's fingertip circled the freckle under Jac's left eye. "You don't have tattoos. I thought all bikers did."

Jac blew a raspberry. "Oooh, you're stereotyping. I quite like tattoos—on other people. I'm too chicken to get any myself—I've heard they hurt. Caitlin said she screamed the parlour down when she got hers."

"So, she has only one, then?"

"She has four. Apparently, it's like childbirth—you forget the pain. Not that Caitlin has any kids."

"Do you want kids?" Maren stared up at Jac, a question in her eyes.

Jac froze. A second comment that sounded more than casual. Or was she reading too much into this? "I like my life the way it is, and I don't think a baby fits in with that. I know thirty-five isn't too old, but I honestly can't see myself being a mother. Unlike you."

"Unlike me," Maren echoed. "I don't regret for a second having Orli, but it did change my life. It paused my career for a few years—which is why I'm older than the average newsreader now."

"It doesn't seem to have done you any harm."

Maren licked her lips and, fascinated, Jac watched the swipe of Maren's tongue across them.

"No, but if I don't give Ethan an answer soon, it might. After all, my current work situation directly results from motherhood. It was easier in Melbourne. Marcus was there for most of Orli's childhood, and Janelle was almost a second mother figure to them." She sighed. "I miss Janelle. But she's wanted to do an around-the-world cruise as long as I've known her."

"Will she come back to work for you?" It seemed luxurious, having a housekeeper for two people, but if Maren went back to work, then maybe it would be necessary.

"The offer's open. She's on six months' long service leave from me at present. The ship is now heading toward Africa. It's up to her. She's also welcome to come back and live with us with no need to work." Maren pressed her hips into Jac's. "Are we going to keep talking about Janelle, or are we going to get up and go to Austinmer, or are we going to do something far more decadent and exciting?"

The pulse of blood in Jac's sex seemed heavier, sultrier, a slow surge of arousal. "I think we should take advantage of your empty house, and then go to Austinmer." She lowered her head and her lips found Maren's.

For long moments they kissed, soft and slow, then a gradual build to demanding and fierce. Jac's nipples rubbed against Maren's breasts, and the feeling was so intense it was as if her bones had turned to wax and melted from the closeness of the sun that was Maren. She broke the kiss and settled her lips against Maren's neck, sliding her way down to Maren's breasts, kissing first one, then the other. Silvery lines feathered over them, and Jac traced them with her tongue. "Are they from breastfeeding?"

"Yes. My badge of honour."

"I love them. They're like the fingers of the moon."

"Very poetic. Maybe you haven't seen the darker ones on my stomach."

"Oh, I have, and I love them, too. They're part of you, Maren, and part of what has made you who you are."

"Thank you. I like them, too. And as long as I still look slim and beautiful in a suitable outfit for TV, no one cares what I'm like underneath."

"I care." Jac traced the silver web on her other breast. "And I very much like what I see."

She moved lower, and her fingers strummed along the darker line over Maren's stomach, the slight puckering of skin. "The beauty of experience, right here on your body."

Maren rolled her neck and stared at Jac through slitted eyes. "You say the best things."

Jac pushed at Maren's thighs until she parted them, then Jac moved down to settle between her legs. Her tongue touched down.

"And you do the greatest things… Oh!" Maren's words ended on a gasp.

Jac smiled as her tongue explored. She doubted there would be any more words for a while.

A couple of hours later, Maren parked her car at the Austinmer sea baths. Carrying their towels, they walked across the rocks to the edge, then shed their clothes to reveal their swimmers. She eyed Jac's body as she stood on the edge of the pool. Her simple black one-piece was as practical and unfussy as Jac herself. Maren looked down at her own swimmers: a one-piece like Jac's—she'd never wanted bikini photos of her in the press—but with high cut legs and a scooped neck. She traced the lines of Jac's legs, lean and strong, and her muscled arms and shoulders. *Nice.* A low burn started down in her belly at the thought of Jac and her naked in bed together earlier.

Maren padded over the wet rock to the ladder and lowered herself into the water. "Come in! It's…bracing! Oh!" She gasped as the swell from an incoming wave lifted her up.

"You took the chicken route." Jac's words ended in a splash as she leaped in from the edge.

The water sprayed up, drenching Maren. "Horror. You did that on purpose." She splashed Jac.

"Might have. Or not." Jac swam up to her and, taking her hands, towed her out to the middle of the baths. "There's too many people around to kiss you. Unfortunately."

Maren glanced around. While the few people there in the middle of a weekday appeared to be minding their own business, swimming laps, or doing some sort of aerobic workout, Jac was right. Unless she was willing to come out, but even the thought of that made her curl inside.

"Let's stay in the friend zone here."

The warm light vanished from Jac's eyes. "Sure," she said after a beat. She put her hands on Maren's shoulders and heaved herself out of the water, attempting to duck her.

Maren dipped away instead, and Jac plunged back down like a breaching whale.

She surfaced, laughing, and looked around for her. "Sneaky."

"Can't catch me," Maren said in a sing-song voice, and took off in a smooth Aussie crawl to the far end of the pool. It had been a couple of months since she'd swum any distance or speed, but it seemed she still had it. She reached the far end and clutched the rock wall.

Jac approached in a splashy and inefficient crawl and rested her elbows on the side of the pool. "I thought I was fit. You've left me for dead."

Maren turned on her back and floated in the salt water. A strand of seaweed brushed her toes, and she kicked it away. "Swimming was my main exercise back in Melbourne. But in an indoor pool most of the year. Sometimes in the bay." She trod water and slicked back her hair. "You don't need to worry how you look in your swimmers."

Jac paddled closer. "That's what I was thinking about you. You're gorgeous, Maren. Every bit of you."

For a long and charged moment, their eyes met. Jac's flamed with desire. Maren's limbs turned to jelly, and she wished they'd stayed in bed and loved each other again. She shook her head and pushed her wet hair from her eyes. "Race you back to the other end. Loser buys lunch."

Without a word, Jac took off in her splashy overarm crawl.

Of course, Maren had won their impromptu race, but she'd insisted lunch—their date, she'd called it—was her treat anyway.

They sat on the bench by the window of the Pacific View Hotel, bodies angled toward each other, although, Jac supposed, to the casual observer, it would look as if they were admiring the view of the ocean.

Away out to sea, the tankers lined up, and closer to shore, seabirds wheeled and darted over the waves.

Jac sipped her beer and watched Maren. The view was amazing as ever, but it was Maren she watched. Maren held a glass of no-alcohol gin and tonic but was yet to take a mouthful. Maren had called this a date. The knowledge thrummed in Jac's bones. Did that mean Maren was reconsidering the way forward for her—for them? Maybe even coming out?

That reminded her of something. Some of the joy fled the day, but she couldn't not mention it. She set her beer down on the table, carefully aligning the coaster underneath. "I need to tell you something."

Maren arched an eyebrow. "Oh?"

"The other day, I had an unexpected—and very unwelcome—visitor. A journalist who'd somehow identified me and tracked me down as the mystery woman you kissed on the beach. He offered me money for my story."

Maren's face lost all expression. "What did you do?"

"Didn't say a word in confirmation or denial and threw him off my property. Lucky you weren't on your front deck—I don't think he knew you lived next door. He left a card in my letter box. I was going to rip it up, but I kept it, so we can find out if he does print anything. Peter someone."

Maren twisted her glass in her hands. "Could be anyone. There's so many legitimate press, and even more wannabes. What's worrying is how he found you."

"He didn't say and I didn't ask. I wanted him gone."

"He was able to find you from one photo. Surely he would have found out where I live, too. Did you see what he drove?"

"Some forgettable sedan. Old. Silver, I think."

"Did you get the registration?"

"No, of course not. He took a photo of me, but I turned so he didn't get my face, and then he was gone."

Maren set her glass down and pleated the hem of her T-shirt. "We both need to watch for that car. He knows where you live. He could follow you—or me— hoping to get compromising photos. He could approach Orli." She rubbed her forehead. "There's no law against this, unless he trespasses. We'll both have to be extremely careful."

Jac frowned—surely that was an overreaction. "I run a public business—I can't vet my clients to see if they're paparazzo. He came, he didn't get what he wanted, he left. Why would he waste time returning?"

"You don't get it, Jac. Life in the public eye means dealing with things like this. No doubt he wants a scandalous story with an attention-grabbing headline."

That was exactly what he had wanted, but now was not the time to joke about that with Maren. Jac bit her lip.

Maren reached out a hand. "I'm sorry. I don't want to fight with you about this, and I don't expect you to understand how it is. I've hidden my sexuality for half my life. To consider going public is difficult for me. Even today. It scares me," she said in a low voice, "and the thought of someone like that reporter taking my autonomy is terrifying. I'm trying to get to that point: for you, for us, but mainly for me."

Jac's heart melted. Maren was fighting her dragons, and although she could support her, she couldn't slay those dragons for her.

"Are you going to call him back?" Maren asked.

"No way! I don't want my life disturbed like that, let alone yours."

A glimmer of a smile appeared on Maren's face. "Thank you." She set her glass down and twisted her hands in her lap. "I know what you're thinking, Jac. How much easier it would be if I was just out, and the world be damned. How little it would matter in a few days. And you're right."

"Orli asked me about us," Jac admitted. "I said we were friends, and they should talk to you if they had questions."

"They're more accepting than I thought they would be. After their initial huff...well, they seem pretty cool about it—although they think we're in the friend zone. Maybe they think I'm questioning—I don't know. I guess them coming out as non-binary brought it home to them."

"There's still Channel 12." Jac took a mouthful of beer. Why was she pointing out the difficulties to Maren instead of rejoicing that she seemed more open to the idea of coming out? Her hand shook, and she set her glass down carefully. *Because I care. Because I want Maren to be happy and comfortable with her decision. Because it's not just about me.* Her gaze locked on Maren. When had that happened? Sometime between dealing with her rebellious teen—who was easing into being happier within themself—and their connection over shared interests. Well, Maren was not just a neighbour and a friend anymore. Jac licked her lips. She didn't know what she was, couldn't find the words to describe. What were the words for more than friend, lover, but not yet a person she loved?

What was love, anyway?

"Jac?" Maren waved a hand in front of her face. "You okay? You looked a million miles away then."

Jac snapped her gaze back to Maren and forced a smile. "It's nothing. Just dreaming for a moment."

But it was very much something. She just needed to determine what.

CHAPTER 34
WHO HAS A SAY?

"Maren, it's Ethan. I'm following up on our earlier conversation. I'm being pushed as to whether you're interested in those couple of days a week from the Sydney studio."

Maren's stomach sank. Ethan's offer simply hadn't been at the forefront of her mind. Oh, she knew she had to respond, but every time she'd thought of it, she'd been no closer to a decision.

"Changes are happening," Ethan continued. "I don't know if you've kept abreast of the ratings, but Luka and Zoey have now equalled the ratings of you and Luka at your peak. I know she hasn't been too friendly to you, but Zoey's professional and incredibly ambitious. The station recognises that. They've offered her a long-term contract—replacing you."

And there it was. She'd always known that Zoey wanted her job. Even Nas had mentioned it, although how she knew was anyone's guess. The thing was, what—if anything—did she want to do about it?

"That's not unexpected," she said. "What are my options? Can I insist on returning to my position? I'm still a full-time employee—my time there predates the move to contracted working."

Ethan sighed. "It's not that simple. Yes, you're guaranteed a full-time position upon your return, but it doesn't have to be the same position. Indeed, it almost certainly would be a lesser position, albeit on the same salary."

"Comparable work?"

A silence on the line. "If it's available," Ethan said at last. "Which right now, apart from the two days in Sydney, it's not. Maren, I'll be honest with you. I pushed for you to be offered the two days. If you turn it down, the position is gone. Yes, you're guaranteed a job, but you could find yourself reporting from the regional areas. That would mean a lot of travel. Any full-time, studio-based position would most likely be as a production assistant or researcher or similar."

"They'd do that?" Her voice took on a crystalline sharpness—her newsreader voice. "They'd make Australia's favourite newsreader re-search stories?"

"They can't invent a position for you. There's been cuts already. Marika from the Melbourne team has gone, so has Felippe in Perth. You'd probably get the fill-in jobs when someone's sick or on leave."

"If I take the Sydney position, what happens at the end of the year when I move back to Melbourne?"

Ethan's silence was even longer than the last time. "That's where it falls down. If you take the Sydney position, you'll be considered to have moved locations—and there's no guarantee you'll be able to transfer back in any capacity. The upside of the Sydney position is that it keeps you in the loop, keeps your face in front of the nation, albeit less often."

Oh, this is not good. In fact, it was as bad as it got as far as she was concerned. Effectively, the station was shuffling her out of the door. If she stayed, it would be career suicide: she'd likely never rise again to the elite rank she'd occupied, even at another station. Channel 12 must realise that and was hoping she wouldn't take the demotion and would leave of her own accord.

Which was very tempting. But what would she do instead? So much of her identity and self-belief depended on her TV persona. Who would she be without it? Over twenty years in the industry and it came down to this.

"When do you need my decision?" she asked.

Ethan gave a short laugh. "Yesterday. But you can have until Monday. No longer."

"I understand. Thanks, Ethan." She ended the call.

She'd have to think hard. It wasn't just about her career now—it was also about Orli. Would they want to stay in Sydney? Did Maren? An image of Jac flashed into her mind: naked in bed, the sheet in a knot around her feet, her sun-browned face, eyes crinkling as she smiled. Her skilful hands and what they did to Maren's body.

Jac was a reason to stay in Sydney—at least for now. But for how long?

Orli rushed into the house like a whirlwind, shedding school bag, hat, and gym bag as they went. By the time Maren caught up with them, Orli had their head in the fridge.

Maren waited until they closed the door, poured themself a glass of orange juice, and cut some cheese to go with crackers. "Don't rush off just yet. I need to talk to you about something."

Orli froze, the glass halfway to their mouth. "I've done nothing you need lecture me about. I'm positive."

"You've done nothing wrong. It's about being here in Sydney."

"Oh?" Orli sat on a stool and hooked their feet around the rungs. "I've kinda got used to it here."

"You like your school?"

They shrugged. "School's school."

"You've got less than two years until Higher School Certificate. Thing is, the station wants me to take a two-day a week job here in Sydney, but if I do, it effectively kills any chance of moving back to Melbourne. What do you think? Do you want to stay here, or move back to Melbourne at the end of the year as we planned?"

Orli made a multilevel pile of cheese and crackers and shoved it into their mouth in one go. They spoke through a mouthful of cracker crumbs. "Why are you asking me? Why not just decide as you always do and tell me later?"

"Leaving Melbourne was necessary, and you didn't get a say in that. You do get one here. So, I'm asking: what do you want?"

Orli chewed steadily, their eyes never leaving Maren's face. They must have seen something to convince them, as they said, "Okay. I want to stay here. I like working with Jac and the bikes. I want to get my learner's permit and then a bike. School's okay, and I like Mackenzie. And volunteering at Banksia Farm is kinda good, too." They took another bite, and said, "Mackenzie wants to go to uni in Melbourne. I thought I might do that too—if I get in. So, I'll be in Melbourne in another two years, anyway."

Nerves twitched in Maren's stomach. Orli's choice made so much more come into focus—and made so much more potentially possible. The Sydney position—if she wanted it. A closer relationship with Marcus and Rick. A more settled teen.

And Jac. Maybe there would be more with Jac.

Maybe.

CHAPTER 35

IN TIME NOW

JAC LOOKED AT THE TEXT on her phone.

I know this sounds like a booty call, but Orli's out clothes shopping & won't be back until late afternoon. The house is empty. It's 2pm on Saturday & all I can think about is you naked. Want to come around & let me see the reality? Okay, this totally is a booty call. :)

Jac's senses sprang to red alert, and instantly her body was molten. Her lips twitched. Who'd have thought that cool and poised Maren would be texting for a quick middle-of-the-day bed session? Although, so far, few of their times together had been quick. Slow and sensual, or hot and horny. Seldom quick.

Jac picked up her keys and headed down the hall, but her feet dragged. Was this the right thing to do? Keep jumping when Maren called? Keep seeing her, sleeping with her, even though a tiny part of her died whenever Maren talked about keeping their relationship from Orli, from Channel 12. From everyone, really.

She halted. Closed her eyes. Tossed her keys from hand to hand. Her breath shuddered out of her. There was no choice. Her body thrummed an urgent rhythm and thoughts of Maren filled her head. It might end in heartbreak later, but for now, she was committed to this course.

The door swung open as she walked up Maren's steps, and she continued on, straight inside. She barely remembered to push it closed with her foot before she was in Maren's arms, their lips sealed together, tongues already meshing.

Jac ran her hand up Maren's side, stroking the side of her breast through the thin T-shirt she wore. "You're not wearing a bra."

"Thought I'd save you the trouble of taking it off." Maren broke the kiss and yanked her T-shirt over her head.

Jac's gaze went to her breasts—her pale, perfect breasts, small but perfectly formed, with just those faint, silvery lines. She covered them with her hands, letting Maren's nipples poke through between her fingers. She squeezed gently. "Your hall is drafty."

"I don't care." Maren's eyes were huge.

"And the floorboards are hard. If I kneel to put my tongue between your legs, my knees will hurt."

"That's the best reason for moving to the bedroom." Maren took Jac's hand and led her to the large bedroom, already so familiar with its white cotton quilt, and silvery-green paint that Maren had chosen as part of her redecoration. The room was cool and elegant, just like Maren.

Jac stripped naked as fast as she could, heart thrumming in anticipation of her fingers inside Maren, her mouth between Maren's legs, how Maren looked, the small noises she made as she came, how she looked with her eyes closed, her head thrown back. And then how Maren's mouth would feel on her breasts, how her nipples would stiffen in a way that was nothing to do with the cool air and everything to do with Maren.

It was all about Maren. It was all Maren.

Here. Now. Later.

In time now, and in time to come, for as long as she was able.

An hour later, Jac and Maren sat at the kitchen counter, big glasses of wine in front of them, and a plate of crackers and cheese.

Jac pulled the borrowed robe tighter around her body. "It seems sort of wrong to be dressed like this here."

"I dress like this all the time." Maren's robe gaped open as she leaned forward to snag a cracker.

"It's your house." The hairs on the back of Jac's neck prickled, and she glanced around. "What if Orli comes home? They might learn way more than you intended."

"Relax." Maren chased the cracker with a mouthful of wine. "The shopping centre doesn't close until six, and then they have to get the train. They'll call for a lift from the station."

"Hope so." Jac swallowed her disquiet and leaned in to meet Maren's lips. "I respect your decision to keep it quiet." *Even if it's unsettling, as if I've regressed, gone back in time to when I was with Talia.* But the alternative—no Maren in her life—was worse. "The last time I was sitting like this—in someone's kitchen in my underwear—her housemate came in and wanted to join us."

"What did you do?" Maren's eyes lit with interest.

"We politely refused. The housemate was lovely, but it didn't feel right. There was no problem. And Dix and I teased each other about it afterwards—should we have said yes?"

Maren rose and went to the fridge, before returning with the wine, and topping up both of their glasses. "Got plans for tomorrow?"

"Back-to-back bike tours. Liz is helping with the second, and Orli is coming for a couple of hours in the morning to help get the bikes ready. They're very good at the detailing—better than me."

"Pity they don't give their room the same attention. It looks like the lion cage at the zoo."

Jac laughed. "It's all about motivation. They keep asking me to take them back to the road safety course. I will, but right now, finding the time is the problem. I've got tours booked every day for the next ten days."

"That's great. Although I was going to ask if you wanted to come with me and Orli to Bondi Beach tomorrow. Orli wants to strut their stuff on the sand."

"And you?"

"I'll stay covered up and let them have their fun. Afterwards, they get to pick the restaurant for dinner. I think they want soup dumplings in Chinatown."

"I wish I could join you, but I don't think I'll be finished before six, by the time I've settled everything."

"Next time."

Next time. The words held a promise and a tantalising glimpse of what might be.

"For sure. There'll be soup dumplings in your—" Maren halted. "Did you hear footsteps?"

The front door rattled with the sound of a key, then opened and slammed shut.

"It's Orli." Maren stood clutching the front of her robe together with white knuckles.

Jac surged to her feet. What to do? Did Maren expect her to hide in the closet like some '70s farce? Even if there was time to get there—

"Hi, Mum." Orli stood in the doorway, hair blown every which way, and laden with shopping bags. "Jac?" Their gaze moved from one to the other. "What the hell?"

Maren went to hug them, but Orli shifted away at the last moment. "Are you... You're sleeping together. Jeez." They dropped their bags and jammed their hands on her hips. "You told me you weren't. And you"—they swivelled to face Jac—"when did this start?"

"That doesn't matter to you," Maren said. "I treat you as an adult, which means we're two adults in the same house, entitled to our privacy. That means you don't get to interrogate Jac, or me, for that matter."

"You didn't treat me like an adult in Melbourne. I was fucking Raz, and you asked me questions. You took my laptop. You cut me off from my friends. Talk about a lack of privacy then."

"You've grown up a lot since," Maren said. "Back then, you thought you were pregnant but hadn't even done a pregnancy test. That wasn't the behaviour of a responsible adult. I also did not pass an opinion on your choice of partner. Now, I'm asking you again for the same respect."

Jac shuffled her feet. "I should go."

"No need on my account," Orli fired back. "Finish your wine, have a shower, maybe fuck my mum once more."

"*Orli!* You will apologise to Jac for that." Maren stood in front of her teen, white to the lips.

For a moment, the two faced off, then Orli dropped their gaze. "Sorry," they said to Jac. "That was a bit off. You've always been decent to me. But it's one thing knowing Mum's queer, another to have this"—they waved a hand at the two of them—"shoved in my face."

"You see Dad and Rick together. How is this different?" Maren said.

"I dunno. It just is. And Rick wasn't my friend before…" Their face twisted.

Jac looked to Maren. There was no logic to what Orli said. But then it seemed Orli was a creature of impulse. Someone who acted before they thought. Maybe, once the surprise had eased, they'd settle down once more.

"I need to go anyway," Jac said. "I have things to get ready for tomorrow."

Orli faced her. "Do you still need me tomorrow?"

"Of course." Jac raised an eyebrow. "Unless something's changed and you can't work tomorrow?"

"I'll be there," Orli mumbled.

"Good." Jac tightened the belt of her robe. She'd said she had to go, but what was the protocol for situations like this? Was she supposed to walk out barefoot wearing a robe and go home? Or disappear into Maren's bedroom and get dressed? Would that antagonise Orli all over again? There was no way she was going home dressed like this. She turned and went back to Maren's room.

The bed was in disarray, the quilt thrown back in a splash of snow white, tangled with the sheet in the middle of the bed. Jac spent a couple of minutes making the bed, so that if Orli looked in, it was less abandoned-boudoir-sex and more calm mother's retreat. Ha! Who was she fooling? Orli was sixteen, not six, and knew what went where in matters of sex. She shed the robe, pulled on her clothes, then returned to the living area.

Orli was sitting at the counter eating a bowl of cereal and scrolling on their phone. Maren, still in the robe, sat on the couch, her hands twisted in her lap. Jac went over and leaned in to press a quick kiss to her lips. There seemed little point in hiding now. She resisted the urge to see Orli's reaction—if indeed, she'd even noticed.

"I'll see you soon?" she murmured to Maren.

A quick nod, and Maren took Jac's hand and held it to her cheek for a moment. "You will. I'm sorry about"—her hand sketched the air—"all of this."

"No worries. I'll let myself out." She faced Orli and projected her voice. "Bye, Orli. See you tomorrow."

"Bye." Orli didn't look up from their phone.

Jac clattered down the stairs. A sick feeling swelled in her stomach, like coffee when the milk had gone sour. The things Maren worried about were happening. Her job was under threat. Her teen was struggling to come to terms with their mother's sexuality. And although Maren had implied they'd catch up soon... Would she change her mind when the 3 am night demons inevitably came to haunt her sleep with what-ifs?

Jac reached her house and went straight through to her kitchen. She took a tumbler from the shelf and found her bottle of Patron Anejo tequila that hid at the back of the cupboard and poured herself a stiff drink. This back and forth with Maren was messing with her head. Was it even worth it?

Right now, she didn't know.

CHAPTER 36
HOUSEWIFELANDIA

ORLI SHUFFLED INTO THE SHED the next morning. They jammed their hands in the front pocket of their hoodie. "Mum says I have to apologise."

Jac pulled out the leather cleaner and a rag and set them near Orli. "Do you want to?"

"Yeah. No. Maybe."

"That's decisive."

A flicker of a smile appeared on Orli's face. "Mainly, yeah. I wasn't very nice yesterday. I thought I was okay with you and Mum, but seeing you, both naked—"

"Naked in thick flannel bathrobes. But apart from that, naked."

Their shoulders raised. "So nearly naked." They picked up the cleaner and went over to the BMW and started applying cleaner to the leather, staring down at the dark seat as if it held the secrets of the universe. "Mum and I talked. She told me she really likes you. Not just as a friend, but—"

"No, Orli, please don't repeat it. That's for your mum to tell me if she wants. She trusts you—don't break that trust." Jac's fingers trembled. What had Orli been about to say? That Maren saw them in a relationship? As partners? Or had Maren given Orli a sex-positive talk about respectful casual sex? For a moment, she wished hard that Orli had finished the sentence—although how wrong that would have been to let her.

"You're right. Even though I bet you, like, want to know what I was going to say."

She shrugged with a casualness she didn't feel. "Really, that's not my business. I don't ask you about your private stuff. If you want to tell me, that's great, but I don't expect it. That's how it works."

"I told you I was non-binary."

"You did. Thank you for sharing that."

"And you told me you were a lesbian."

"I did."

"Thank you for sharing that." Orli's grin peeped out. "Now that's out of the way, can we get back to the bikes?"

"Of course."

Was that it? Jac looked at the top of their bent head as they polished the BMW's seat. Were they all one big happy family now? Was Orli now instantly fine with seeing Jac in Maren's robe? Would they cook eggs for breakfast together, and relax on the couch in a huddle?

No. That was all a few dozen steps too far. But it was a start.

Maren glanced through the blinds at Jac's house. The light was on in Jac's kitchen and Maren had glimpses of her as she moved from the fridge to the stove, preparing food. It had been two days since Orli had sprung them, and in that time, Maren had only waved to Jac from the car as she'd taken Orli to school.

Jac had texted, asking if she wanted to come play pool with her and her friends, but Maren had refused. Quiet night in, was how she'd put it, but the reality was she was acting normal for Orli. She sighed. Acting described it perfectly. What she was doing was playing a part: that of a devoted stay-at-home-mum, one with no life of her own except as it danced around her kid. What sort of example was that setting? A poor one, was the answer. If that was what someone wanted in life, of course, that was wonderful. But it wasn't what Maren wanted.

Today's looming deadline with Ethan was a fixture in the front of her brain, too. And she still didn't know what to do. She longed to talk to Marcus, to her friends in Melbourne, and ask for their advice, but something held her back. This had to be her decision and no one else's.

The clock on the wall ticked past four. She had an hour to get back to Ethan. He'd given her enough time, so she doubted he would call her. If that deadline passed, he would assume she was turning down the offer. But she owed him the courtesy of a reply.

Maren rummaged in the odds-and-ends drawer until she found a twenty-cent coin. Maybe it was as simple as tossing the coin and leaving it up to fate. Heads, and she'd take the job. Tails, she'd tell Channel 12 to go screw itself.

She tossed the coin. Heads.

Maybe the best of three.

The second toss was also heads.

That's not right. Best of five.

The third and fourth toss were tails. Fifth and final had it. She took a deep breath and tossed. Heads.

No, no, no, no… Abandoning the coin, Maren sat on the stool and put her head in her hands. There was her answer, right there. Her visceral horror at the coin-toss result told her everything. She had to turn down that job. She didn't want it. Didn't want to be an occasional player in a team where she'd been the lead. Didn't want to see Zoey's smug face as she and Luka bantered out the last minutes of the news.

And then there was Orli. Her teen, who'd surprised her and wanted to stay in Sydney. That should have been a tick in the "accept the offer" box, but it wasn't even a factor. They would stay in Sydney. That was now a given. But she was better than Channel 12's offer. She was worth more. And she was damn good at what she did. There was something out there for her; she just had to find it.

She glanced through the blinds once more. Would that something else include Jac? She didn't know. But as she'd told Orli the other night, she wanted to explore what they had. Find out. Be bold, be brave, be free.

It was as if chains were falling away from her chest, freeing her from expectations—her own and other people's. Her life was once again her own. She turned her face to the ceiling and laughed. It wasn't just these past two years she'd been trapped—it was the past twenty

225

years. Her marriage to Marcus—for all that she loved him—was its own sort of prison. And while she wouldn't change those years for anything—after all, they had brought her Orli, the greatest person in her life—to suddenly be mentally free made her feel light, airy. Joyful.

"I am my own person," she said to the empty room. "Finally, and completely, and utterly."

Orli had gone to a new friend's place after school. They'd told Maren they were doing their homework with Zuzanna, but Maren thought, more likely, it was just to hang out, and Orli would do their homework in their room later. But whatever the reason, she was glad Orli was settling in. Making friends.

When Orli arrived home, Maren waited until they were sat at the counter with a tall glass of orange juice, then pushed across a plate of cookies. "Try these. Peanut butter and chocolate chip."

Orli took one and stuffed it into their mouth. "Not bad," they said through the crumbs. "Not as good as Janelle's, though."

Ouch. But also accurate. "They're not," she agreed, "but they're better than store bought."

"Yeah." Orli took another. "Can I take some with my lunch tomorrow?"

"Of course. We got a postcard from Janelle today. It's on the fridge."

Orli wandered across to look. "Muscat, Oman. Cool. Although who sends postcards anymore?"

"Janelle, apparently." Maren waited until Orli had put it back on the fridge, then said, "I turned down the offer to work at the Sydney studio."

Orli whirled around. "Does that mean we're going back to Melbourne?" Their voice rose. "Who'll teach me to ride a bike?"

"We're not going anywhere—we're staying in Sydney."

Orli opened the fridge and pulled out the OJ to refill their glass. "Good."

Good? Is that all they have to say? Good, as in Maren wouldn't be racing off to work, would be home for Orli? "Good in what way?

Orli shrugged. "'Cos you're better than a two-day a week job. You're better than Zoey. The way she flirts with Luka… Ugh."

"I didn't know you watched the news."

"Sometimes. Can I have another biscuit?"

"Sure." She shunted the container across again.

"So, what are you going to do? Not sit at home still? Although the decorating you did is cool, and the house is, like, super clean."

"Except your room. You know where the vacuum is." She hadn't thought Orli had even noticed the house.

"Later. Got homework."

So, she was right; no homework had been done with Zuzanna. "I haven't figured out what I'll do yet. I only turned down the job today. Maybe I'll write the next great Australian novel. Or a tell-all memoir about the secrets of the TV industry."

"You hate writing."

"I'd hire a ghostwriter." But she wouldn't. It didn't appeal, and she wasn't going to burn her bridges in the industry just yet.

"You wouldn't. You're too much of a control freak." Orli chugged their juice.

Maren watched her teen absently while she mulled over what they'd said. They were growing fast. Their ankles already stuck out like sticks below their jeans. Or was that how they wore jeans these days? Orli was right; Maren did like control. Look how she'd reacted to Orli's rebellion in Melbourne. You couldn't get more controlling than taking them away from everything they knew. And that was one major reason for turning down the Channel 12 offer: because she wouldn't have control over what she did at work. Not that she'd had complete autonomy before, but she'd had enough input to satisfy her.

The answer came to her gradually, forming in front of her eyes as she stared unseeing at Orli. One minute, she had no idea of her future, except that she couldn't stay at home compulsively cleaning the house. That would end with a slow descent into the bottom of a bottle of gin. She wanted something that utilised her TV experience, her presenter skills. Something to get her teeth into. Something meaningful, or that could be, if she made it that way.

"I'm going to explore options for news documentaries. A current affairs program. The major issues affecting Australians, and the world. Interview people who make a difference." Saying the words aloud made the idea coalesce in her head. She'd need a co-presenter. Maybe another woman to get away from the accepted binary. One show each week, in the prime-time evening slot.

Orli blinked. "That sounds good. Better you than chanting the news. Certainly more you than trying to be Mrs Mop and Betty the Baker." They took another cookie. "What's for dinner?"

Maren covered a laugh. Orli supporting her new career and then in the next breath, punting it right back into housewifelandia with their question about food. But what did Maren really expect from a permanently starving teen?

CHAPTER 37
STARTING TO FEEL LIKE NORMAL

Jac stared at Maren's text.

Orli's at Marcus and Rick's. Want to come around. Bring your PJs. Except you won't need them. ;)

The text should have her bouncing out of her skin, lit from within at the thought of a night of pleasurable activity with Maren, sex that would set her body on fire and leave her sated, boneless, and drifting into a dreamless sleep. Instead, she was restless, and her skin seemed too tight for her body.

I'm not sure I can do this anymore. She typed the text, then deleted it unsent. She sprang to her feet and went out to her back deck where Maren wouldn't see her.

When had sizzling sex not been enough? *Since Maren.* Her mind supplied the answer almost before the question had formed in her head. Since Maren had barrelled into her life with her request that Jac take on Orli. With her gin and tonics and casual dress, so different from the perfectly presented TV personality. With her joy at bike riding, with the ease with which she fitted in with Jac's friends. Jac's life.

Jac's heart.

She froze, clutching the railing. When had that happened? But it had, and there was now more at stake than great sex and bike rides.

She wanted more. She wanted to wake with Maren every morning. Have breakfast, disagree over the best milk to have on cereal: almond or full-fat dairy. Help her and Orli get their bike licences. And then, at some point in the future, there would be rides together, the three of them. Almost like a family.

Whoa! That was about one hundred steps too far.

But with Maren...she wanted it all—with her. And that was the problem. Because as long as Maren remained in the closet, that couldn't happen. There'd be no strolls on the beach, hand in hand. No drinks at the Pacific View Hotel, bodies angled toward each other, knees touching. Maren touching Jac's thigh to make a point, Jac capturing that hand and holding it to her leg. The secret smiles that couples shared, smiles that shut out the whole world and promised everything to each other.

Love.

Was it love? Jac's heart slammed against her ribs with painful intensity and suddenly she couldn't breathe. Love. *Love?* Her instinctive, "Oh, hell no" withered away.

Because it was. She, Jacinta Fowler, loved Maren McEvoy, and that was one hell of a problem.

She looked back at Maren's text. Her finger hovered over the reply button. She wanted to, oh, how she did. And if it was this, or nothing... Well...she chose this. Again. She hit reply.

Depends if dinner's on offer.

It seemed to take an age before Maren's reply came through: *Thai takeaway? Mild or spicy?*

Jac grinned.

Nothing about you is mild, Maren. Spicy, of course!

Ten minutes later, she was in Maren's hall, her lips welded to Maren's, their bodies pressed together. Jac pushed her hand into Maren's hair, holding her even closer. Her other hand ran down

Maren's body to her waist. She pushed her hand under the T-shirt, delighting in Maren's soft skin and her shudder and soft gasp.

Jac slanted her mouth over Maren's, teasing her lips apart with her tongue. Maren tasted of gin and lemon, sharp and addictive. Maren's hands mapped Jac's body, skimming her sides, her waist, down, lower to cup her buttocks as she thrust a thigh between Jac's legs.

Jac ground down on Maren's leg, then broke the kiss. "Have you ordered the food yet?"

"Not yet."

"Then let's order it…afterward." She pressed another hot, deep kiss to Maren's mouth.

"Best idea I've heard today." Maren broke away and walked toward her bedroom, pulling her T-shirt off as she went. She spun it on a finger and flicked it away. It landed on the back of the couch.

Jac watched, fascinated, as Maren's coral-pink bra followed, landing on top of a floor lamp.

Maren flung her a heavy-lidded glance over her shoulder. "Has someone planted you in that spot?"

Energy flowed back into Jac's legs, and she followed Maren into the bedroom, coming to a stop at the sight of Maren facing her, her fingers hooked into the waist of her linen shorts. She undid the button, then eased the zip down.

Jac swallowed hard as the top of matching coral-pink undies came into view. They were silky and sheer enough that the crinkle of hair was visible through the material. Then Maren pushed the shorts and undies away in one go, and fell back on the bed, legs apart. She raised her head. "Are you trapped in an invisible cage?"

Jac walked toward the bed, shedding her own shirt and bra, then shorts and undies. "No. Just appreciating the view."

And then her mouth was over Maren's, and the kiss was deep enough to drown in. Maren's fingers between Jac's legs were knowing and soft, and her orgasm washed over her in too short a time. But there would be more. They had never stopped at just one.

Later, they put on the robes and went out to the kitchen. Maren opened a bottle of riesling and ordered Thai food. She seemed to order way too much for two, but as she said, sex always made her hungry.

Jac cupped the stemless wineglass in her hand. Her newfound knowledge—that she cared for—*loved*—Maren unfurled in her chest, the words straining to be set free. But how could she say that, now, when they didn't even have an acknowledged relationship? Just this. Just company and friendship, and amazing sex. Just shared times, and time together with Orli.

If that wasn't a relationship, then Jac didn't know what was. But a relationship was also a public acknowledgment. And that seemed a long way off—if it ever happened. But knowledge settled firmly in her chest. She'd told Maren to be true to herself, to do what was best for her, and here she was, ignoring her own advice. Even if it broke them apart, she had to say something.

"I like this, with you," she said. Her voice settled softly in the space between them. "You and me. Together."

Maren reached out a hand and covered Jac's. "I like this too."

"I want more, Maren. You and me. No more sneaking around. It feels wrong to me, winds me up inside. Like I'm not true to myself."

Maren bowed her head. When she raised it again, her eyes were damp. "I can't...not yet. But I promise you I'm working on it. On coming out. Maybe not with an announcement, but on being open with you. I've hidden myself for so long, to come out... It still scares me, even though I know it shouldn't." She took a breath. "But what we have feels like a relationship to me."

The words, a mirror of those in Jac's head, made her catch her breath. She stared at Maren, her thoughts of earlier coalescing into words, trembling on her lips. Words she hadn't said except to Talia. *And look how that ended*. She hesitated.

Maren gazed at her a moment longer. "You don't have to say any-thing. I thought we were heading toward the same thing. But I un-derstand your reservations. Until I come out—*if* I come out—it's not right for you." She drew a quick breath and picked at a loose thread on her robe. "I quit my job. Well, I'm still technically on a year's leave, but I turned down the two-day per week offer. I thought hard, and it feels right to do it. More than right."

Jac leaned forward and took Maren's hand. Relief shuddered in her throat and her words of earlier dissipated. This she could reply to. For this, she could be the caring girlfriend, all concern and support. The other... Not yet. "It's your decision. No one else's. You must do what's right for you. How did your boss take it?"

"Ethan wasn't surprised. He'd given me plenty of warning of how things were heading, and time to think it over. I wish Luka and Zoey well, but I've already moved on. It's not my circus anymore, and I'm good with that."

"Do you have plans?" What if Maren took a job in another state? Went back to Melbourne. Her words of earlier curled into a smaller ball and lodged in her chest where they couldn't fly free.

"Not really. And I'm lucky I don't have to rush into anything. I'm going to put out feelers. I'd like to work on a current affairs program. Documentaries. One or two in-depth stories per hour, not simply reading the day's happenings. It's a tight market for that in Australia, but I'll put my name out there and see what happens. But it will have to be in Sydney, or no more than a couple of days per week travel. Orli will do the HSC in less than two years. It's not good to move them, especially now they're settled and starting to do well. So, we'll be here in Sydney, at least until then."

The warmth in Jac's chest exploded into a smile. "I'm glad, Maren. Really glad. So, what will you do in the meantime?"

"Orli's already told me I need more than playing Mrs Mop and baking cookies. And while decorating the house passed some time, it's not really my thing. I'm going to get my bike licence. I already know a teacher." Her smile twitched at the edge of her mouth. "And past that, I'm going to get fitter, work on settling myself into this community more. I'll still be there for Orli, of course, but I'm here for me as well. Maybe I'll volunteer somewhere. Explore the region. Travel a bit. I'm probably the only Australian who's never been to Bali."

"You haven't missed much if you mean the tourist resorts," Jac said. "But away from them, Indonesia's a wonderful country."

For long moments, they stared at each other. Maren's gaze rested on Jac's face. Jac swallowed hard and picked up her hand, sandwiching it between her own. Her thumb stroked the back of it. *Just say it. Tell her what she's starting to mean to me.*

The doorbell shrilled, startling Jac.

Maren removed her hand. "That will be the food. I hope you don't mind, but I ordered it in your name. Would you mind getting it?" She gestured at her own robe. "I don't want this image of me in the next gossip rag."

"Sure." Jac slid from the stool and went to the door to collect the food.

When she returned, Maren was putting out plates and bowls on the counter. Chopsticks and forks lay next to them. She went to the cupboard and grabbed various sauces.

Jac put the food down. "Suddenly, I'm starving. I hope you ordered spicy noodles."

"I did." Maren started pulling containers from the bag. "Let's eat."

And the moment where Jac might have said more disappeared into a haze of normality, of food and wine, and lighter conversation that didn't touch on what they might mean to each other.

Jac didn't know whether to be relieved or sorry.

CHAPTER 38
LOOKING IN THE MIRROR

Marcus dropped onto the stool at Maren's counter. Maple whined to be picked up, and he bent and pulled her onto his lap, then looked over at Orli, who was practically vibrating.

"Got something to show you, Mum." They put down a magazine on the counter. "My interview's out. Nas told me it would only be online, but it's made the print edition, too."

Maren glanced at Marcus and raised an eyebrow.

His small nod reassured her there was nothing too awful in it.

"Congratulations, Orli. Nas must have thought you were really interesting."

"Read it." Orli turned away to fiddle with the coffee machine.

"I'll have a cup, since you're making one," Marcus said to them.

Maren pulled over the magazine. There was no mention of Orli on the cover, but then why would there be? Orli wasn't a money-spinner in their own right, except as Maren and Marcus's teen. She flicked the pages until a photo of Orli caught her eye. They were half-smiling into the camera looking slightly away, a baseball cap backward on their head, their hoodie zipped to their neck. Maren recognised the photo as one Rick had taken when they'd visited Banksia Farm. *On Coming Out as Non-Binary*, the headline read.

The name Orli Coffey isn't known to many people, but sixteen-year-old Orli is the child of newsreader Maren McEvoy and rugby great Marcus

Coffey. I talked to Orli about their realisation they were non-binary and their acceptance and coming-out process.

Maren looked at Marcus who gave a discreet thumb up. Maren read on. Nas had done a good and sensitive job. The article focussed on Orli's thoughts on gender, on presentation, and their gradual realisation that they were non-binary and what it meant to them. Most of it, Maren recognised as being distilled from Nas's interview, but some parts were fresh.

Maren was present when I talked with Orli, the article continued, *but she didn't interfere, simply let her teen speak.*

The article continued with Orli talking about being unsure how their parents would take the news. Maren sucked a breath. Was this where Nas would talk about the photo of Maren and Jac kissing on the beach?

"Mum and Dad have supported me," Orli said. "I'm lucky like that. I've always been brought up to be honest and true to myself. My parents are divorced, but they're still really good friends, and I like that."

Maren's hands shook, and she smoothed the magazine to steady them. Yes, she and Marcus had encouraged Orli to be honest and true to themself. But when she applied that to herself... She swallowed hard and met Marcus's sympathetic gaze. She resumed reading.

Marcus Coffey now lives with marketing executive Rick Curtis in inner Sydney, and Orli divides their time between them and Maren's house in southern Sydney.

Orli was honest about what brought them to Sydney from Melbourne, where the family used to live. "I didn't have too good a time the last year in Melbourne. I had friends—and they're still my friends—but together we got into a bit of trouble. The dynamic between us meant we were always trying to outdo each other. I got arrested for carjacking. It was stupid, and I really regret it. I'm still paying back my parents—they paid for the car I wrecked.

"But I was figuring out my identity, sexuality, gender. And it felt like I had no one to talk to about it all. That wasn't true. Turns out there were lots of people I could have talked to, but I didn't realise it at the time. Anyway, Mum moved us to Sydney. I hated it at first, as I knew no one."

Maren sucked a breath. None of this had been in the interview with Nas that she knew of. Orli must have talked with her again or messaged her. Was this where she mentioned Jac? Mentioned Maren's sexuality? She glanced at Orli as they set a coffee in front of both her and Marcus.

Orli worried their lower lip with their teeth.

They were nervous, worried about her reaction. "I'm still reading. But it's great so far. You've been really open and honest. And Nas writes well."

"I messaged her a few times after. I'm sorry I didn't tell you, but I wasn't sure I could tell you about how I felt. It seemed easier to tell a stranger."

A pang. Her teen couldn't talk to her? But then what teen did confide fully in their parents? That was part of growing up—making your own decisions, working through things in your own time, your own way. And she had to let Orli do that. "I understand. If you ever want to talk to me, you can. About anything. But sometimes it's easier with someone less close."

Orli's eyes shone, and they lowered their head. "Thanks. I couldn't talk to Dad either. I did sorta talk with Rick—when we went to see Mia Raines—and hinted at it to Jac. They were both great."

"I'm glad you could do that." She lifted the magazine. "Let me finish reading." Her pulse buzzed as she read on. Her teen, her difficult and rebellious teen, was growing and maturing in their own way.

A couple of minutes later, she set the magazine down again with a sigh. There was nothing about her sexuality. Indeed, she was barely mentioned as Nas had promised, except for a quote when she said she supported Orli and loved them unreservedly. There was nothing about Jac or the damage Orli had done to Jac's bike, only a couple of sentences about how Orli intended getting her bike licence as soon as she was able.

"Nas did you proud." Maren stood. "Can I hug you?"

With a choked cry, Orli flung themself into Maren's arms.

Maren wrapped her arms around Orli's shoulders and looked at Marcus over their teen's head. Their precious, difficult, awkward teen, who had caused them so much angst recently. It seemed they would now be okay,

When Orli had disappeared into their room, Maren raised an eyebrow at Marcus. "I don't know about you, but coffee isn't really cutting it." She held up a bottle of cabernet. "Despite Nas's assurances, I was still worried about what she'd write."

He nodded. "Me too. But she did a good job."

"She respected my wishes. Kept the focus on Orli." She twisted the screw cap on the wine and poured them both a glass.

"What about you, Maren?" Marcus took a sip and set his glass down on the counter. "Now that you're no longer in the talons of Channel 12, are you going to do something similar?"

She sucked her lip. "It's not that easy. I know, realistically, that most people don't care anymore. There'll always be the haters—"

"Yes." Marcus's lips twisted. "I remember only too well. And some of my haters were men I'd played rugby with for years. But you can't pander to the haters, or you'll never be true to yourself."

"I know that. I really do. When I said my hesitation was because of Orli, because of Channel 12, I was fooling myself. Yes, they were a factor, but not *the* reason." She looked down into the rich red wine, swirling it absently in her glass. "The real reason was me."

Marcus waited, his eyes on her face. He'd always been like this. Giving her time and space to form the words, to work through her issues without pushing her or trying to direct her choice.

"I was married to you for eighteen years. It's two years since we split. And in all that time, I buried who I really was. Back then, it mattered more. For you, definitely, but for me too. Twenty years ago, both our careers would have suffered. And then Orli might have suffered too."

"You married me because I asked," Marcus said. "I know it was mainly for my sake that you did." He bent and kissed Maple on top of her curly head.

She nodded. "And I don't regret that. How could I? My best friend, our teen. We were happy together."

"We were. But Maren, toward the end of our marriage, it became uncomfortable for me. Not with you, never with you, but because I wasn't being myself. And I think you felt the same, although you've never really said."

She licked her lips. Perceptive Marcus. "It wasn't like that, really. I simply buried that part of me—the sexual side. And I had the companionship of women, friendships—"

"But you shouldn't have had to settle for that. And now, maybe you don't."

"When you've spent so many years hiding, when so many friendships and relationships know me as one way... To change, to come out... It makes me feel exposed," she ended in a whisper.

"Orli is already coming around," Marcus said. "She looks up to Jac, respects her. And she loves you. Why wouldn't she want you to be happy?"

"I know. I was hiding behind her and Channel 12. I'm getting there, Marcus. Jac doesn't want to hide, and I'm afraid I'll lose her if I keep doing so."

"You can't come out for Jac, though. It has to be for you."

"I know."

"It doesn't have to be an announcement. Just be seen together. Go on dates. Walk on the beach holding hands. Go somewhere together with Orli. Be normal."

"You saw the sensationalist headlines about that beach kiss."

Marcus was silent. "What would have happened then if you'd shrugged and carried on?"

"I couldn't because of Orli. Because of Channel 12."

"Back then, yes. But now?"

She took another sip of wine, her heart slamming against her sternum. Her fingers trembled on the glass and she tightened them to stop it. "But now, nothing. Except to do so now will take the focus from Orli. And I don't want that."

"So, wait a week. That's the lifespan of such things."

She nodded. He was right. To think otherwise was self-absorbed.

"Remember when I came out? The macho bullshit. Blokes I'd played with for years, saying they now couldn't feel safe in the changing room?" He snorted. "As if I was focussed on anything except rugby. The speculation as to whether I would out anyone else. How long did that furore last? About five days. Sure, there's the occasional rumble now, or comment about gay ex-rugby league player Marcus Coffey, but that's it."

"It will drag it all up again for you if I come out," Maren said. "People will question our marriage."

He shrugged. "Let them. It's none of their business." He tapped her hand where it lay on the counter. "I know it's hard, Maren. I agonised over it for a long time before I took the plunge. And I didn't have a partner to stand by my side then. You were great, supporting me publicly, but I didn't have someone to hold my hand, be my person. Maybe you'll have Jac."

Maybe she would. And wasn't that mostly what this was about?

CHAPTER 39

SODDEN

MAREN STARED OUT OF THE window. Rain hammered down, lashing against the windows in waves. She pressed her nose against the glass like a kid, trying to see out. It was supposed to clear soon, although there didn't appear to be any slowing. Her legs twitched. Orli's school had a pupil-free day, and they were at Marcus and Rick's. Maren had planned a bushwalk in Royal National Park, something that would burn off her energy and settle her nerves. A walk to let her thoughts float free, and clear her head. Maybe even make some decisions about her life.

It had been a few days since the magazine article about Orli had been published. Orli had taken the magazine to show Jac, but Maren hadn't seen her. Was she simply busy, or was there a different reason? Such as she couldn't be with someone closeted.

Her head pounded with the what-ifs. She rubbed the window clear of the fog from her breath. Maybe the rain was easing. Well, rain or not, she was going out anyway. She whirled around and went to her room to change into jeans and hiking boots and pull her rain jacket from the cupboard. Sure, she'd get wet, but she could come home to a cosy house, order in food, and curl up with a hot chocolate and a book for the evening.

The rain had eased to a drizzle. She went down the steps to her car.

Jac stood by her mailbox, riffling through her mail. Maren stopped and wound down the window. "Hi!" To her ears, her voice sounded artificial and too bright. "How are you?"

Jac came over to the car. "I'm fine. Frustrated because of the rain. Today's riders cancelled. Can't say I blame them."

"I'm the same, but I can't sit still any longer. I'm going bushwalking in Royal National Park." She hesitated, the words thrumming on her tongue. "Want to come?"

Jac bent and peered into the car. "We'd get drowned. Have you looked at the rain radar? This drizzle is only a temporary reprieve."

"Waterproof jacket. And, to be honest, I don't care. I need to get out." She put the car into gear. "I understand you want to stay dry. I'll see you later."

"Wait." Jac's voice was sharp. "I'll come, if you can give me five minutes to change."

Warmth trickled through Maren's chest. "I'll give you all the time in the world." She turned off the engine.

Their eyes met, and the connection between them leaped into life once more.

Maren's breath caught in her throat as a glimmer of hope surfaced.

With a nod, Jac jogged back to her house, before returning a few minutes later dressed in jeans, hiking boots, and a waterproof jacket. She dropped into the passenger seat. "You realise we'll still be saturated. We'll probably turn amphibious."

"We'll be outside, in wild Australia—"

"On a gravel track."

"Kilometres and kilometres from anywhere—"

"Maybe ten."

"Surrounded by ravaging beasts."

"Kyra got kicked by a swamp wallaby once. Does that count?"

"You're destroying my iron-woman fantasy." Maren put the car into gear and drove out onto the road.

They were silent for the short drive to Royal National Park. Maren parked at the visitor's centre and got out. The rain sluiced down, and she flipped up the hood of her jacket.

Jac joined her. "My gills are sprouting."

Together they walked over the bridge to Currawong Flat Picnic Area and turned up the Robertson's Roundabout Trail. They squelched along in single file as the trail wound higher, patches of mist lending an eerie feeling.

Maren walked fast, arms swinging, avoiding the wettest parts of the track. Somewhere, a black cockatoo called its mournful cry into the mist.

The rhythmic thump of her boots on the soft ground and the pitter patter of rain on her waterproof jacket were strangely soothing. Maren marched along, letting the physical exertion soothe her hyperactive mind. Jac huffed along behind her, her breath loud in the forest's soft air.

After thirty minutes, they reached Robertson Knoll lookout. Maren halted and stood looking down through the trees at the Hacking River partially visible through the mist.

Jac came up alongside her. "This is wonderful. Wet, but wonderful. My boots aren't as waterproof as the manufacturer claimed."

Maren laughed. "Mine neither. But the exercise feels fantastic. Nothing better than a walk to help you work through things."

Jac tilted her head. "Is it working?"

"Maybe." She said no more. Instead, she turned to face the path. "Shall we continue? It's downhill all the way now to the carpark."

"Sure," Jac said. "I feel I've earned a beer."

Fifteen minutes later, they arrived back at the picnic area. Maren slowed to let Jac draw alongside. She took her hand, twining their fingers together.

Jac's hand stayed immobile in her own. "There's people here." She jerked her head toward a couple sitting under a shelter eating sandwiches.

"They're not paying us any attention." *I can do this.* Still clasping Jac's hand, she ambled along the path to the bridge, passing close to the couple. Her pulse raced with more than the exertion of the walk. What if they recognised her? What if they had a camera? She steadied her tumultuous thoughts. With her rain jacket hood up, her own mother wouldn't recognise her.

"Nice weather for the ducks," she called to the couple, who smiled in response. The tightness in her chest eased; she and Jac were just another crazy couple out in the rain.

She didn't release Jac's hand until they were back at the car. They shed their wet jackets and dropped them into the boot.

Once inside, she turned to Jac. "Do you want a drink somewhere? Maybe some bar snacks? Somewhere overlooking the water?"

"Sure. There's a place on the foreshore near Cronulla. That should be quiet."

Considerate Jac, no doubt thinking of her wish to remain hidden. But was it still important? *Maybe not.* She took a deep breath and started the car.

Jac directed her to a small and intimate cocktail bar. They were lucky, and secured window seats that looked out over the gusty foreshore to the wind-whipped slatey sea. Jac went to the bar and returned with a beer for her and a gin and tonic for Maren. They clinked glasses.

"To us," Maren said. Her eyes held Jac's, and she held her breath, waiting for her response.

Jac sipped, her gaze never leaving Maren's. "To us, with what conditions?"

Here it was. Could she do this? *Yes. Yes, I can.*

"Organically out."

Jac's eyes crinkled. "Like free-range eggs?"

Maren snorted, and her gin and tonic splashed over the glass. "That's one way of looking at it. I'm not hiding anymore, Jac; I'm ready to be me. Be free. The things that held me back before either aren't important, or are changing. I have the support of my family. Your support, too, if you'll have me."

"You do." Jac picked up Maren's hand and held it between her own.

Jac's palms warmed her own clammy hands. Was that nerves or just the cold?

"I'm not going to announce anything—yet. But I'm not hiding either. I want to hold your hand as we walk on the beach. I want to kiss you in a quiet cocktail bar."

Jac looked around. "There's the bar person, a group of people by the far wall, and a couple by the other window. Is that quiet enough for you?"

Maren leaned across and took Jac's lips with her own. Jac's lips curved into a smile under her own, then softened, letting Maren direct the kiss.

She deepened the kiss, her tongue darting between Jac's parted lips, then withdrawing. She sat back, her lips tingling from the touch.

Jac took a discreet look around. "The group didn't pay us any attention. The couple just smiled at me. Is that okay?"

The concrete casing around her soul collapsed into dust. Her shoulders tightened, then relaxed, the knot of tension at the base of her neck softening into nothing. "That's okay. More than okay."

Without breaking her stare, Jac picked up her beer and took two big gulps. "Strikes me, we shouldn't be here. We're wet, we're chilled." She shivered dramatically. "We should probably get out of these wet clothes."

Maren pushed aside the rest of her gin and tonic. "We should."

There was something so different in making love to a woman she cared about. Jac nibbled her way along Maren's body, along the impossible softness of her breasts, lingering over her nipples. She grazed her fingers along the undersides, then down over the slight mound of her belly.

Maren's sigh wafted over her ears.

Jac's hook-ups, single nights with someone passing through Sydney, were nothing compared to this. *Nothing.* For a moment, she rested her head on Maren's belly before moving lower, down to between her thighs. Would she ever get used to this with Maren? Touching her, tasting her, being inside her? Maybe not, and that was the way she wanted it.

Maren came in feathery little flutters around Jac's fingers. Jac stayed where she was, lazily tasting and touching until Maren came a second time with stronger shudders.

And then Maren took control, pushing Jac onto her back, straddling her, playing with her nipples, touching her side, cupping her small breasts as if they were something magnificent. Jac came once at the touch of her tongue, a second time when Maren used her fingers, and finally the echo of a third time, a lazy little aftershock.

When they were lying together again, facing each other, arms around each other's waists, faces close enough to lean in and kiss, Jac drew a deep breath. Words hovered on her tongue, so full she could taste them. The words she'd been so close to saying to Maren once before—but hadn't. Now though. Was now the time?

"You're happy with us?" Maren asked. Her breath wafted over Jac's cheek. "You're okay with us being together, no hiding, but no announcement?"

She nodded. "Yes. The no hiding part is the big one. The rest is up to you. Although it's always been up to you."

"Not anymore," Maren said. "Now it's up to us. And as long as Orli gets consideration and care, then I'm yours." She touched Jac's cheek. "You're important to me, Jac. What we have…it's special. You're more than a friend, more than a sex partner. I hope you know that."

"I'm beginning to." Jac mirrored the gesture, running her fingers over Maren's cheekbone. "I have words for it too: caring, happiness"— she sucked a breath—"love."

"Love," Maren echoed. "Love. Yes."

Jac leaned in to kiss her again. Her heart pounded hard and heavy, a drumbeat that reverberated around her entire body. "I love you. So you don't doubt."

"And I love you too."

Then the words and declarations, kisses, and caresses started again, and Jac's body lit from within, fiery from Maren's touch.

Her woman. Them together.

CHAPTER 40
WHAT YOU HAVE TO DO TO GET PIZZA

Three months later

"IF I GET MY LEARNER'S permit, will you buy me a bike?" Orli huddled in the back seat of Marcus's car as he drove them, Maren, Rick, and Jac, to the test centre.

Jac stifled an amused smile. Orli had told her she was going to ask this.

Maren nudged them, where they were sandwiched in the back seat between her and Jac. "No. You're still paying off that car you wrecked in Melbourne. But I'll lend you the money."

Marcus met Maren's glance in the rear-vision mirror. "You could be up for a big loan. Aren't Nortons expensive bikes?"

"They are," Jac said. "Not a learner's bike either. Start on something that it doesn't matter so much if you ding it or drop it."

"I'd never do that!" Orli said in affronted tones.

"Honeybun, if you treat a bike the way you treat your dad's car, the bike won't stand a chance. I found half a sausage roll down the side of the seat yesterday," Rick said.

"Sorry. I thought I'd eat it later and I guess I forgot." Orli chewed a thumbnail. "What if I fail my learners? What if I do something stupid?"

"You won't." Jac found her hand and squeezed it. "Haven't you practiced the test manoeuvres for weeks now? You could do it in your sleep."

"I'm more likely to fail than you," Maren said. "Being old and stiff with no balance."

Marcus laughed. "Bollocks. You'll both pass. Many people won't have been on a bike. You'll both ace this."

"You better both pass," Jac said. "I'm counting on the pizza feast your dad and Rick have promised all of us tomorrow when you do. I'm going to have a lamb, rosemary, and tzatziki pizza, then a capricciosa with extra olives and anchovies."

"Eww." Orli wrinkled their nose.

"That one's all yours," Rick said. "Those smelly little fish are gross."

Jac laughed. "If I'd known how easy it was to get you to keep your hands off my pizza, I'd have ordered them weeks ago."

"We're here." Marcus turned into the motorcycle school. "Now, you two behave yourselves. We're taking Jac to look at paint charts for our kitchen."

Jac's jaw dropped in pretend horror. "You never said that! You said we'd catch a movie."

"Since when have we ever agreed on a movie? Paint charts it is. You can look at power tools or something."

Marcus stopped the car in front of the school, and they all got out.

Jac hugged Orli. "You have so got this. Today will be a breeze. Tomorrow will be even easier, and then you'll have those big yellow L plates. You'll just need a bike to put them on."

Orli managed a nervous smile before Marcus swallowed them up in a hug.

Maren came up to Jac. "Do I get a good luck hug, too?"

"You get more." Jac palmed both sides of Maren's face, drawing her close to kiss her.

Maren's lips were soft under her own as she returned the kiss.

"You're not worried, are you?" Jac said when they broke apart. "Because this is just one step above a formality."

"I realise that. It's all good. You'll get your pizza feast." She raised her voice. "I hear hot pink is the new trend in kitchens."

Rick's and Marcus's twin expressions of horror made them all laugh.

Orli and Maren had both got their learner's permits, and the days and weeks slid by. Jac asked around and found a couple of decent second-hand bikes. The small Suzukis were zippy enough to keep Orli happy, but steady enough to reassure Maren.

Whenever they all had a day free, they'd ride out together, exploring the coast and the Illawarra region, visiting small towns, and touring winding rural roads.

Orli's friend Mackenzie came along sometimes, riding pillion behind Jac.

More often, it was just Jac and Maren. They'd explore longer and further, occasionally staying overnight somewhere. Then Maren showed her love of luxury, booking them into boutique hotels and unusual Airbnbs: a tree house in the forest canopy, a modern steel-and-glass house secluded and private on a clifftop overlooking the ocean, a perfectly furnished art house, where every wall, every surface was painted to a theme.

Now that Maren had been out of the public eye for some months, few people recognised her, especially not in bike leathers, her hair longer and windswept. One day in late autumn, when the days were getting cooler, they arrived at an Airbnb, riding up on the bikes. The owner greeted them and kept shooting them curious looks as he showed them the beach house. As he turned to leave, he slapped his forehead.

"Now I know where I've seen you before," he said. "Maren McEvoy. I used to love seeing you on the news." He glanced at their linked hands. "Any chance you'll be returning to the slot?"

"No," Maren said. "I've moved on from that, and Zoey is filling my boots very well."

"I hope you'll do something new." He turned back again to leave. "Enjoy your stay. Please call me if there's anything you need. And you must get asked all the time, but if there's any chance of a selfie with you in the morning, my wife would love that."

"There's every chance," Maren said with a smile. After he'd left, Maren said, "I'm not sure what surprised him most: that I was holding hands with you, or that I was in bike leathers."

"Probably the bike," Jac said. "I mean, who wouldn't want to hold hands with me?"

Maren laughed and thumped Jac's biceps. "Modest woman. For that you can show me exactly why you're so irresistible."

And they closed the blinds against the amazing view and prying eyes and Jac showed Maren exactly why that was true.

CHAPTER 41
SHOUTING OUT

Six months later

"We don't have to do this." Jac sat next to Maren, their knees touching on Maren's—no, *their* couch. "We can keep on keeping on. Being ourselves, being open and affectionate in public. Smiling enigmatically when people ask us about our relationship."

"We could," Maren agreed. "But I don't want to. This is only my second time to move in with someone—"

"Technically, I moved in with you." Her business was still next door, and she'd rented the house to a young couple who didn't mind her coming and going to the shed.

"—and my second time to agree to marry someone. I want to tell the world about us."

Jac brushed her palms over her jeans. "I've never given an interview before."

"There's nothing to it. Smile, be friendly. And if there's a question you don't want to answer, just incline your head and don't say anything. If it's recorded—which it will be—Nas will move on."

"You'd better do most of the talking. After all, you have the most to talk about—the success of *Our Australian World* and how you're 'filling a viewing gap between straight-out factual documentary, life stories, and pure entertainment.'" She made air quotes. "At least that's how the TV guide puts it."

"This is mostly about us, not my career."

"My partner, the most in-demand current affairs journalist in Australia." Jac leaned in to kiss her, and she pressed her palm to Maren's cheek. "Have I told you how happy I am to be with you?"

"You did this morning. Has anything changed since then?" Maren inclined her head with a smile.

"Nothing."

"Then all's good with the world."

Jac fidgeted with the seam of her jeans. It was all very well for Maren to be cool and calm about this. The only journalist Jac had ever spoken to had been the pushy one she'd thrown off her property after the photo of her and Maren kissing on the beach had surfaced. And nothing had come of that—luckily. Maren had received an e-mail from Nas Caspian some weeks after the article about Orli had been published. Nas had told her the journalist had attempted to sell the story to *Out and About*, but once they'd found out he'd obtained his information by illegal means, and had trespassed on Jac's land, *Out and About* had not only refused the story, but told him that if it surfaced anywhere else, they would report him to the police for illegally obtaining information. Nas said that *Out and About* was strict about not outing anyone without consent.

It was this that had made the choice of journalist for Maren's story easy.

Maren rose from the couch and flicked on the coffee machine. Her engagement ring glinted in the overhead light. For a moment, Jac wished she'd allowed Maren to buy her one too—but expensive jewellery and motorbikes didn't mix. She'd wait for the plain gold wedding band.

"Nas will be here any minute." Maren looked Jac up and down. "You look amazing. The photographer will love you. Except…"

She returned to Jac and kissed her mouth again. "Now you've got no lipstick on."

"Which I'm happy about. Before today, I don't think I've ever worn any makeup that isn't Chapstick."

"Lipstick is better for the photographs. But we can redo that later."

The doorbell rang, and Jac tilted her head, her heart thrumming in double time. This was it. Although she and Maren had often been seen together in the past few months, Maren had steadfastly refused to discuss their relationship. Until now.

"Are you ready to come out to the world?"

"As ready as I'm ever going to be."

Jac stood and held out a hand. "Then let's tell the world about our love."

Hand in hand, they went down the hall to answer the front door.

OTHER BOOKS FROM
YLVA PUBLISHING

www.ylva-publishing.com

A HEART FULL OF HOPE
Cheyenne Blue

ISBN: 978-3-96324-955-6
Length: 275 pages (88,000 words)

When executive Imogen's elderly uncle has a bad fall, she steps in to run his life. She doesn't count on his friend, handywoman Hazel—who has one leg, two jobs, and a lot of opinions. Worse, now the meddling old man is match-making them!

What could an icy, driven career woman have in common with a cute butch with charm to burn?

Opposites attract, repel, and bicker like fools in this adorable small town lesbian romance about finding what truly matters in life.

FLIPPING HEARTS AND HOMES
Chris Zett

ISBN: 978-3-96324-952-5
Length: 227 pages (78,000 words)

When smalltown handywoman Rowan inherits an old house, it's a great chance to flip it to pay off her mom's debt. She never expects to meet adorably nerdy Maia, a big-city radiologist staying in town to heal a broken heart.

While undeniable attraction sparks between them, what future could they ever have for two people with such different goals?

A heartwarming, low-angst lesbian romance about finding a home and family in unexpected places.

JUST FOR SHOW
Jae

ISBN: 978-3-95533-980-7
Length: 293 pages (103,000 words)

When Claire, an overachieving psychologist with OCD tenden-
cies, hires Lana, an impulsive, out-of-work actress for a fake relationship, she figures the worst she'll have to endure are the messes Lana
leaves around. It's only for a few months anyway. And it's not as if
she'll enjoy all those fake kisses and loving looks. Right?

A lesbian romance where role-playing has never been so irresistible.

RESCUE ME
Michelle L. Teichman

ISBN: 978-3-95533-762-9
Length: 272 pages (94.000 words)

Kristen Bailey of the Royal Canadian Mounted Police has it all figured out, until she meets Ashleigh Paige. Beautiful, naïve, and trusting, Ashleigh is the perfect lead for her case. Only she's a paramedic,
and in Toronto, EMTs and cops don't mix, and the closer she gets
to Ashleigh, the more the line between informant and intimate gets
blurred.

ABOUT CHEYENNE BLUE

Cheyenne Blue has been hanging around the lesbian erotica world since 1999 writing short lesbian erotica which has appeared in over 90 anthologies. Her stories got longer and longer and more and more romantic, so she went with the flow and switched to writing romance novels. As well as her romance novels available from Ylva Publishing, she's the editor of *Forbidden Fruit: stories of unwise lesbian desire*, a 2015 finalist for both the Lambda Literary Award and Golden Crown Literary Award, and of *First: Sensual Lesbian Stories of New Beginnings*.

Cheyenne loves writing big-hearted romance often set in rural Australia because that's where she lives. She has a small house on a hill with a big deck and bigger view—perfect for morning coffee, evening wine, and anytime writing.

CONNECT WITH CHEYENNE

Website: www.cheyenneblue.com
Facebook: www.facebook.com/CheyenneBlueAuthor
Instagram: www.instagram.com/cheyenneblueauthor
Twitter: twitter.com/iamcheyenneblue

Sometimes We Fly
© 2025 by Cheyenne Blue

ISBN: 978-3-69006-015-8

Available in paperback and e-book formats.

Published by Ylva Publishing, legal entity of Ylva Verlag, e.Kfr.

Ylva Verlag, e.Kfr.
Owner: Astrid Ohletz
Am Kirschgarten 2
65830 Kriftel
Germany

www.ylva-publishing.com

First edition: 2025

Credits
Edited by Sarah Ridding and Sheena Billet
Cover Design by Ronja Forleo
Print Layout by Streetlight Graphics

Made in United States
Troutdale, OR
04/27/2025

30924177R00156